I KNOW
YOU
REMEMBER

ALSO BY JENNIFER DONALDSON

Lies You Never Told Me

I KNOW YOU REMEMBER

JENNIFER DONALDSON

RAZORBILL

RAZORBILL

An imprint of Penguin Random House LLC, New York

alloyentertainment

Produced by Alloy Entertainment
30 Hudson Yards, 22nd Floor
New York, NY 10001

First published in the United States of America by Razorbill,
an imprint of Penguin Random House LLC, 2019
Paperback edition published by Razorbill, an imprint of Penguin Random House LLC, 2020

Visit us online at penguinrandomhouse.com.

THE LIBRARY OF CONGRESS HAS CATALOGED THE HARDCOVER EDITION AS FOLLOWS:
Names: Donaldson, Jennifer (Young adult author), author.
Title: I know you remember / Jennifer Donaldson.
Description: New York : Razorbill, 2019. | Summary: After moving back to
Anchorage and discovering the mysterious disappearance of her best friend,
high school senior Ruthie embarks on a search that reveals dark secrets.
Identifiers: LCCN 2019011070 | ISBN 9781595148544 (hardback)
Subjects: | CYAC: Missing children—Fiction. | Secrets—Fiction. | Mental illness—Fiction. |
Best friends—Fiction. | Friendship—Fiction. | Anchorage (Alaska)—Fiction.
Classification: LCC PZ7.1.D644 Iak 2019 | DDC [Fic]—dc23
LC record available at https://lccn.loc.gov/2019011070

Paperback ISBN 9781595148551

Printed in the United States of America

1 3 5 7 9 10 8 6 4 2

Text set in Kepler, Tiempos Headline, and Adelle Sans

To Crystal Rice McDonald

CHAPTER ONE

THE URN IS SMALLER than I expected. It's green—her favorite color—and made of aluminum, and even though it's less than a foot tall it's heavy. Dense with her ashes. With her body.

With my mother, broken down into a million crumbling pieces.

It sits on a small altar at the front of the little chapel, and I can't take my eyes away from it. Even with the funeral director standing at the lectern, reading some poem I'm sure I okayed in the meeting we had a few days ago. Even with the sound of weeping behind me. The urn takes up all my vision, soaks up all the light in the room. The green is dark, the same color as the Douglas firs she loved. The color of the mossy stones in the shadows of the Columbia River Gorge.

The thought makes me close my eyes tight.

It's been a week since the accident. My body isn't a body anymore, it's a machine that I have to operate through force of will, pulling levers with all my might. I'm somewhere inside of it, tiny and exhausted. I have to shout to be heard from in here, and so sometimes it's easier not to speak at all. Sometimes it's easier to close my eyes and sit in stillness. But everyone seems to want something from me, and so I keep having to guide my machine-body through the motions.

For instance. Next to me, I feel Ana Maria putting her hand on mine. She's my case worker. She's nice enough. I don't have any family in Portland, besides my mom, so Ana Maria's been helping me make all the arrangements. She helped me set up the funeral, helped me make a reservation for the flight to Anchorage tomorrow night, helped me close out Mom's accounts, her credit card and the utilities and the apartment lease. She's definitely one of those people that believes in meditation and support groups and grief counseling, and she's already given me a book called *Present in Loss: Surviving the Death of a Loved One through Mindfulness.* And even though I just feel numb, and tired, I have to force my machine-body to move yet again, so that she doesn't think I'm just some kind of monster who can sit here during her own mother's funeral and stare out in space. I open my eyes and look down at my lap and let her take my hand.

The room is packed, but that's only because it's such a high-profile death. The women from her office sit in a row just behind me, crying into their handkerchiefs. There are college kids in the crowd—Mom was a well-liked registrar at Reed— and a handful of my schoolmates, though I hardly know most of them. All around I hear the quiet rustle of people shifting in their seats, craning their necks to get a glimpse of me or of the urn or of the blown-up photo on the easel at the front of the room that shows my mom, smiling her dimpled smile. Even in the midst of all these people, all these well-wishers, all I want is to talk to Zahra. But she's a world away, and I'm alone, and surrounded.

"And now, Lori's daughter, Ruth, will play one of Lori's favorite songs for us," says the funeral director, nodding toward me.

I make my robot-body get up and walk onto the dais. I don't look out into the crowd. My guitar is already set up next to a chair; I pick it up, hook the strap around my shoulder, and take a breath. Then I start to play.

It's an old pop ballad from the nineties, and I'm playing an instrumental arrangement—I'm not a singer—but everyone recognizes it. I can see people moving their lips to the unspoken words. In the arms of an angel. Mom used to sing it off-key every time it came on the radio. I remember her in the little trailer where we moved after she left my dad, crooning while she did the dishes. I remember rolling my eyes at Zahra as we breezed past her on the way to my room, the two of us laughing hysterically over her earnest, yearning face. I remember every part of that sun-drenched summer when I was fourteen, when my mom fluttered at the edge of my vision like a mildly irritating moth. When I ran free with Zahra, the two of us writing stories and roaming the woods, turning our jeans into cut-offs and eating mountains of candy.

It feels like forever ago, even though it was just a little over three years.

All I want to do is go back. That girl I was—she seems impossibly young, impossibly innocent. She takes so much for granted. She has no idea how much she stands to lose.

The song comes to an end. I sit still for a moment, cradling the guitar. My machine-body feels frozen, and I realize I'm not sure whether to get up and go back to my seat or not. Nobody moves.

My eyes light on the urn again. And now there are more memories to deal with: my mom, sipping from a Nalgene bottle on a high promontory in the Gorge. Below us stretches the river. Mountains bare their jagged teeth against the horizon. This is her favorite place, and she is peaceful.

I want to stop there, but I can't. My muscles seize up now, my fingers curling anxiously around the guitar's neck, because it happens again and again in my memory, and I can't stop it or change it, because it's done. The next moments come in choppy fragments. She takes a step. She's so close to me. If I'm fast enough I can put out my hand to stabilize her and stop it all from happening. But I'm not. I'm not. Her foot twists and the water bottle flies from her hand, out over the cliffside, and my eyes follow it as it spins around and around into the vertical drop. And then I look back at Mom. She's leaning backward over the empty air. Her eyes are so wide, so wild. And then she's gone.

———

I AM ONLY VAGUELY aware of time passing. I shake hands, hug classmates, talk to people who knew her. She was shy but warm, my mother, and the people around her were drawn to that. But it strikes me that there are no dear friends here. No one who knew Mom's stories and her tics and her jokes. We kept to ourselves the last few years, and these people all worked with her or knew her superficially. The thought hits me with a pang, and I think, *am I finally going to cry?* Am I finally going to feel something besides exhaustion?

Then it passes.

Three hours later, I'm back at the apartment. I kneel on the floor of my living room in front of three boxes (donate, throw away, keep), sorting through our piles of belongings. I've been holding a throw pillow for twenty minutes, trying to decide where to put it.

"How you doing in here?"

Ana Maria stands in the hallway, a box of half-used shampoo bottles in her arms from cleaning out the bathroom. She's a short, round woman, still in her funeral clothes. For once I can see the tattoos she usually covers up with her cheap work blazers: birds flying, flowers bursting into bloom. I usually feel like tattoos are supposed to make you look tough, but on Ana Maria they somehow look vulnerable, and the phrase *wearing your heart on your sleeve* keeps popping into my head.

"I'm fine." I shove the throw pillow into the donate box just so I don't have to look at it anymore. "Just a little distracted."

"Of course." She sets the box down and sits on the sofa,

watching me closely. "Maybe it's time for a break. Want to go get coffee? Or ice cream?"

"Thanks." I give her a weak smile. "I just want to get this done."

She's so shabby and so earnest, and I don't know why but some tiny part of me despises her for it. There is too much pain in the world to live like that. She'll get hurt, and it'll be her own fault. I want to tell her to toughen up. I want to hug her close and then shake her.

She picks a piece of fuzz off her skirt and idly rolls it between her fingers. "Are you nervous about seeing your dad again after so long?" she asks.

I look down at the pile of clothing on the floor—Mom's clothes. I know immediately I'll donate most of them, but I pick up a fuchsia cardigan and pretend to examine it so I don't have to meet Ana Maria's eyes.

"I guess, a little," I say. "I talked to him on the phone. He sounds . . . different. He's been sober for almost three years now, so that's good. But it's going to be weird to see him again."

We've barely spoken since the day Mom packed up our clothes and moved us out of the house at the end of eighth grade. He went to rehab not long after, and I guess it took, but Mom had had enough by then, and I guess I had, too. We talk on the phone a few times a year, and he always sends a gift card at Christmas. Last year I missed his wedding to Brandy, some woman he met in AA (and yeah, I had a good laugh about her name). "But I'm glad I get to go back to Anchorage," I add. "I miss it."

I glance up to see that familiar look of interest in her eyes. Everyone reacts like that when they hear I was born and raised in Anchorage. It's either, *oh wow, what was that like? Cold? Dark? Did you ride a dog sled to school? Did you see moose walking down the street? Are you an Eskimo?* (Yes/yes/no/yes/ that's actually a slur, and no, I'm obviously not Inupiaq.) But Ana Maria just nods.

"I've heard it's beautiful," she says. "I've always wanted to go."

That's the other reaction. People have seen footage of the cruises and the bus tours. Calving glaciers, frolicking otters, grizzlies catching salmon, jagged peaks. All of which is a part of it. But living there is different. Living there means shoveling snow and getting up in the dark to go to school and practicing regular earthquake drills. Still, I miss it. I miss the long summer days, the honey-colored light stretching into midnight. I miss the mountains across the east and the dark glitter of stars in the winter. I miss the inlet and the lagoon and the creeks and lakes and streams.

I miss Zahra.

"Mom didn't miss it at all," I say. I throw the sweater into the donate box. "She hated the dark and the snow. It made her depressed."

"I can understand that," Ana Maria says. "It's hard to imagine what that's like."

"It never bothered me too much." It's not totally true—but I do have some good memories, of curling up with a book and some hot chocolate, of watching the neighbor's Christmas lights make colorful patterns in the snow. Darkness is like that. It can make you tired and sad, or it can make the bright spots stick out even more.

"Well, it's going to be a big adjustment," Ana Maria says gently. "And . . . look, Ruthie, I'm not here to tell you how to feel, but . . . there are a lot of different ways to grieve. Some people cry and scream and suffer out loud. Some people . . . some people need a little bit of time, to process everything. And whatever you're going through, whatever you're feeling, it's okay. It's not wrong. Just make sure you listen to your heart and give yourself room to heal."

I look up at her, startled. I thought I was putting on a good show for her. But suddenly I realize Ana Maria isn't quite as oblivious as I thought. I feel seen, which is both scary and soothing. Is she saying it's okay that I'm numb? Okay that I'm feeling flat and robotic?

"Grief unfolds over time," she says, making an opening-book gesture with her hands. "It changes day by day. Today you might be going through the motions. Tomorrow it might all hit you, or the day after that. Just be kind to yourself, no matter what. Okay?"

I feel my lips start to tremble. And I realize, this is what I needed. Permission. Validation. It's okay to feel nothing. It's okay to feel tired.

"Okay," I whisper.

I glance at the urn where it rests on the kitchen island. I think of my mom that day in the Gorge. She loved hiking but she usually went alone. We'd grown apart over the past few years. I suppose a part of me resented her for moving us down here. But that day, I'd decided to go with her, on a whim. And I'm glad. Because the look on her face when I offered to come made it worth it. She'd been surprised, thrilled, her eyes lighting up. "Oh, Ruthie, I can't wait. It's a perfect day for it. Here, you can wear my boots."

Yes. I'm glad I went. Because even though it's not the goodbye I would've wanted, it's the closest I have.

I look back at Ana Maria.

"Would you mind if I finished up on my own?" I say. "It's almost done. I just want a little time alone with her things." I tug at the end of my braid, twisting it around my fist. Ana Maria's gaze softens.

"Are you sure?" When I nod, she looks around the living room. "Well, the bathroom is done, and the bedrooms are mostly empty, I think. This is the last of it. Arc of Multnomah County will be out tomorrow morning to pick up whatever you don't want. Are you sure there's nothing else I can do to help?"

"I'm sure. I'm just going to order pizza for dinner, get through this last little bit."

She chews her lip, then nods slowly. "Sure," she says. "If you need me, you can text me."

"Of course."

I hold back as she gathers her bag and jacket, half afraid she'll change her mind. But then she's gone, and I'm finally, blissfully, alone.

I turn back to the almost-empty apartment. Really all I

9

want to do is curl up in the pile of my mother's clothes and rest. Instead, I start to gather up armfuls of her things. Her work clothes, her jeans, her exercise gear. The one snug blue cocktail dress she never had a chance to wear anywhere. I shove them all into donate. The box isn't big enough but I don't care. I shove shirts and skirts and slacks on top until it looks like some kind of clothing volcano, exploding in color.

I pick up the urn and again think how strange, how unlikely, that this is the entirety of her body, made into a small, portable object. It doesn't feel like her. It feels like a thing—one more thing that I have to pack.

Our balcony looks out over a narrow strip of landscaping to a busy street beyond. My downstairs neighbor isn't home, which is good; I don't want them to freak out about what I'm going to do next.

The cremains smell strangely earthy. The pieces are bigger than I expected, but they crumble easily in my hand, into a fine powdery ash. I hold out a handful and the breeze catches most of it, though some rains down on the hedges below. I'm not sure if human remains are good for the soil, the way some kinds of ash are—but I like to imagine that they are. That she'll make the trees grow big and strong, that they'll house baby birds and squirrels. I honestly don't know if Mom would approve of this or not. We didn't understand each other. But I do know she wouldn't want to be stuck in a vase.

The urn is light and empty, and I feel that way, too. I feel more focused, more centered. I go back inside and put it into the throw away box. Then I pull out my phone and pull up Zahra's number.

Arriving in Anchorage this Sunday, I type. Can't wait to see you.

I hit send.

I'm ready to go home.

CHAPTER TWO

I<small>T'S NEARLY ELEVEN IN</small> the morning when my plane lands in Anchorage. I barely slept last night, and I was too nervous to sleep on the flight, so I have that stretched-thin, almost hallucinatory sensation you get from exhaustion when I step into the terminal. Everything is too bright, too loud, too strange, after the hushed darkness of the plane.

I adjust the grip on my guitar case and follow the rest of the crowd toward baggage. Before I leave the secure area I stop in one of the restrooms to brush my teeth. I barely recognize myself in the mirror—this girl with her long, serious face and dull skin, the color of old lace unraveling. Or maybe that's just the cruel fluorescent glare of an airport bathroom. I comb my hair and wipe smudges off my glasses and splash water on my cheeks. It's the best I can do. Will Dad even know me? What did I look like three years ago? Shorter, with more pimples, with chubbier cheeks. But he hardly ever looked at me that last year Mom and I were with him—so maybe he doesn't even remember that much.

I've stalled as long as I can. I have to leave sometime—though for a moment I imagine living in the terminals, spreading my coat in the darkened corners to sleep, eating from vending machines and Cinnabon. Riding the moving walkways back and forth all day. The thought makes me smile, and the face in the mirror suddenly gentles and becomes me again. I pick up my guitar case and my backpack and head out past security.

My eyes twitch back and forth over the waiting crowd. I want to see him before he sees me. I'm not sure why—it's just that the idea of him watching me as I approach, being able to size me up before I can do the same to him, makes me anxious.

Then I think I see him, and I have to stop and blink a few times to make sure. Because he's the same, and he's different.

The last time I saw him was the end of middle school, when Mom moved us out. And he'd been in bad shape—drunk by the time I got home from school, brooding in his armchair and flipping through channels on the TV. He'd always been a drinker, but it got much worse after he was laid off. He'd started to look somehow both flabby and sunken, and his skin had been raw and red all the time.

The man just beyond security looks like that father, but from an alternate dimension, one where he'd never collapsed under the weight of his own addiction. He's tall and broad shouldered, with just a little flab at his waist, and while his cheeks are still ruddy, it looks more like a healthy flush than a drinker's bad skin. He's clean-shaven and his button-down shirt is freshly pressed.

His eyes meet mine, and neither one of us moves for a second. Then he waves at me, a nervous smile twitching across his lips. I can't pretend I didn't see him there. I walk toward him, my mouth dry as sand.

"Your hair's gotten so long, I almost didn't recognize you," he says as I approach. He looks down at me like I'm a puzzle he can't figure out how to put together.

"It's always been long," I say abruptly. When I see his face I realize it sounds like an accusation, so I add, "But I used to keep it in a ponytail."

He nods. Then, before I can say anything else, he pulls me into a hug. I'm still holding my guitar case, and it knocks awkwardly against his leg, but he doesn't let go.

"I'm so sorry about your mom," he says into my ear. "We ended things badly and I never had a chance to make things right. But she was a special woman, and I'm so sad that you've lost her."

I'm pressed against his shoulder so I can't speak, which is just as well, because I don't know what I'd say. Make things right? How would he make things right? Travel through time? But suddenly he's wiping tears from his eyes, and I don't know what to do. I'm disoriented, and tired, and I've never seen my dad cry before. I look down at my feet.

He straightens his back and takes a deep breath. "Sorry. It just brings up so many memories. So many regrets."

"Tell me about it," I mumble. The vision of Mom's foot, slipping a bare half inch on that mossy stone, hovers at the edge of my consciousness; the image of her eyes, wide and wondering, as she tilts backward . . . but I shake my head and it clears.

"We should get your luggage," Dad says. He leans down to take my guitar case from me, but I pull it away. He doesn't say anything, just turns and leads me down the escalator to the carousels.

We stand close to each other in the crowd around the conveyer belt as floral old-lady-tourist suitcases make the rounds next to duct-taped fishermen's coolers and canvas military duffels. I can feel Dad next to me, wanting to say something, so I keep my eyes determinedly on the bags until I see mine. I know I will have to figure out how to talk to him sooner or later, but right now it all seems so fraught. I just want to feel my feet on the ground for a few minutes first.

On our way out, we pass one of the airport's taxidermied polar bears, snarling on its hind legs. A cluster of hipster tourists gather around it, taking selfies. I remember seeing the bear as a little kid—along with the musk ox and the trumpeter swans and the beaver in different displays around the airport—and feeling like it was a fluffy, friendly presence, the way you think of a teddy bear. Now, though. Now I can only see it as a trophy. It's a wild thing that was killed and put under glass, transformed into a curiosity. It breaks my heart.

He loads my stuff into a beat-up old Honda—that, at least, looks as shabby as I expected. The radio is set to a Christian rock station and it's not long before the yearning power ballads grate on my nerves. Since when does my dad listen to stuff like this? Since he started recovery, I guess. I wonder what else I don't know about him.

The drive is just as surreal as everything else. I'm so tired the world vaguely sparkles, with little vision tracers popping in the corners of my eyes. This is the place I've thought of as home all my life—but I haven't seen it for three years. It's like having a dream where you're walking through a building you know well, but the layout is just a little bit off, or there's a room you never noticed before. I look out the window and tick off the things that are the same and the things that are new. The old salon Mom took me to—still there. But the bakery where we used to get croissants after? Gone, replaced with a CrossFit. The trees look small and ragged compared with the ones in Oregon; the lots we pass are choked with weeds, and I notice a lot of shuttered businesses. The sky is low and gray. Mid-September weather.

I sneak a look at my phone. Zahra still hasn't replied. My heart gives a little twist of anxiety. Our contact's been erratic for the past few years—we text and email every so often, but she's not great at staying in touch. She doesn't really do social media, either, so I can't keep up with her that way. It's hard to know what her life's been like. But I was sure the news that I was coming home would get a reaction.

My dad's voice interrupts my thoughts.

"So, your stepmom and Ingrid are at the house waiting to meet you," he says, clearing his throat. "They're real excited."

The house. Not "home." I've never been to my dad's new place; he sold my childhood home after the divorce. But I know he and Brandy bought a place together, not far from the woods where Zahra and I used to hang out.

"Okay," I say. Then I realize he's probably waiting for something more. "I'm looking forward to it."

It is the furthest thing from the truth. I have never been good at getting to know people. Sometimes I just want to hide, or withdraw, rather than risk the awkwardness. Dr. Karadzhova, the psychiatrist mom found for me, called it social anxiety, and he was probably right, I guess. He always told me I just had to realize how little other people actually cared about me and I wouldn't worry anymore, which is a very Eastern European way to comfort someone.

But now I have an insta-family, and I'll have to figure out how to deal with them. With Brandy, and her daughter, Ingrid. All I know about them is that Brandy is a recovering drug addict, and Ingrid is my age, two months into her senior year at Merrill High.

We pull up to the rear of a dark blue house surrounded by chain link. Brandy and Ingrid are in the yard, sitting at a beat-up picnic table and watching for us, and I feel a tightening in my shoulders. I stay in the front seat while my dad grabs the suitcases from the back. It looks like they've got a brunch spread on the table, which is sweet, but all I want to do is go to sleep. Now there will be cantaloupe *and* small talk to deal with, and I just don't know if I have the strength. But when Ingrid jogs over to beam at me through the car window, I open the door and let myself out.

"You're here!" She comes in for a hug without hesitation, ignoring or not noticing the tension in my body as she wraps her arms around me. I've never been much of a hugger. "I'm so glad I finally get to meet you."

She's a plump, pink girl, neatly dressed in a fluffy white sweater and a yellow skirt. Dark blonde hair hangs in a straight line on either side of a bland, clean-scrubbed face. If anyone ever looked like an Ingrid, it's this girl.

"Um. I'm Ruth," I say. Then I feel stupid, because she obviously knows who I am.

Her smile just gets wider. "'And Ruth said, entreat me not to leave thee, or to return from following after thee, for whither thou goest, I will go, and where thou lodgest, I will lodge; thy people shall be my people, and thy God my God.'"

I stare at her.

"It's from the Book of Ruth," she says. "In the Bible. One of my favorite sections. It's all about loyalty and friendship. Women taking care of other women. It's very empowering."

"Oh," is all I can think to say. I'm way too tired to try to deal with someone who has a favorite section of the Bible.

"Hi, sweetheart." This is Brandy. She looks like a more weather-worn Ingrid—or, I guess, Ingrid looks like a less weather-worn her. She's come around the other side of the car, and I feel a little like I've been caught in some military maneuver, a pincer snare or something. Another hug: Brandy's body

18

is bonier than Ingrid's, and there's a warm, sweet smell to her, like bread. "Welcome home."

My dad comes out from behind the car, dragging both of my suitcases. He hands me the keys.

"It's yours now," he says. "Well, yours and Ingrid's. You guys will have to share. But she doesn't have her license yet."

"I failed the parallel parking test," she says cheerfully. "It's okay, I don't mind riding shotgun. I like playing with the radio."

I hope she has better taste in music than my dad, but it doesn't seem likely.

"Thanks," I say, turning to Dad. The keys feel foreign and clumsy in my hand. I look again at the little car with new eyes. I've never had one of my own—in Portland I had to ask to borrow Mom's. The Honda's not much to look at, but it's mine. Well, ours.

"You're welcome." It sounds almost formal, but when I look at him he's smiling. "You'll need to be able to get around. It's on you girls to keep gas in the tank, though."

"Hungry?" Brandy asks. "Or do you just want to get a little sleep? You must be wiped out."

"I'm pretty tired," I say. "But you went to the trouble . . ." I gesture toward the table.

She shrugs. "It's nothing that won't keep until later. Ingrid, why don't you show her to her room? Rick and I can unload the car and you can go downstairs to rest."

Ingrid doesn't even wait for me to reply. She grabs my backpack and slings it over one shoulder. "Come on, Ruthie, you're downstairs with me."

"Are we sharing a room, then?" I try to keep the trepidation out of my voice. She laughs.

"Just a bathroom. We've both got our own rooms on either side of that." She opens the door onto a small landing and points up the stairs. "Mom and Rick sleep up there," she says. "We sleep in the semi-basement but it's kind of nice because we have privacy."

We descend into a big open room with windows set high in the walls, looking out on the flower beds at ground level. There's a TV and a dumpy old sofa on one side; the washer and dryer rumble softly on the other. A pool table takes up the middle of the room, serving the function pool tables always serve in rec rooms: a folding station for clean laundry and a surface on which to stack random boxes. A dark hall leads down to our rooms.

"Rick had me decorate your room," Ingrid says, sounding suddenly shy. "I mean, obviously you can change whatever you want now that you're here, but I wanted you to feel welcome." She pushes open the door to reveal walls painted with pink glitter. The curtain and bedspread are white with black stripes. My name decorates the wall over my bed in black vinyl decals. There's a gallery of framed typography art on another wall— LOVE and DREAM and WISH spelled out in gold-leaf script.

"Wow," is all I can say. I've always hated random word art. It feels like a command. And I wonder how hurt she'll be if I paint the walls right away. They remind me of Pepto-Bismol, and it leaves a nauseated, chalky feeling in my throat.

But she's beaming with pride. "I'm glad you like it!" She

bustles over to the bed and actually starts turning down the sheets.

Now that I'm here, in my room, all the adrenaline that's been keeping me going has dried up, and I sway a little, waiting for her to go. It seems to take forever. She smooths my sheets—which I see now are pale pink and threaded through with gold—and fluffs my pillow. I close my eyes and almost immediately see the deep grayish dark that usually means I'm falling asleep.

Finally, she straightens up again. Her bright blue eyes meet mine.

"I've always wanted a sister," she says.

If I can just say something banal and noncommittal like, "Me too," or "I'm glad I'm here" she will leave and I can go to sleep. But all possible words stick in my throat. The moment drags out—it's maybe ten seconds of silence but it's time for me to simultaneously fret over hurting her feelings, resent her for saying such a weird thing, and then recursively wonder if it's not weird at all and if I'm the weird one, failing to handle normal human social cues.

Social anxiety is nothing if not brisk and efficient.

But she finally just smiles a little. "Anyway. Rest well, okay?"

And then she leaves.

Finally. I pull off my jeans and slide down between the sheets. The room swirls around me a little. Quick snaps of the last few days' events flash across my vision. No—I don't want to see it.

My gaze falls again on the type art. HOPE, says one of them, in flourishing cursive.

"Fuck off," I mumble out loud. "You can't tell me what to do."

Then I turn my face into the pillow and slip away from the world.

CHAPTER THREE

WHEN I WAKE UP it takes me a minute to remember where I am. Then I see the pink walls, my bags on the floor, the neat row of pansies outside my window. My father's house.

My phone says I've been asleep for almost four hours. It also shows that Zahra hasn't texted me back yet. I open my suitcase, pull out a change of clothes. The air is cold; I pull my jacket on over my sweater.

No one's in the downstairs rec room. I'm not sure if they're all upstairs or if they've gone out, but I'm grateful. I'm not ready to see anyone yet. I sneak up the stairs and through the back door.

Outside the sky seems big and flat. The space around me is so jarringly different from that in Portland—after two years surrounded by towering trees I feel a little exposed by Anchorage's smaller ones. But my heart does a little heel-kick throb at the sight of the mountains cradling around the edge of the sky.

My dad's house is on a quiet lane just a few blocks from Russian Jack Springs Park, the sprawling woods where I used to wander with Zahra. I step around a bollard with its red reflector, onto a trail carpeted with dead leaves. There's a rich smell of rot and rain in the air.

Just a few feet down the trail the woods close in around me. I can still hear the distant sound of traffic—but there are parts of the park where it feels like you could be hundreds of miles away. At the height of summer the hike-and-bike trails get crowded, but by autumn they're quiet. There's a low twitter of birdsong, a far-off shout from the neighborhood kids at the elementary school playground, but not much else to tether me to the world. I set off along the rising and falling hills.

Every step takes me closer to a memory. Walking here with Zahra. Talking about the books we loved—mostly fantasy books, sword and sorcery and escape—or, later, writing our own. There was something almost haunted about those woods. The trees, the shadows, the long beams of sun working through at eleven or twelve at night in the summer—they shimmered with something close enough to magic.

Our novel took place in a world we called "The Precipice." In it, the sun was always perched on the edge of the sky, streaking gold and red, like our own midnight sun. A young witch known only as the Starmaiden and a warrior named Lyr from a clan of Amazonian women journeyed together to stop an evil force called the Elodea—we'd gotten the name from an invasive plant—from choking the life out of their world.

A lot of it was derivative. No surprise, we were fourteen

and fangirls and it was our first attempt at writing. There were hints of Middle-earth, of Garth Nix's Abhorsen books, and Tamora Pierce's Song of the Lioness. But it felt so powerful to make something of our own. To let our alter egos struggle and triumph. There were moments it felt more real than anything else in my life.

I can still hear Zahra's voice—not her normal speaking voice, but her written voice, the particular rhythm and stress of it. I wonder if it's always the case that writing with someone makes you close, that their voice becomes one of the voices in your head forever after. Some of her sentences have lodged in my mind and become a kind of music to me over the years. *The Starmaiden felt the power of the heavens flow from her fingers.* Or: *In the misty morning, the Dark-Dancers came up from the depths of the pond.* She liked alliteration, liked smashing two words she liked together into a new one. She liked for things to be beautiful and for good to prevail.

I still look at our old notebooks sometimes. I tried to keep writing the story when I moved to Portland, but without Zahra it just didn't work. I was the discipline—I kept the plot moving, I kept us diligently working every day—but she was the vision. She was the one who breathed magic into the book—into my life.

Almost without thinking about it, I step off the paved portion of the trail, toward a barely visible break in the bushes. The trail cuts up a steep hill. Sticker bushes and yarrow crowd around my shins. I keep my eyes peeled for devil's club, the brutally spiny shrub that grows thick out here. And now I'm on the other side of the crest, heading down into a small valley cut through by a stream. I cross an old, disused gravel road, and the woods open up to reveal the playground.

It's long abandoned. Sometime in the last thirty years the city rerouted the paths and closed off this little road to the public. They partially disassembled the equipment, but they didn't bother taking it all out of here—I guess it must have been too expensive to bother with. Zahra used to call it "Pedo Park" because the idea of a playground surrounded entirely by trees, set back from the road, seemed so dangerous.

Now I take a few hesitant steps into the clearing and look around. It's almost entirely as we left it. The merry-go-round sits cockeyed against its base, the nuts and bolts removed. Three spring-loaded animal rockers sit on their sides where they were wrenched from the ground, and a huge truck tire filled with sand smells of rotten rubber and faded urine.

There's a mostly intact play structure with a few platforms and a slide down one side. A tattered, weather-beaten sheet flutters where it's hung. It's that sheet that makes my heart squeeze. I remember it: we'd put it up for shade, an old flannel flat sheet with Ninja Turtles printed across. We used to sit side by side under it while we wrote. Now it's torn and frayed, trembling in the breeze.

I know, then, that no one's been here since I left it, three years back.

The quiet feels breathless around me. I look around and see more evidence of our existence. Over that summer different treasures, found or stolen, had accumulated out here. Mason jars of colored sand or bowls of pretty stones— now overturned and cracked from three years of snow. A makeshift vanity under the ancient slide, a magnetized locker mirror clinging to the metal. A coffee tin full of now-dried-up nail polish and lipstick. A stack of pillaged lumber we were going to use to make a bookshelf. We never did finish it.

Sharpie scrawls cover the wood and metal equipment: drawings of flowering vines, of butterflies, of birds. Nothing complex; we'd never been good artists. But there, where I remember it, I see Zahra's loopy faux calligraphy across the frame: THE PRECIPICE. The names of our protagonists— Starmaiden and Lyr—are etched to either side.

I stand for a moment longer, and then I head back toward the main path and continue my hike.

On the other side of the park from my father's current house is a busy commercial road. On the other side of that is Walker Court—the trailer park where my mom moved us both the February of my eighth-grade year.

It hasn't changed much. When I first moved there I was freaked out—Mom accused me of snobbery, which was probably a little bit right. We'd never been rich, but a trailer park? But Walker Court is like any other blue-collar neighborhood: a mixed bag. A place where lots of different kinds of people live. East Anchorage is the most diverse part of the city, and the families in the trailer park are white and black, Hmong and Samoan, Latino and Laotian. There are neat little yards and potted flowers; there are muddy driveways and cars on blocks. There are noisy, boisterous houses full of noisy, boisterous kids. There are meth-heads and alcoholics and junkies. There are people with regular jobs who like to grill on the weekends.

I stand outside Zahra's trailer for a few minutes, my fingers fidgeting against one another. It suddenly occurs to me that her family could have moved. The yard is choked with weeds, and the teal-and-white paint job is peeling away. I don't remember the place being so run down.

But then I see their two enormous shaggy mutts, Deshka and Yukon, ranging across the yard, wrestling over a Kong toy, and I know they're still here.

I can't keep the grin off my face as I jog up the steps to the door. Even with everything that's happened, even with my mom's death, I'm excited. I've played this moment in my head for three years. I knock at the door, and then clasp my hands together, waiting.

Footsteps behind the door. A man's voice shouts something; someone responds from deeper inside. Then the door swings open.

It's Zahra's dad—Mr. Gaines, though he always told me to call him Ron. He looks down at me blankly for just a moment before his face flashes into the wide, easy grin I remember.

"Ruthie Hayden! What the hell are you doing here?" It'd be weird to hear any other parent I know say that—but from Mr. Gaines, it's just a jovial welcome. Zahra's parents are what my mom used to call "free spirited." Her dad, a stocky black man with long, neat locks, paints houses under the table. Her mom, a sweetly plump white woman, seems to cobble together a bunch of hobbies that may or may not make money—she sews stuffed toys and beads earrings, puts together astrological star charts and cans pickles. She sets up booths at the fair and the farmer's markets every year. They're a raucous, odd, funny family, loud when they laugh and when they fight. Zahra talked to them like they were friends or irritating roommates, nagging at them to clean up after themselves and pay the bills on time even when she was a kid.

"Hi, Ron." I let him hug me, getting a pleasant whiff of his musky aftershave.

"Come in, kiddo, come in." He opens the door wide. "Charity, you'll never guess who's here."

The living room is much as I remember. A cotton tapestry with a celestial pattern hangs on one wall; the TV chatters softly, turned on for noise and then forgotten. A lanky teenage boy is draped over the sofa, staring at his phone; it takes me a moment to recognize Zahra's little brother, Malik.

"Wow," I say. "Malik, you've grown." I realize immediately that I sound like a grandma. It's a stupid thing to say. But he doesn't even look up. I feel a little pang of disappointment—when he was younger, he used to laugh and banter with me. Now he just gives a sullen little nod.

Charity, Zahra's mom, comes to the door of the kitchen, wiping her hands on a dishtowel. Her eyes widen a little. "Ruthie?"

"Hi." I give a shy little wave. "It's good to see you."

She comes in and hugs me, too. "What are you doing here? Are you visiting your dad?"

"No, I . . . I'm back." I hesitate. "My mom passed away last week."

"Passed away" doesn't feel right; "passed away" describes a quiet death, a gentle release after a long decline. For a moment the image of my mother tipping into the chasm comes back to me. I blink it away. Charity looks stunned. She stares at me for another second, then hugs me again.

"Oh, baby, I'm so sorry. That's . . . awful. I never knew your mama well but she seemed like such a nice lady."

"Yeah," I whisper into her shoulder. "Thank you."

"So you living with your dad now?" Ron gives a little frown. I realize they probably remember some of the stories about him. I nod.

"Yeah. But he's sober. He's doing good." I lick my lips. "Anyway, I'm just happy to be home."

"Come on in, sit down." Charity leads me into the kitchen, where the big oval table takes up most of the room. "Can I make you some tea? I've got rose hip, peppermint, chaga . . ."

"No, thank you, I'm okay." I glance around. "I was hoping to catch Zahra. Is she home?"

Ron and Charity exchange glances. There's a moment of tension that passes so quickly I'm not sure if I imagined it.

"No," Charity says. I can't read the tone. "She's been gone all weekend."

"I think she's camping with her friends," Ron says. Charity shakes her head.

"I told you, her tent's still in the shed," she says. She gives me a tense smile. "She didn't tell us where she was off to. She's probably off with her boyfriend."

Boyfriend. She has a boyfriend. It's not a big deal, of course, but it annoys me that I didn't know.

"She didn't tell you where she was going?" I ask.

Charity purses her lips, but Ron just gives a little shrug. "She's old enough to make her decisions," he says.

I nod. Even at thirteen her parents gave her a lot of freedom. She didn't have to check in every few hours the way I did. They didn't pay attention to what she read or watched; I had to borrow all George R. R. Martin's books from her and hide them because my mom thought they were too "sexy." So it's not such a surprise that her parents don't know where Zahra is. Still, it feels like there's something they're not telling me.

"Um . . . how's she been?" I ask, glancing from one of them to the other.

Another little pause. Then Charity smiles. "Oh, you know. Typical moody teenager." Her tone is light but I can feel something fraught beneath it. I glance at Ron.

His eyes are sad, but he gives a little shrug. "She's good. Keeps busy with school and her friends and all that. Always got something going on."

I nod. I guess I get that. In Portland there were full days when I didn't see my mom, between school and music rehearsals. But I'd never been as close to my mom as Zahra had been to her parents. And "typical moody teenager"? That had never been Zahra's thing. If anything she'd always been mellow, easy to talk to.

"Hey, do you mind if I leave her a note?" I ask. "I've been texting her but it's been a while. She might not have my number anymore."

"Of course." Charity nods toward the hallway. "You remember where her room is?"

I stand up. "You don't think she'll mind?"

"Nah, go ahead," Ron says. He hesitates, then he pats me on the shoulder. "Glad you're back, Ruthie, even under the circumstances. Things haven't been the same without you."

Zahra's room is at the very end of a cramped hall. For a moment I think it must be the wrong room. Nothing about it feels familiar. I freeze a few steps in, feeling like I'm somewhere I shouldn't be.

Three years ago this room looked like an extension of Zahra. The walls were dark gray, with white twinkle lights tacked around the edges. She'd made an impromptu canopy with some spare pink tulle from one of her mom's crafting projects. She'd drawn flowering vines all over one wall with colored chalk, and scrawled across another, in wide looping letters, a quote from *The Hobbit*: "Even dragons have their ending." Zahra was the only person I'd ever met who was reflexively creative—she didn't spend a lot of time planning or thinking or analyzing; she just made things, because the desire took her. I'd come over to her place and find her cutting up a T-shirt into a strappy halter, or gluing glitter to a plastic barrette. I always asked where she got the idea, and she'd just shrug. "Dunno," she'd say. "I was just messing around."

Now, though, there's no sign of that Zahra. No twinkle lights, no tulle, no uncapped paint pen drying out on the desk next to a half-drawn sign. The room is small and tidy, the bedspread smooth across the mattress. A utilitarian lamp sits next to the bed; the one small window is covered with blue-and-white striped curtains. There are no stuffed animals, no empty cups or art supplies or scented candles.

But weirdest of all, there are no books.

The last time I'd been in this room, every surface had been stacked high with books. Old crusty paperbacks she'd inherited from her parents, cheap book-fair copies of chapter books, water-damaged picture books. It was a riotous, haphazard collection. For some reason she had three copies of *A Light in the Attic* but had to borrow my edition of *Where the Sidewalk Ends*. She had the second, fourth, and fifth Harry Potter books but was missing the rest; she had a stack of true crime books and a copy of *Alaskan Bear Tales*, filled to the brim with terrifying stories of people being mauled to death, and an ancient stack of Sweet Valley High books from her mom's own childhood. She read like it was breathing, like she had to do it to live. She read everything she touched, without pausing to consider if it was relevant to her interests or not.

Now, the only books I see are a stack of textbooks on her desk. *U.S. Government, Fundamentals of Physics, Intro to*

Psychology. For a few heartbeats I stand in the middle of the room, feeling almost dizzy.

Maybe she got an e-reader, I think. *Maybe she threw all the books out*. But this room feels like a stranger's room.

The one personal touch is the French bulletin board, photographs laced under the straps. I step close to it and check out the pictures. They're all candid, but well composed, obviously taken with a good camera and developed with care. They're all of people I don't know—a few kids laughing at something in the hall at school, several action shots of snowboarders. A girl with a beanie pulled down over her red hair, smirking playfully. A boy with a short black Mohawk, sitting on a dock and staring moodily out over a lake. I try not to be hurt that there's not one of me.

I take a deep breath and pull a notepad from my purse.

STARMAIDEN—

I'M HOME FROM THE GREAT BEYOND! GIMME A CALL WHEN YOU CAN, CAN'T WAIT TO SEE YOU.

<3

LYR

I think about crumpling it up for a moment and starting again, without using our old fictional alter egos. She might think it's cheesy, embarrassing, at this point. The girl who lives in this impersonal room surely would. But instead, I leave it on her desk. Maybe she'll see it as self-deprecating, playful.

Or maybe, I think, barely daring to hope for it. *Maybe it'll remind her who she really is.*

CHAPTER FOUR

"And Lord, we ask that this meal provide sustenance to our bodies and give us strength to enact your will."

It's the next morning. My first day of school. Dad and Brandy got up early and put together an enormous breakfast. Eggs, bacon, pancakes, fruit—the works. Which would be really sweet of them, if they'd just let us eat it.

"We ask that you give your blessing to our family, and let these two young women flourish under your guidance," he goes on. "Give them the wisdom and fortitude to make good choices, and the humility to follow your teachings."

Darkness pushes in at the windows. I'd forgotten how heavy an Alaskan morning could feel, how smothering the sky gets as the days shorten. Waking up on those cold black days feels like a fight against your own body. Like a kind of violence, even, forcing yourself out of the warmth of bed and dream. Mom used to play music to wake me up. She'd start with something gentle—Chopin, maybe—but if I stayed in bed too long she'd blast the opening number to *Oklahoma!*, which never failed to send me tumbling out of bed, scurrying to turn it off in irritation.

The thought makes me close my eyes tightly over my clasped fingers.

"Lord, we ask that you give us strength against temptation." His voice doesn't waver, but I can hear a subtle shift in it. A sharp, metallic note. "Thank you for another day of sobriety."

I sneak a glance around the table. Dad never used to be religious, but I guess it's part of what's helped him stay clean. I know he, Brandy, and Ingrid go to Victory Evangelical, the biggest fundamentalist congregation in Anchorage. I'm personally not a big fan. Victory's pastor, Dale Worthen, is old-school fire and brimstone. They used to go out and protest every pride parade, every ballot initiative that would protect LGBTQIA rights. Mom hated the guy—I still remember her gearing up for a counter protest, painting a sign that said GOD IS LOVE in rainbow colors.

"In Jesus's name," Dad says, "amen."

"Amen," Ingrid and Brandy say in unison. I say it, too, a half second too late.

Silence lingers over the table for a moment. Then Dad gives an awkward little smile. "Well, let's eat, everyone. Before it gets cold." He picks up a platter of hash browns and starts to serve himself. Brandy and Ingrid take that as their cue to dig in, too.

I don't know if it's the darkness, or the prayer's strange

urgency, but I'm not very hungry. I poke listlessly at a pancake, then give up and pour myself a cup of coffee.

"Did you sleep okay, Ruthie?" Brandy asks, taking a bite of hash browns. "It sounded like you were up pretty late."

"Oh, I . . . I'm sorry if I bothered you," I say. "Just nerves, I guess." This morning I woke up in yesterday's clothes, my well-thumbed copy of *The Hobbit* splayed on the bed next to me. My go-to book for new beginnings. I always go back to see if Bilbo will have the courage to set foot out his door and on that trail once again.

"No, no, you didn't bother me." She has a smile that borders on fragile, a tremulous little curve of the lips. "I just want you to know you can always come upstairs and hang out if you want. I'm a night owl, too."

"Chronic insomniac, more like," Dad says.

"Well, either way, I make good hot chocolate," Brandy says. "And I like company."

Ingrid's got my schedule in one hand as she pours syrup over her plate. "Hey, we have economics together!" She sounds delighted. "With Mr. Thatcher. He's really nice."

"Oh," I say. "Good, yeah." I take a sip of the coffee; it's burnt and bitter. I lean across the table for the sugar bowl. I'm not sure how I feel about sharing anything with Ingrid. A class. A car. A bathroom. I don't go from zero to besties at the best of times, and now I have a roommate there's no way to dodge.

"And you're in yearbook?" she says. "I've heard that's fun."

"Actually," I say, setting down my mug, "I'm going to drop that." Dad was the one who signed me up for classes—which he did without knowing anything about my academic history. I'm in a solo and ensemble class in the music department, which is fine, and economics is required. But he also put me in regular biology and English, so I'll need to talk to a counselor sometime today so I can switch to AP. For some reason he put me in intro to Russian, so I'll have to change that to French IV. And then, with one elective left, he stuck me in yearbook, which just goes to show how little he actually knows about me.

"That's too bad," Dad says, frowning. "You used to love to write. I remember you were always filling up those little journals . . ."

My hand squeezes convulsively on the handle of my mug, sloshing coffee over the side. "That's not the kind of thing I write," I say. My voice comes out strangely shrill. I look up to see Dad's face go pink and startled.

I take a deep breath and say, more calmly, "Yearbook's just not my scene. It's all . . . fluff pieces about popular kids."

He looks confused. "I just . . . I thought it'd be a good way to meet people, since you've been gone so long."

"I already *have* friends, Dad. But thanks." I fight to keep the venom from my voice, but my mouth feels tight with anger. Little journals. Could he have been more condescending?

He doesn't even know what I wrote in those notebooks. He doesn't know anything about me.

IN THE CAR, INGRID sets the radio to a pop station and starts immediately singing along. It's a relief. Maybe we'll make it the ten minutes to campus without talking. In the middle of the song, though, she turns the radio off with a snap.

"It's not my business," she says. "But your dad's been really good to us."

She's looking out the window. We're driving down a commercial strip, lined with car washes and fast food joints. Her hair hangs in a neat, straight line, hiding her profile.

"I mean, I get it. My mom was a meth-head for, like, half my life. There's a lot I'm still trying to forgive her for. I'm not trying to say you have to let everything he did wrong go. I just . . . I guess I just want you to know how hard he's worked to change. I hope you can give him a chance."

I realize I'm squeezing the steering wheel in both hands and force myself to lighten my grip.

Easy for Ingrid to tell me my dad's a "good guy." She wasn't there for the screaming matches between him and my mom. She wasn't there the day he drove over my bike and then swore at *me* for having the nerve to be upset about it. She wasn't there for the long sullen silences after, when he disappeared into a guilty fog of vodka.

And hearing about what a great guy he's been to some other family? Not exactly the most comforting thing in the world. Actually, it pisses me off. Because why was I the last to get the benefit of this new and improved Dad?

We're at the turn to the school. I take a deep breath, and even though there's only a few moments left of the drive, I turn the radio back up.

Inside, we're swept into the crowd. Red-and-black laminate floors stretch down the hallway like a checkerboard. The harsh, bright odor of chlorine hovers around the entrance, near the pool, and then fades as you go up the stairs, absorbed into the swirling currents of BO and cheap body spray.

I've been dreading this part. I'm the new student, almost a month into senior year. Almost everyone will have a foot out the door already, thinking ahead to graduation and college. I recognize a few faces in the crowd—at least, I think I do—but it's been a long time, and I didn't really have any close friends in middle school. Back then I had a hard time talking to other kids—that was when things at home were really falling apart, and it took all my strength to keep up a normal front. I didn't have a lot of extra energy to make small talk about Miley's dance moves or whatever. I doubt anyone will remember me.

At least I have Zahra. I hope. All the photos on her wall left me uneasy. What if there's no room for me in her life anymore? What if she's changed in ways I can't even imagine?

"You want some help finding your locker?" Ingrid asks, half-shouting to be heard over the crowd. Her sleek blonde head disappears for a second as a hulking boy in a letterman jacket passes between us, then reemerges a moment later.

"Uh, that's okay. I can find it," I say. "I'll see you fourth period."

She looks like she wants to say something else, but then just gives a little wave and heads down a side hall. The English hall, I think. I spent last night staring at a map of the school, trying to memorize where my rooms are. I don't want to look like a lost tourist on my first day.

I've only been to Merrill High once before, when Zahra and I came together to register for classes and get our student IDs. We hadn't been in school together before—I'd gone to Northern Lights Middle School, and the trailer park was zoned for Mountain View—but we'd both go to Merrill, and I was excited about that. Excited to, for once, have classes with a close friend.

It'd come as a shock when Mom announced that we'd be moving to Portland to "make a fresh start" just a few days after that.

The hall is busy and echoing, kids jostling each other and laughing loudly. I hear snatches of different languages—Merrill High is one of the most diverse high schools in the country, and I recognize fragments of Spanish, Tagalog, and what I think must be Hmong.

I shake my head to clear it, and find my locker. I stand there for a moment, staring into its soothingly empty metal interior, before I sling my backpack off and start to unpack.

I don't know what it is that gets my attention—an oddly pointed silence to my left, maybe, or just an odd tingle on the back of my neck. I pause in the middle of putting my lunch on the top shelf, looking around. And there he is—a boy, standing a few lockers down from mine. His eyes track my every move with a strange intensity. Something about it leaves my cheeks burning.

I swallow hard, then dart a glance at him, trying to see if I know him. He's parchment pale, his jaw lined with dark stubble. Skinny. Sharp featured. I busy myself hanging up my coat, organizing the few scanty things in my locker, but eventually I have to look up again—and he's still there. His pupils flare as I turn to look at him.

"Hi," I say.

He recoils then, as if I've slapped him. Then, before I can say anything else, he slams the locker shut so hard the door vibrates in its setting and strides away down the hall.

My mouth falls open. I watch his retreating form, hunched in a dingy-looking jean jacket. Wondering if I know him. Wondering if he thinks he knows me.

I glance around the hall, looking to see if anyone noticed the odd interaction. But the crowd's starting to thin out, everyone scattering toward class. No one's even looking my way. Whatever the hell that was, it wasn't part of the official Merrill High Welcome Committee.

I shut the locker and twirl the lock, turning to head to class. But the memory of his eyes still burns my skin. I feel it all the way down the hall . . . almost as if he's in some dark corner, watching me go.

CHAPTER FIVE

I DON'T HAVE TIME to make it to the guidance counselor's office before first period—so I have to sit through yearbook, at least this once. I find the classroom, a small room with computer stations against the walls. People are already sitting around a large rectangular table when I get there, but I don't know if seating is assigned, and I don't see anyone who looks like a teacher. So I just stand off to the side and wait.

It's a surreal feeling, being somewhere familiar and strange all at once. When I started my freshman year at East Multnomah High in Portland, that at least was a clean start. I didn't know anyone. I didn't have any idea of the social order—the cliques that reigned, the messages that your choice of sneaker or your hairstyle might send. Down there I couldn't tell if a kid in a gemstone sweater was wearing it ironically or in dead earnest, or if the girl who wore a Pikachu headband every day was a hardcore Pokémon fan or some kind of arty hipster.

Here it's different. Here I can look around the room and get a read on most of the kids I see. They're all clean-cut, in North Face or Columbia, in shearling-lined boots and leggings, their bodies strong and sporty. I'm willing to bet at least a few of them still have lift tickets dangling from the coats in their lockers. There are all kinds of outdoorsy types in Anchorage, but these are the ones with enough money to make it look stylish.

The bell rings. There's still no sign of the teacher. A few kids look up at the door and frown, but most of them are caught up in their own conversations.

And then I hear her name.

Zahra.

The name cuts through the murmur of talk around me, like it's somehow amplified. Like I'm wearing headphones and it's being piped right into my ears. Everything focuses very sharply. My eyes dart around the room, looking for the source. Then I see her—the girl from Zahra's pictures. The redhead. She's wearing a chunky knit hat and a sleek puffer vest, and one foot jiggles up and down with nervous energy. She's sitting at one corner of the table, talking to a couple of boys.

". . . haven't heard from either of them since the party," she says. There's a note in her voice that sounds half airy, half mad. "So I have no fucking idea."

One of the boys smirks. He's black, short but muscular,

his red Merrill High hoodie bright against his skin. "They're probably off making up," he says. "Out at the lake or something. In a nice cozy cabin. You know how they do."

The other boy is taller, white, with shaggy blond hair. "Maybe," he says, uncertain. "But that fight was messed up. I've never seen Ben that mad. I almost thought he was going to . . ."

"Would you shut up, Jeremy?" the girl snaps. I suddenly realize she's looking at me. Her eyes are almost the same shade of amber as her freckles, hard as stone. "It's all just gossip. Not everyone needs to know Zahra's business."

"Seriously, Tabitha?" The shorter boy shakes his head. "You of all people don't have room to talk."

"I'm just saying." She tugs at the edge of her knit cap, still looking at me. "Some of this is private."

My cheeks flare hot. I look down at my sneakers, but not before I see the boys glance in my direction.

"Hey," says the shorter boy, suddenly friendly. He cocks his head at me a little. "New girl?"

"Uh . . ." I say. "Yeah. I'm sorry, I didn't mean to eavesdrop, I just heard . . . are you talking about Zahra Gaines?"

Tabitha's mouth is a small, tight button, but the shorter boy nods. "You know her?"

"She's my best friend," I blurt, before I can think twice. Then I feel my cheeks get even darker. "I mean, she used to be. Before I moved to Portland. I used to live down the street from Zahra in middle school."

"Oh," Tabitha says, as if that explains everything. "In the *trailer park*."

I frown. I know it's supposed to be a dig, but I can't tell if it's at me or at Zahra. But before I can decide how to respond, the shorter boy speaks again.

"I'm Marcus. Marcus Wray," he says. His eyes are warm, and there's a sly little smile on his lips. It's suddenly oddly familiar.

"Did you go to Northern Lights for middle school?" I ask.

"Yup," he says.

"I remember you. You were in my English class." He'd been one of the pranksters in the back, loud and constant-ly wisecracking through lectures. "Weren't you the one that managed to get everyone chanting 'Kill the pig' during our *Lord of the Flies* unit?"

"Oh, yeah! Ms. Lautermilk actually gave me extra credit for that because it was a good object lesson on mob rule," he says. He squints at me, cocking his head. I can tell he doesn't recognize me.

"I was really shy," I say, to let him off the hook. "You might not have noticed me."

"No risk of that now," he says with a grin.

I feel my cheeks turn red again, but I'm actually kind of pleased. Good to know I've gotten a little more memorable in the last three years.

Tabitha rolls her eyes. "Very smooth," she says caustically to Marcus.

"I'm just being friendly!" Marcus holds up both his hands. "She's new, she doesn't know anyone."

"Lucky her." Tabitha doodles idly in the corner of a notebook. I wonder if I've blundered into the middle of something— if Tabitha and Marcus are an item, having some kind of quarrel. But Marcus just gives a little shrug and grins.

"I'm Jeremy," says the blond boy, reaching out to shake my hand. He has a dimple in his left cheek. "Nice to meet you."

"Hi." I smile shyly. "You guys all know Zahra?"

"Yup," Marcus says. He nods at the empty seat next to Tabitha. "She's usually sitting right there."

My eyes fall on the plastic blue chair. I try to imagine her, but for some reason it's hard. She flits in and out of existence like a ghost, her face a blur.

"No one's heard from her since Friday, though," Marcus says. Tabitha gives him a murderous look, but he pretends not to notice. "But if you know Zahra, you know about her famous disappearing acts."

I don't want to admit that I have no idea what he's talking about, so I just nod. "Sure," I say.

"I love Portland," Jeremy says. "It's so pretty around there. Why'd you guys move?"

"I, uh . . ." I don't know if he means why I moved there, or why I moved back, but I'm pretty sure dropping my dead mother into a getting-to-know-you conversation is not going to make things less awkward. "My parents got divorced and Mom wanted a new start."

"That sucks," Marcus says. "I'm a military brat. We used

to move a lot, before Dad took a command on base. I always hated it."

"Yeah, it was . . . not easy," I finish vaguely.

"But at least Portland's got good hiking spots," Jeremy says. "Did you ever go out to the Gorge?"

I hesitate, then nod. I think absently about the word "gorge," how it can mean different things. How it can be a noun or a verb. To gorge oneself; to eat. I picture my mother disappearing down the canyon's rocky throat.

The door swings open. I exhale softly, relieved.

A youngish woman, crisply dressed in a blazer and black-framed glasses, comes inside. There's something fumbling and absentminded about her movements. She leaves the door open behind her, coming to a halt in front of us and looking around the classroom, almost as if she's lost.

"You're tardy, Ms. Yi!" Marcus says gleefully. "I'm gonna write you up."

His tone is easy and playful. It makes me think that maybe, on a normal day, this is a fun, playful classroom, that Ms. Yi lets them joke with her. But now she just turns to stare at him. The room goes very, very quiet.

Marcus swallows, looking suddenly nervous. "Uh. I mean . . ."

The teacher's voice is slow and soft.

"There was an emergency staff meeting," she says. She blinks a few times and I wonder if she's fighting back tears. "There's some bad news."

The silence stretches out for what feels like forever. I look down and see my fingers are like shards of bone, white and sharp and cold as they clench around my notebook. At the table Tabitha leans forward, staring intently at the teacher.

Ms. Yi turns a stunned look on the classroom, like *we're* the ones who've surprised *her*. But when she speaks again, her words are almost deathly calm.

"Zahra Gaines," she says. She takes in a sharp breath. "Zahra . . . is missing."

CHAPTER SIX

I STAND VERY STILL while everything falls apart around me. I watch as the other kids react. Jeremy almost falls out of his chair. One girl gasps audibly.

Tabitha shakes her head.

"No," she says simply. "No, Ms. Yi, that's not possible."

Ms. Yi looks down at her, helpless. Marcus tries to touch Tabitha's back, but she shakes him off.

"It doesn't make any sense!" Tabitha says. Her voice cuts loudly through the room.

"Tabitha, I understand what you're feeling, but . . ." the teacher says, but Tabitha interrupts with a laugh.

"She's not missing. She's with Ben," Tabitha insists. Ms. Yi shakes her head.

"No, she's not," she says, her voice trembling. "That's why her parents called the police. Ben Peavy came back late last night and he had no idea where she was."

Her words land in a pool of silence so complete you can hear the ticking of the clock. My breath is quick but even, a hot pain in my chest. I turn the idea over and over again in my mind. *Zahra's missing. Zahra's missing. Zahra's missing.*

Tabitha shoots to her feet. I catch a quick glimpse of her face as she runs to the door, starkly pale beneath her freckles, her mouth a twisting knot. She shoves through the door and is gone.

Marcus gets up to follow, but Ms. Yi holds up her hand. "I'll go after her," she says. "The rest of you, please, just stay here. I'll be back and we'll talk more about this, okay?"

Marcus sits back down. The kids all seem too shell-shocked to answer, but Ms. Yi seems to take that as a tacit agreement. She hurries into the hall after Tabitha, and we're all quiet for a half second before the room breaks out into a rumble of conversation.

I finally take a few heavy steps toward the table and sit down. I do it partly because I'm suddenly so exhausted, and my bones feel so heavy. And partly because I want to stay close to these boys who know my best friend, who saw her just a few days before. Who might have some kind of information.

"I bet she's just embarrassed," Marcus is saying. There's a note of bravado to his voice, like he's trying to convince himself. "Everyone saw that fight. So maybe she's just off somewhere hiding."

Jeremy doesn't answer. He's frowning down at his hands, long and pale against the table.

Marcus's voice goes on, more urgently this time. "Remember last year on the Fairbanks trip, when they had that dumb fight and Zahra woke Tabitha up at two in the morning and made her drive her all the way back to Anchorage?"

Fairbanks to Anchorage is a seven-hour drive. He's making it sound like some little spat, but the Zahra I knew wouldn't have flounced off like that for something minor.

"What did they fight about?" I ask. They both look up, just now noticing me listening. "When they fought last Saturday, I mean?"

Marcus shifts his weight in his chair. "I don't know. I just caught the tail end. It was at Tabitha's house. There was a party, and we all kind of . . . we all went out on the deck to listen in when word got out they were fighting. She was crying and he was pissed. He told her it was over. Then he left, and she went back in the house."

"They didn't leave together?" I ask, looking from Jeremy to Marcus and back again.

Jeremy shakes his head. "Nope. He got in his truck and peeled out of there after the fight. She sat in the yard crying for a while and then came back in."

"And proceeded to get *fucked up*," Marcus says. "She was already drunk when they fought, but she doubled down after that."

I frown. "But when did she leave the party? Why did everyone assume she was with Ben?"

Marcus gives a little shrug. "I don't know. After the fight I lost track of her. She was with Tabitha most of the night, and then she just kind of disappeared. It was a big party."

I glance at Jeremy, and he looks uncomfortable. "I left at one and she was still there," Jeremy says. "I saw her in the line to the bathroom."

"But she and Ben fight and break up and then get back together all the time. It's kind of their whole thing," Marcus insists.

So an emotional, obviously drunk Zahra vanished from a party full of kids after a fight with her boyfriend and hasn't been seen for two days. And somehow, it didn't raise alarm bells for anyone. It seems odd. But then this is a Zahra that seems odd to me, too—one I don't recognize, anyway. Maybe this is her new normal.

I close my eyes. The words are still ping-ponging around inside me—*Zahra's missing. Zahra's missing.* But she's already been missing for years now. At least, she has been to me. What happened to the sun-kissed, smiling girl I knew? What happened to change everything?

I remember the first time I ever talked to her. It was March—just a few short weeks after I'd moved to the trailer court. I'd been keeping to myself, hiding in my room—I was pretty shut down back then. But a watery sun warmed the air that day. The winters in Alaska are long and dark and claustrophobic, and when the light comes back it's like a blanket being lifted up off your head. I couldn't resist; I sat on the rickety steps to our mudroom with my book, wiggling my bare toes.

"Whatcha reading?"

I looked up to see a brown-skinned girl with corkscrew curls, standing just beyond the uneven fence. For a second I wasn't sure how to answer; most people only ever asked that question so they could tease me about it. But she leaned her forearms on the fence, eyes wide with curiosity.

Behind her hovered another girl, shorter, with tangled blonde hair and raw-looking pink skin. She shifted her weight, a basketball against her hip. Where Zahra's gaze was even and interested, the other girl's darted wildly, like a woodland creature looking for a direction to run.

I finally just held up my book, since I didn't know what else to do. My cheeks went hot as she squinted to make out the title. I fought the urge to hide my face.

"Is it any good?" she asked.

"Yeah. If you like fantasy, I mean." My body was tense, waiting for her to make a face, to snort, but she just nodded.

"Have you read the Abhorsen books? Those are my favorites," she asked.

I almost thought I was imagining it for a moment—it seemed too miraculous, too remarkable, that she might love something I did.

"I love Garth Nix," I said. My voice came out strangely high, and I cleared my throat.

"I couldn't read the last one. My library card got suspended." She grinned then, revealing teeth with a small gap between them. I was almost relieved to see it—otherwise, she was almost too beautiful to be standing here face to face with me.

"I've got it in my room," I said. I gestured stupidly to the trailer. "If you want to borrow it."

Later on I'd question the wisdom of offering to loan a book to a stranger who'd just admitted to a library account in arrears—and for good reason, because every book I ever loaned her came back dog-eared and stained—but at the time, I was blindsided by this fascinating girl who liked to read, and who wanted to talk to me.

The other girl, the one behind her, scowled. She moved the basketball from left arm to right.

"Come *on*, Zahra, I thought we were gonna play."

"All right, all right," Zahra said, waving her hand at the girl. She turned back to me with that same unapologetic grin. "Bailey likes some guy who hangs out at the park. We gotta go. See ya."

And then she was gone, and I spent the rest of the day trying to figure out how to find her again. Could I just sit out there with a book, like a fisherman trolling, hoping she'd bite? But I didn't have to go looking for her. She showed up at my door the next day, as if we were already friends. As if all the awkwardness and strain of getting to know someone could magically be bypassed. "Hey, you got *Clariel* for me to borrow?"

She made it so easy to like her. She made it easy to step down off the steps of the porch and back out in the world, because her courage made me brave, too. She wasn't afraid of the other, bigger kids in the trailer park. She wasn't afraid of the woods across the street, the place with all the stories about murders and homeless camps and ghosts. She wasn't afraid to paint on her bedroom walls, to write in a library book, to cut up a T-shirt, to argue with her parents. When I was with her, I felt like anything could happen.

So what, exactly, has changed?

And if I figure it out—will I be able to help bring her home?

CHAPTER SEVEN

I PULL UP OUTSIDE the Gaines's trailer, right next to the blue-and-white cop car parked on the street.

It's just after noon. By lunchtime it was obvious I wasn't going to make it through the day. And I wasn't the only one. The news cut across all the social strata, shaking everyone. There were kids crying in the hallway. The teachers kept telling us that the counselors were on standby, if anyone needed to talk. So I just slipped out after fourth period, got in my car, and drove straight to the trailer park.

Malik's sitting on the steps outside the trailer, his jaw jutting forward tough-guy style. His legs are long and skinny under the basketball shorts a certain kind of Alaskan boy wears year-round. I pause at the base of the steps and try to meet his eye, but he won't look at me.

"What's going on?"

He gives a wordless shrug.

Two years ago, Malik was a wisecracking sixth grader with a loud and easy laugh. But like his sister, he's changed. Become unrecognizable to me. Has something happened to them, to their family? Or is this just how time passing looks?

"Are your parents inside?" I ask. He nods.

I walk up the steps and pat his shoulder a little as I walk past.

I hear their voices in the kitchen and linger in the doorway, not wanting to barge in.

Charity sits at the big round table, her face in her hands. Ron is behind her. There's an officer sitting across from them, a youngish Samoan American guy with close-cropped hair. His nameplate says SAPOLU. He has an untouched mug in front of him. I get an earthy whiff of one of Charity's weird hippie teas.

And at a fourth chair, between Ron and Sapolu, is Tabitha.

She sits there silently, looking miserable. In the classroom her body had been an athletic sprawl, but now it looks oddly small, like she's retracted back into herself. She picks at a spot on the oilcloth cover while she listens.

"Does Zahra have a history of any drug abuse that you know of?" Sapolu asks, looking up from a notepad.

Ron shifts his weight. "We busted her with some of our weed last summer," he says. I give a little start, then remember—just like Oregon, Alaska's got legalized marijuana now. It's still weird hearing someone talk casually about drugs to a cop. "We grounded her for two weeks. But that's the only time I've ever caught her with anything."

"But she's so secretive," Charity says. Her voice comes out in a raspy sob, her eyes almost pleading. "It's hard to say for sure."

Sapolu nods, makes a mark on the page. "Any mood swings, changes in behavior in recent months?"

They're both quiet for a long moment. I see Ron's fingers twitch on the back of Charity's chair.

"Nothing new," Charity finally says. "She's always a deep feeler. But I haven't noticed anything in particular going on with her lately."

"She's in the middle of her running season. She's been at practice a lot and we haven't seen much of her," Ron says.

"But she's seemed fine," Charity says again. I wonder if she's trying to convince Officer Sapolu or herself.

Sapolu gives a little nod, checks something on his pad. "Okay. Well, the other thing is that we're still trying to put together a timeline. We've gotta talk to the kids at the party, and that might take a little while. Tabitha, you said Zahra and Ben fought around nine, right?" Sapolu looks down at his notebook. "Mr. Peavy left in his truck after that and Zahra came back inside."

Tabitha's voice is soft and small. "Yeah. Um. She got kind of drunk." She looks desperately over at Charity and Ron.

"It's okay," Charity says gently. "We need to know everything."

"She was upset. I sat with her for a while and tried to cheer her up but she was just . . . beating herself up. I don't know what they fought about but she was blaming herself for it. Then she decided she wanted to go for a walk."

"At two in the morning?" Sapolu asks. His voice is mostly neutral but I can hear the faintest note of judgment.

Tabitha shrugs. "My house is right by the Chester Creek trails. We walk and run out there all the time. She had her phone, and I thought she'd just go find a place to sit and cry and come back."

"But she didn't come back," Sapolu says. Charity gives a little sob.

Tabitha's eyes fall again.

"No," she says. "She didn't."

"And when did that fact register with you?" Sapolu asks.

Tabitha shakes her head. "I don't know. I was kind of . . . it was a party, you know? I guess I got busy. I woke up around noon the next day and texted her. I texted Ben, too—I wanted to make sure he was okay. And neither one of them answered so I just kind of assumed they were together."

"I've never liked that kid," Ron says. His mouth tugs downward. "Little hotshot thinks he can get away with whatever he wants."

"Ben's fine," Charity says. "Ron wouldn't like any boy messing around with Zahra."

"I know the feeling," Sapolu says with a smile. "My daughter just turned thirteen and I've been pricing all-girls schools. My wife tells me I'm crazy." He looks at Ron, serious again.

"But for real, is there anything about him that raises a red flag for you?"

"Just a gut feeling," Ron says. "What'd he say when you questioned him?"

"Says he saw her Friday night like everyone else, and then he was camping for the rest of the weekend," Sapolu answers. "He got back late last night. So far he's cooperating."

"But no one saw him," Ron says. "Camping. No one can back him up?"

"We're looking into everything we can, Mr. Gaines," Sapolu says. Then he looks up and meets my eyes. "And who's this?"

The sudden attention takes me off guard. I didn't realize that he'd noticed me.

"Ruthie," Ron says. He takes a step toward me, then stops, his hands hanging awkwardly at his sides. There's a moment where his posture reminds me almost of my mother's, so helpless and heavy, as she tumbled back over the side of the cliff. I sway on my feet for just a moment, feeling queasy, and then clutch at the doorjamb to steady myself.

"Come sit down, baby," Charity says, holding out her hands. I step into the kitchen and squeeze her fingers, then pull out a chair and sit. I can feel how closely Tabitha's watching, her gaze suddenly hard.

"You're a friend of Zahra's?" Sapolu asks, taking me in.

"Yes. But I've been living in Oregon until last week. I haven't seen her since I got home." I look around the table at everyone. "I don't know that I'll be much help. Zahra only texts or emails every so often, so I don't really know what's been happening with her."

"When was the last time you heard from her?" asks Sapolu.

"August twenty-third," I say, without hesitation.

Sapolu gives me an odd look, like he'd expected me to have to look it up. I pick up my phone and scroll through the messages.

"I remember because I checked when I heard the news," I say. "It was just a short message. *Senior year about to start. Good luck.*"

Reading it out loud, I hear how empty it is. It's the most superficial text—nothing about her feelings, her fears, her boyfriend, her family. Nothing personal. Nothing intimate.

Was she hiding something? Or was she truly that busy?

Or had we grown apart more than I'd realized?

I'm braced for more questions—more questions I can't answer—but then Sapolu turns back to the Gaineses.

"Now, are there any other relatives she might reach out to? Friends of the family, cousins, whatever?"

"My family's all in Texas," Ron says. He glances at Charity. "And Charity's sister lives in Nepal."

"Nepal?" Sapolu looks a little surprised. "Huh."

"She's a missionary." Charity's voice sounds strangely muffled. The faintest hint of a smirk hovers around her mouth. "She's doing the Lord's work."

Sapolu gives Ron an uncertain look. Ron takes a deep breath. "Charity's family's pretty involved in the church," he says carefully. "We don't have much contact with them."

"Dale Worthen is my dad," Charity says flatly.

Sapolu and I both do a double take at that.

"Dale Worthen?" I say. "From Victory Evangelical? Zahra never . . ."

"Like I said, we don't have much contact," Ron says shortly.

"Zahra tried living with him and my mom for a little while a few years ago," Charity says. Her voice is still strangely hollow. "I don't know why. Something got in her head and she thought she wanted to be born again. It didn't last. She was home with us heathens inside a month."

Sapolu nods, writes something down. "Okay. Well, I'm working on a list of people to check with, so if anything occurs to you just give me a call or send an email. I just want to make sure we look into all our options."

My mind scrambles to sort out the new information. It's hard to imagine Charity in the same room as Dale Worthen, much less related to him. I remember catching parts of his big multimedia Christmas pageant (with live animals! And angels flying over the audience!) on the television as a kid, before I'd inevitably get bored and start searching for cartoons. He was a short man, built like a fireplug with broad shoulders and a square-shaped face flushed red. Even on a day like Christmas he yelled and slammed the pulpit, stern and charismatic all at once. Charity, warm and messy and scattered, is nothing like her firebrand of a father.

But even as I think that, I can see the resemblance. Something in the shape of her jaw. A hard, stubborn line in the middle of an otherwise round face. Something unbending in both of them.

"So, what's next? What can we do?" Ron asks.

"Well, we'll work on retracing her steps," Sapolu says. "We're already talking to the phone company to see if we can ping her location. And we're looking around the neighborhood of the party to see if there's any security footage that might show her leaving. The Morgan family doesn't have a system, but a neighbor might." He stands up from the table and puts his hat back on his head. "As for what you can do . . . keep getting the word out. Someone knows something. We've just gotta track that someone down."

Ron gives a helpless nod and rubs Charity's shoulders. I'm suddenly aware how cold it is. I left my jacket at school, and there are goosebumps up and down my arms.

The officer is almost to the door when Charity speaks again, her voice soft and almost distracted.

"I can't stop thinking about that little girl that went missing a few years ago," she says. "Bailey Sellers. Remember, Ron?"

The memory of her floats up: the malnourished, grimy girl who used to follow me and Zahra around. She was a year ahead of us but tiny, and it was easy to treat her like she was younger. Mom didn't like me going to her place, but she didn't have to warn me off it; the one time I went inside, it smelled like cat pee and unwashed laundry.

Sapolu's brows furrow low. "I'm sorry, I don't know the case."

"Y'all treated her like she was just a runaway, is why," Ron says. He looks down at Charity, his expression troubled. "She lived down the street. Used to play with Zahra when they were kids. Her mom was a piece of work, so maybe she *was* a runaway."

"Or maybe she wasn't," Charity says. "What if . . . I mean, what are the odds of two girls going missing from within a few blocks of each other?"

The question turns something over deep in the pit of my stomach. I look up at Sapolu, a shudder moving in slow motion up my back.

He pauses in the doorway, half-turning to look back at us. He seems to choose his next words carefully. "I'll pull up that file when I get back to the station, just so it's on my radar. But look, I work a lot of missing-teen cases, and most of them are kids who've run off for a few days and come back when they've cooled off or sobered up. Try to keep positive, keep calm. I'll let you know as soon as I know anything, okay?"

Charity gives a frail nod. Ron moves to walk the officer out.

When they leave, the room is very quiet for a moment.

I reach out to take Charity's hand. Her fingers are cold and shaking, but she smiles weakly up at me.

"Thank you, Ruthie," she whispers. "For being here."

"Of course," I say.

Across the table Tabitha is still looking down, her nose crinkled. She's fighting tears, I think.

"Mrs. Gaines . . ." she says.

"I told you, honey, you can call me Charity."

She nods a little. I realize suddenly that she doesn't spend much time here, in the trailer, with Zahra's family. Whatever the nature of their friendship, either Zahra doesn't share this part of her life, or Tabitha doesn't want to see it.

"Charity. I'm . . . I'm so sorry. I shouldn't have let her . . ." She trails off, her voice choked. Charity gets up and goes around the table to put her hands on Tabitha's shoulders.

"It's okay," Charity whispers. "Whatever happened, it's . . . it's not your fault. It's not."

I look away from them. Maybe it's not Tabitha's fault—but some part of me isn't willing to let her off the hook. She let her drunk, heartbroken best friend wander into the darkness. Alone. I would never have done that. If I'd been here . . .

But then I don't know how to end that thought. If I'd been here, would I have kept her safe? Would I have even been at that party? Would we have been friends, still, given all the ways she's changed, given all the *things* that have changed?

"I'm going to head home," I say. "But will you guys let me know if you need anything? Anything at all?"

Ron pulls me into another hug, and I let him. His wrinkled flannel shirt smells like peppermint and cigarettes.

"You girls be safe out there, okay?" he says. "Be careful."

Tabitha follows me out to the front steps. Malik's gone.

I wonder if he's in his room, or if he's off roaming the neighborhood with the other kids, slow-pedaling on a rusty BMX or dribbling a basketball. Hiding his feelings behind teen-boy toughness.

Tabitha nods at my car. "Do you mind giving me a ride home? I ran here."

"Sure." I unlock the door. The car's old enough that there's no power lock, so she has to wait for me to let her in. When she climbs in, she rests her head back against the seat and closes her eyes.

"Fuck," she says.

I'm not sure what to say to her, so I pull away from the curb. She looks legitimately scared, but there's something else in her expression, and I don't know how to place it or what to ask.

She passes the rest of the ride without speaking except to give directions. Her house, paneled in gleaming cedar, is in a subdivision with streets named after colleges, lined with old trees and new cars.

She sits in silence for a second before turning to look at me.

"Look, my family's out of town right now and I don't want to be alone. I've got a couple people coming over tonight to help make some flyers. Marcus and Jeremy'll both be there." She looks me in the eye, maybe for the first time. "You want to come, too?"

I bite the bottom of my lip. "Yeah. That sounds good. What time?"

"Come around dinner, we'll get a pizza." She gets out of the car, then leans down to peer at me across the seat. "Thanks for the ride."

"No problem."

I watch her walk up to the garage and punch in the code to let herself in. She straightens her spine, runs her fingers through her hair. The worried lines smooth out of her expression as she disappears through the door.

And I wonder—was she putting on a show at Zahra's? Trying to look scared and sad and vulnerable? For Zahra's parents? For the police?

For me?

CHAPTER EIGHT

WHEN I GET HOME, Dad's outside, spreading mulch around an aspen sapling. When he sees me he waves. The twinge of dread tugging at me makes me feel guilty; I'd been hoping to slip downstairs without notice, without having to talk to him. But here he is, with that earnest, hopeful smile.

"Would you look at this little guy?" he asks as I approach. "Made it through the aphids. Now if I can keep the moose off it through the winter it might just survive."

I nod a little. Dad never used to care about yard work, but now he's out here, trying to get his plants ready for winter. God and gardening: Dad's sobriety hobbies. There are worse options, I guess.

He kneels down and starts coiling up the hose. "Last year I tried planting apple trees but they only ever turned into apple shrubs." He gives an awkward dad-joke laugh. "I think

I planted them the wrong time of year. I'm still learning." He finally looks up at me, and his expression shifts, turning uncertain. His eyes squint as if I'm far away. "You okay?"

"Yeah," I say. Then, "No. Not really."

He stands up quickly. "What's wrong?"

"Zahra." I don't like looking at him while I talk. It makes me feel vulnerable. So instead, I look down at the plants, fresh and green and bright, watered and nurtured by a man who once drunkenly threw a shoe at my head. "My . . . my best friend. She's missing."

His pupils flare. He carefully puts the hose down, then straightens up to look me in the eye. "Missing?"

I nod automatically. "Since last Friday. They announced it at school."

He pulls me into a hug. I don't fight it. I close my eyes.

"I'll pray for her," he says. "For both of you."

DOWNSTAIRS, I GO STRAIGHT to my room and shut the door. Not much natural light makes it through the sunken windows, and the bright pink walls look flushed and feverish in the glow of the lamp. Words and letters swirl all around me. *Peace. Hope. Gratitude.* I stand frozen in the center. Then I move quickly, quietly around the walls, taking it all down. When I'm done the walls are almost bare, except for the vinyl decals spelling my name.

Then I lie on the bed and pull out my phone.

Ingrid's texted a few times, but I dismiss the alert without checking. Instead I open the internet browser. There's nothing on the news about Zahra being missing, but Tabitha's already posted FIND ZAHRA GAINES all over her own social media accounts. Her most recent Facebook update is a long rambling post about her: Zahra is the best friend I've ever had and she has been there for me through thick & thin. If you have seen her or have any information call the police at . . .

She's attached a picture. I barely recognize Zahra. She stands with a red solo cup, wearing a short yellow dress. Her hair is gone. Not gone-gone. Just short, chopped into a shaggy pixie that makes her look sharp and angular. She's beautiful. She always was—her long limbs graceful instead of gangly, her eyes a light-filled hazel surrounded by dark lashes. But with the hair gone, with the lines of her face left so starkly exposed, she's haunting.

There are already over a hundred comments, and it's only been twenty minutes or so.

OMG I can't believe it, where is she?

Zahra babygirl come back we need you

I had a dream about her last night and I woke up with the worst feeling . . .

I skim through them. Nothing really stands out. Mostly superficial "come home soon" kind of messages. Lots of thoughts and prayers. A few people who rattle off long stories or hint at inside jokes. **I'll never forget the jumpsuit she made for the seventies dance . . . Or, Zahra you still owe me that trip to Portage!**

Zahra!
Zahra.
Zahra . . .

They address the comments to her, as if that will call her back. But if that were enough, I'd have long since summoned her.

I click through some of Tabitha's older posts, mostly just to see if there's anything else that stands out to me. Other posts about Zahra, other pictures that might tell me something about their relationship. But Tabitha mostly reposts aggressive fitspo memes (*Life is hard . . . run harder. Today I do what others won't . . . so tomorrow I can do what others can't*). There are pictures of her running, skiing, snowboarding, rock climbing. Her body is sleek and strong, all force and speed.

Zahra doesn't have a Facebook account—or at least not one that's publicly searchable. I've googled her a few times over the last few years, mostly out of idle curiosity. I've never found much. When I look her up now I get a few hits, none very informative—she's listed on some school websites. Cross-country running, yearbook. I find a picture of her on a community news website; she's in a little group of girls about our age, all of them wearing bright green T-shirts with a coffee mug screen-printed across the front. It looks like they're on one of the trails, enjoying a stroll on a sunny afternoon. *Employees of the Cup and Saucer participate in the annual Walk and Roll for Hope*, says the caption. She's smiling, her eyes hidden behind large aviator shades.

I stare at that one a long time. In a way it's the most familiar of all the pictures I've seen of her. When I knew Zahra she wasn't particularly athletic, but she loved to walk. She walked all over the trailer court, all through the woods, all over the neighborhood, just because the rhythm and movement pleased her. I can see an echo of that in the photo, even though her eyes are concealed from view.

I put the phone against my chest, staring at the ceiling.

Then I pick up the phone again and search for Ben Peavy. Zahra's boyfriend.

Right off the bat I get dozens of hits. I recognize him—he's the boy from her pictures. Full mouth and dark, flashing eyes; black hair shaved close to the scalp along the sides, longer on the top. Turns out he's Merrill High's next great hope for a cross-country win. Last year he came in third in the state, and a bunch of universities are eyeing him. The local news outlets have tons of pictures, his muscles tense with exertion as he pulls ahead of the pack midrace. The *Anchorage Daily News* even wrote a profile on him a few weeks ago. *Tradition, family keep Peavy grounded as he soars*. Next to a picture of him crossing a finish line there's one of him dressed in a beaded moose hide, dancing with a drum.

Like most Alaska Native teenagers, Ben Peavy comes from two different worlds. There's the world of his elders, with its rich history and complex traditions—and there's the world of his peers, obsessed with the latest trends and technology. But for Peavy, bridging those worlds has helped him find balance as he trains toward the coming cross-country running season. It goes on to talk about his background—his paternal grandma's a Koyukon Athabaskan artist known for her beadwork, and his mom's an outreach coordinator for one of the local homeless shelters.

On a dark whim I type in "Bailey Sellers." The girl who vanished from Walker Court a few years ago. There aren't any old news reports that I can find. There's a school picture of her on *NamUS*, the government's missing person site—I recognize her right off the bat. Tangled blonde hair, pinched cheeks. She used to follow Zahra around. She doesn't smile in the picture; I remember she had a badly chipped tooth that she was self-conscious about.

There's not much accompanying information. No one seems to have dug into her case, to find out where she was last seen, or when. I can imagine it too easily—her mom too messed up to be able to answer the cops' questions. The cops putting out a perfunctory search, but no one really bothering beyond that. It's awful. It's unfair. But it's not surprising.

A soft knock comes at the door. I sit up in my bed.

"Yeah?"

It's Ingrid. She's flushed, her backpack still on her back.

For a long moment she doesn't say anything. She just stands there with an odd look on her face.

"Oh. Well. I just wanted to make sure you made it home," she says. "Since I didn't see you after school." Her tone has a forced lightness to it, but I can feel the jagged edge beneath it.

And then I remember.

I left her there at school, without a ride. I didn't tell her where I was going. I didn't even think about her.

"Oh, shit. Ingrid, I'm so sorry, I didn't mean to just ditch you there," I start, but she just gives a little shrug. Her smile doesn't falter.

"It's okay. It's kind of a long walk home, but it's not too cold yet," she says. "If I'd known you were leaving without me I could've taken the bus. But it's not a big deal."

I'm one hundred percent in the wrong. But I've never had any patience for passive-aggressive bullshit. That was what my mom used to do, too. She'd get all wounded, start talking about everything she'd done to make a better life for us. I'd rather us scream at each other all day than deal with that.

So I just stare at her. "Good, I'm glad it's not a big deal."

Taking someone's sulky denial at face value is its own kind of passive aggression, of course, but I just don't have energy to deal with Ingrid right now. So I turn back to my phone. A moment later, I hear my door click back shut, her footsteps fading down the hall.

I'll apologize later. When I'm not so focused on combing through whatever I can find online. When Zahra comes home with a sheepish grin and a weak explanation and we know she's safe and everything is back to normal. I'll apologize to Ingrid, and she can take it or leave it. It won't matter either way.

The important thing—the only thing—is Zahra.

CHAPTER NINE

IT'S AROUND SIX WHEN I haul Brandy's rusty three-speed out of the shed. The brakes squeal and the gear shifter sticks, but it works.

I could take the car. It'd be faster. But the last time anyone saw Zahra she was heading out to the trails. I doubt I'll find anything, but I don't want to pass up the opportunity to retrace her steps. Just in case.

Anchorage has dozens of greenbelts, all with different names, but most of them are connected by bike trails, like emerald beads on a string. Russian Jack is the one closest to both my house and Zahra's, but it links up with Goose Lake, Tikishla Park, the Chester Creek Trail, Westchester Lagoon, and the Coastal Trail beyond. I've always found it kind of comforting, the way you can slip away from roads and cars and feel the trees around you, almost anywhere in town. The way you feel connected to the whole sprawling network wherever you are.

I wish time felt like that. I wish I could feel my past and my future and the way they intertwine with Zahra's. I wish I could sense the way our lives flow together. Instead it feels like something sharp and violent has severed us. Like something happened to her to tear her out of the world.

My breath comes in clouds as I heave up the first few hills of the trail. I wonder if she ran out to the trail the night of the party with the intention of walking home. It'd be a long walk, maybe a couple of hours, but we'd walked those distances plenty of times as kids. We were often out in the woods all night, the light dim but present. It's September, though, and she would have had to rely on the street lights that are only intermittent along the paved trails.

The image makes me tighten my fingers around the handlebar grips. Because while the trails are beautiful, magical even, they're also dangerous. In the winter the moose come down from the mountains and forage, and in recent years there've even been bears. And I grew up hearing all kinds of stories—about the psych patient that shot a bunch of teenagers in Russian Jack back in the eighties, about the teen couple that hid out on the park after a thrill-kill spree. Just last year a man died in a shoot-out with the cops in the middle of a downtown street, and the investigators later matched his gun with a series of unsolved murders all throughout the trail system.

I picture Zahra, in the dark, staggering drunk, the stars obscured by branches overhead. It's easy to imagine her encountering something that night that kept her from coming out the other side.

Of course, the truth could be even simpler than that. It could be the angry ex-boyfriend that everyone saw lose his temper just a few hours earlier. He could have been waiting outside Tabitha's to follow her. Or waiting outside the trailer park to catch her.

I come to a stop at the place where I'd turn off to the Precipice—to our playground. Then I hide the bike in the undergrowth and set off, following the landmarks I know so well. The dead spruce jabbing up like a wounded finger. The heart-shaped boulder with its filigree of moss.

The playground's just as I left it. And I know, as soon as I see it, that she's not here. I knew that before I even arrived, really. If she'd been hiding at the playground I'd have seen some sign of her yesterday. But even still, when I see the barren playscape, the old sheet flapping in the breeze, I'm disappointed.

Part of me, of course, just wanted to find her. But part of me wanted to find her *here*. Because that would mean it still matters. That the world we created together is still meaningful to her.

EVERY WINDOW IS BLAZING with light at Tabitha's house. I walk up the steps to the door and ring. I can hear the bell's distant singsong through the door, but the seconds pass and no one comes. And then I make out the low rumble of voices from inside. I try the door, and it swings easily inward.

The sound is instantly louder, the mumble of conversation over the thump of rap music playing somewhere in the house. I feel out of place the moment my eyes take in the foyer. There's a large oil painting on one wall, of the northern lights shimmering pale green over the mountains. There's a small table that holds a huge bouquet of fresh flowers. Even the light itself looks expensive, coming from cleverly arranged indirect fixtures, or twinkling through the crystals of the chandelier overhead.

For a second I almost turn around. I'm an imposter here. I don't know these kids. I don't know this house.

But Zahra's been in this house, with these kids. And if I want to find out who she's become, I have to follow her. So I take a deep breath, and I follow the sound of voices.

There are ten or fifteen kids in a wide, luxurious living room. Most of them are white, wearing hoodies emblazoned with the words MERRILL HIGH CROSS-COUNTRY. They all stand around holding glass tumblers filled to the brim with liquid. Several bottles stand uncapped on a glass-topped bar, top-shelf vodka and tequila, a few uncorked bottles of red wine, a liter of Coke slowly losing its fizz.

It feels almost like a party. Which seems weird, since we're supposedly here to talk about a missing person.

"Ruthie!" I look up to see Jeremy waving.

"Hey," I say. I head toward him, tugging at the ends of my hair. "I thought we were working on flyers or something."

"Oh, yeah, we are." He's holding a beer in one hand, but his eyes are clear and focused. It's still early, I guess. "I mean, we're gonna." He must see something almost disapproving on my face, because he gives a sheepish smile. "Right now we're all kind of . . . uh . . . commiserating. Can I get you something to drink?"

I hesitate. I'm not usually a drinker. But it sucks to be the only sober person at a party. And honestly, I could do with some commiseration myself.

"Yeah, okay. Thanks," I say.

"Sure." He steps over to the bar and starts to pour. I look around at some of the other kids milling around. There's a trio of almost indistinguishable Nordic-looking guys trying to get a fire going, arguing over where to put the kindling. Another few kids are on the sofa, all looking at a tablet. Near me, a girl with enormous hoops is talking to one with green eyeliner, gesturing emphatically with her hands as she does.

Zahra was here just a few days ago. Probably in this room. On the sofa, by the bar. Maybe leafing through one of the nature-landscape coffee table books. No, wait—she was upset, she was crying. She'd just fought with Ben. Maybe she'd have gone to Tabitha's room to talk quietly with one or two close friends. Maybe she sat on a back porch, staring at the moon.

Was it the same bunch of people here that night? Did she feel out of place here, surrounded by affluent white kids with name-brand outdoor gear? Or had these people become *her* people, her friends? I'm white as hell and *I* feel awkward. But

Zahra was always better at talking to people than I was, and maybe she'd found ways to fit in.

Jeremy comes back with a cup he's filled almost to the top. "Here you go."

"Thanks." I take a sip. It's actually not bad. Fizzy and citrusy, with a little bite.

"Vodka tonic," he says, watching me closely. "Hope it's okay."

I cough a little, suddenly remembering: vodka was always my dad's poison, too. But I throw back another healthy gulp and try to drown that voice. I'm not my dad. I'm not going to live in fear of becoming him.

"Where's Tabitha, anyway?"

An odd look flashes across his face and is gone. "I think she's in the hot tub." He nods toward a clear glass door leading out to a big wooden deck.

I take my drink and head over to the door. It's fogged up but I can see the bubbling hot tub, a deep blue light coming up from its depths. I open the door and go outside.

I recognize Tabitha and Marcus right away. There are two other guys in the tub with them, both white, one with a heavy arm draped over Tabitha's shoulders.

Marcus turns to look, his face lit blue from the tub lights. "You made it!"

"Uh . . . yeah." I give a little wave. "Hey, Tabitha, how're you doing?"

Her head wobbles as she turns to look at me. Her lips are parted, and her eyes don't seem focused. It's obvious she's way, way drunker than anyone else.

"I'm Ruth," I remind her. "Remember? I gave you a ride."

She squints through the steam, then gives a dull giggle. "The trailer park girl."

"Sure," I say. "Yeah, I guess."

"Get in with us," Marcus says, gesturing to the water.

"Oh, I . . . I didn't bring a suit," I say. I'm grateful to have the excuse. Something about the whole thing makes me nervous.

"I've got extra," Tabitha says. She hauls herself up out of the water, climbing over the edge. Her body glints in the hazy light. She staggers a little, then grabs the back of a patio chair to catch her balance. "We're mostly the same size. Except you've got actual boobs."

I feel my cheeks go warm, and carefully avoid looking at the guys in the tub. When Tabitha pads toward the door, I follow.

Conversation goes quiet as we pass through the living room again. I see Jeremy's eyes on us, his expression hard to read. I trail Tabitha back out to the front hall. Water pools on the hardwood below her but she doesn't seem to notice it. We start up the stairs.

"Your sister's cute," I say, looking at the family photos. A little girl with red hair and gaps in her smile beams out from next to Tabitha's senior picture.

"Bethany Beautiful." Tabitha squints at the frame. "Mom and Dad are in the lower forty-eight with her this week."

I can't tell how she feels from her tone—bitter or proud? Or both?

Her room's on the third floor, under the slanting ceiling.

It's not really what I expected. There's a patchwork quilt on the bed. An old gray cat is curled on the pillow, sleeping next to an open sketch pad. Across the room is a mirror-topped dresser, perfume samples and high-end makeup scattered across the surface. A glitter-encrusted GOOD LUCK sign someone made for one of her races hangs on the wall, next to a screen-printed poster for the Alaska State Fair.

I sit down on the bed and reach out to stroke the cat. It opens its eyes and trills softly.

"That's Mr. Pants," Tabitha says. I raise an eyebrow and she shrugs. "I've had him since I was little. No one should ever let six-year-olds name things."

She steps toward the bed and scratches Mr. Pants on the neck. He stands up and rubs his whole face against her palm.

"She's not coming home," she says suddenly.

I give a little jump of surprise. Tabitha's face is still soft and unfocused, but there's something sharp working at the corners of her mouth, an acid-etched sneer. I hold my breath, waiting for her to continue.

"She could. My dad's there to take care of Bethany. But she said it's just too ex-pen-sive." She enunciates the word slowly, syllable by syllable. Her eyes well up, but she wipes the tears away angrily.

That's when I realize she's not talking about Zahra.

"I don't even need her here, but you'd think she'd want to come make sure I'm okay. Or whatever." She brings her face low to press it against Mr. Pants's side. He just lies there, purring evenly. "But it's more *important* to plan for *Bethany's* future."

"Her future?" I ask.

She snorts through her nose. "Yeah, they're touring a bunch of big-time gyms. For gymnastics. Next year when I go to college they're going to move so she can, quote, *'really'* start training."

"Oh, wow." I'm not sure what else to say. But she doesn't seem to need me to say much of anything.

"Right?" she says. "You'd think they'd hop on a plane when they heard about Zahra, but they're somewhere in Seattle, checking out the equipment and running background checks on all the coaches and whatever."

"So you've been alone all week?" I ask. I suddenly understand how "making flyers" turned into a party. It's easy to imagine Tabitha wandering this too-big house in her bare feet, waiting for some update about Zahra. Thoughts spinning out with nothing to interrupt them. She doesn't want to be alone.

"I'm sorry," I say. "That really sucks."

For a moment she presses her face into her cat's fur. Then she sits up. Her expression seems a little clearer.

"You were friends with Zahra in middle school, right?" she asks.

"The summer after. Yeah," I say.

She cocks her head to one side. "So what happened to her, anyway?"

I frown. Her train of thought is drunkenly hopping every track, and it's hard to follow. "You mean the night she left your party?"

"No!" She rolls her eyes, exasperated. "No, back . . . back

when she was a kid. I don't know the details but she talks like something really fucked up happened to her. Every time she has a panic attack or some kind of emotional meltdown, it comes up." She shrugs. "I just thought this was more of that, you know? She has these big dramas all the time. Talks like . . . like she's a big fuckup, like she ruins everything, like she deserves to suffer or whatever. I didn't think Friday was any different. She came in from the fight and was going on about how she deserved to lose him, she deserved whatever happened, blah blah blah. But she's gone now. So. Maybe this time it was different. Maybe this time she . . ."

Tabitha's eyes go distant. Her fingers curl through the cat's long, thick fur as she trails off.

"She what?" I ask. "What do you think happened, Tabitha?"

"What?" Her eyes snap back. She blinks a few times, then gets up and goes to the dresser. She leans over and rummages in a drawer for a moment, then comes up with a wadded handful of purple Lycra.

"Here," she says, shoving it at me. "This should work. Just come down when you're ready."

"But what were you saying about . . ." I ask. But she's already at the door.

I can't tell if she's leaving because she's drunk and scatter-brained . . . or if she just doesn't want to answer me.

I stand there for a moment, the suit dangling lifelessly from my hand, as she leaves. I listen as her footsteps fade down the steps.

So Zahra's been depressed. Anxious. Ever since freshman year . . . right after I left town. For a second I wonder if she just missed *me*. If the loss hit her harder than I thought. But that's just ego talking. No, what Tabitha described sounds more like mental illness. More like a clinical thing.

If she just wandered off in the middle of some kind of episode she might still be alive. She might still be okay.

But if that's what happened, it means we need to find her fast, before she has a chance to really hurt herself.

And really—do I believe it's a coincidence that she had an enormous, raging fight with her boyfriend right before going missing?

I don't know what to think. So much has changed here. So much has happened, and I have to piece it all together from scraps.

I sigh as I put on the swimsuit. She's right—we're similar in size, though the shapes of our bodies are different. I can imagine her, otter-sleek in the racing suit, a triathlon number written across her muscular back. I look at myself in her full-length mirror, a different story entirely—skinny and shapeless, except across my chest. As she surmised, I'm all but popping out the top of the thing. Awkward. But there's nothing I can do about it now. I pull my clothes back on over it. I don't want to walk through the living room like this.

I linger for a few moments, looking around the room. I don't really know what I expected. Trophies, maybe. Sports equipment piled in the corners. Pictures of mountains, as sharp and craggy as her personality. But this room, cozy and almost cute, makes her look . . .

. . . makes her look like the kind of person Zahra would actually hang out with.

I can't decide how I feel about that . . . if it's reassuring to see that there might be more to Tabitha than I thought, or if it's somehow unnerving. I turn to go.

But then my eye falls on the drawing pad on the bed. It's lying open, as if she'd been working on something earlier. Normally, I wouldn't go through someone else's things—someone else's notebooks in particular. But I can't help but see this one.

It's Ben.

It's a drawing of Ben, I should say. Done in charcoal, the lines loose but precise. It's a three-quarter angle, his jaw and cheekbone sculptural, his eyes flashing bright. He looks . . . not angry, but fierce.

Carefully, I flip through the other pages of the book. It's almost all portraiture—a few of Zahra, a few of Marcus and Jeremy. Several of people I don't know. There's one, only half finished, that looks like it was meant to be Tabitha before she abandoned it.

And there are dozens of Ben.

Ben's face at different angles. Ben with different expressions—pensive, tired. One of a playful little smirk. Ben's body, running, sitting.

I put the book back down, suddenly quite sure she

wouldn't want me looking at this. There's something about the pictures that feels strangely intimate. Maybe Ben's just a good model—athletic and handsome. But it feels like something more. I wonder if she's drawn them from memory, or from photos—or if she's drawn them from life. Does he pose for her? Does he watch as she fills in those shadows?

And is she really scared that Zahra's gone? Or happy to finally have Ben to herself?

CHAPTER TEN

BACK DOWNSTAIRS, MORE PEOPLE have arrived. Something has shifted—some threshold of drunkenness crossed—and the noise is now a throbbing chaos. I pass through the kitchen, where a couple of boys in lettermen jackets are pulling things out of the fridge, and make my way back to the living room. The fire's roaring away now. Someone's booted up the PlayStation and there are a bunch of kids on the couch playing a first-person shooter, shouting and groaning every time someone makes a kill. Back by the bar people mill around, refilling their glasses and talking.

It looks like a normal party, kind of. Except there's a weird edge of hysteria to everything. Like you could run your hand over the top of reality and wipe its sheen away to reveal the mottled, damaged surface beneath. Outside on the deck there are a couple of boys wrestling, one in a headlock. Back in the kitchen, I hear something break. There are a bunch of empty bottles perched precariously on the edge of the bar, and the sharp smell of spilled alcohol hovers over the room. It's early, but everything has that exhausted sense that comes at the end of a party.

I go back to the bar and top off my own glass. The tonic's gone. I just pour vodka straight in. All around me I hear Zahra's name—in both what's being said and what's not being said. The kids playing video games, the ones drinking hard, the ones wrestling on the deck. The fear is so heavy it's like a blanket, something stiff and itchy.

"And I still haven't heard from Ben." The girl who says it is the one with the large silver hoops in her ears. I vaguely recognize her from some of the cross-country pictures: Annika, I think. She's standing with the same girl, the one with the green eyeliner, but now they're both a little more flushed, their voices a little more shrill. "As his co-captain, you'd *think* he'd keep me posted."

"Maybe he's in jail," says the other girl, chewing nervously at the end of her hoodie's drawstring. Her mascara is smearing but her green eyeliner is still perfect. "Maybe they just arrested him."

"They can't just arrest him without a good reason," says Annika, but she doesn't look so certain. She takes a big sip of her drink and grimaces. "Do you even know what they were fighting about?"

"ANNIHILATION!" Both girls jump as a voice booms from the screen. A loud chorus of groans and cheers comes from the sofa as a character in cybernetic body armor explodes into a mist of blood. For a moment red fills the screen.

"Would you turn that shit down!" Annika strides over to the sofa and grabs a remote control, aiming it at the screen. "God, have some respect, will you?"

I don't think I'll hear anything else about Zahra's fight with Ben, or who she might have been texting. Quietly, I head toward the door.

There are two more guys in the hot tub. It seems weird—why aren't there any girls? It takes me a minute to realize Tabitha's sitting next to a different guy than before, nuzzling against his shoulder. The first one looks on with an irritated expression.

"There you are!" Tabitha's voice is excited. Either we've become good friends in the last ten minutes or she's one of those girls that gets super effusive when she's drunk. "You get lost on the way back?"

"Sorry." I hang back a little. It feels a little like I'm being served up to these guys, somehow. There's something about the way they watch me, the way they touch Tabitha, that makes it feel almost like they think they're entitled to something. And without meaning to, I picture Zahra in my place. Standing in front of these greedy boys, their eyes raking her skin. Of course they wanted her; she was beautiful.

Did one of them want her enough to take her?

I shudder a little.

"You cold?" Marcus asks. "Come on, you gotta get in."

"Yeah. Okay." I pull my shirt over my head and angle my body away as I shimmy out of my jeans. Then I finish my drink in one long gulp, and I climb in next to Tabitha. My glasses fog up almost immediately. I take them off, and the world goes blurry, and somehow that makes it more tolerable.

"Ruth used to be friends with Zahra," Tabitha says, gesturing toward me. "When they were kids."

The guy on the other side of me, blond with sculptural muscles across his shoulders, grins. "Little Zahra must have been cute."

"Yeah, uh. She was." I don't want to talk about "little Zahra" with these people, though. Little Zahra—who'd never been that little, who'd always had those long limbs—was mine. The world she inhabited, creative and playful and funny and strange, was gone. For all I know, it's because one of these people destroyed it.

I look around at them all. Tabitha's eyes are closed, her hair pinned in a sloppy knot on top of her head. Her head lolls gently against the boy's shoulder. He strokes her arm lightly.

"Tabitha," I say tentatively. "Are you okay?"

She opens her eyes. "Lighten up, Ruthless. Everything's trash. We might as well have a little fun."

The logic isn't exactly sound. But I look around, at their light-suffused faces, at the glittering bottles on a side table, at the moon overhead. And I suddenly want to be with them. Like them. I want to be drunk, and lost, and confused, and not spiraling around in my own head like this is some kind of demented puzzle I could solve with the right pieces. So I grab a bottle of bourbon and tip it back in a long swig. The guys all hoot and crow, watching me, and I feel a weird triumphant rush.

"Can't argue with that," I say.

Tabitha laughs and reaches for the bottle. Soon we're passing it around, and the amber liquid glitters and glitters and is gone, and someone's going inside for another. I'm hyper-aware that the water hits right at the swimsuit line, that my breasts look like I've pushed them up out of the water for display. I keep trying to pull the suit up to cover them a little more. Then at some point, I forget to worry about it. And it's such a goddamn relief.

Every now and then my mind darts back to Zahra. I picture her face and it hits me all over again, sharp and sudden, that she's missing. That she could be in danger right now. That we should be doing *something*. But what can we do? What can I do? Then the thought sinks back under the surface, and I take another swig from the bottle.

The world is pleasantly warm, pleasantly soft. Overhead there's a sharp white crescent of a moon angled in the sky like a weapon. I look up and the sky is so big and black, and it feels comforting. I'm vaguely aware that Tabitha and the boy are kissing now. Something brushes my leg and I giggle. It tickles. I jerk away. It persists, tracing up the outside of my thigh, and the boy whose hand it is grins at me through the steam.

"I'm not . . ." Oh wow, I'm drunk. I edge away from him a little, pulling my suit up. "Sorry, I . . ."

Just then I hear a shriek from Tabitha. My body jerks to

attention. What's wrong? Has someone hurt her? Has something happened?

She's on her feet, water sloshing around her. I follow where she's looking. There's a figure in the doorway, tall, cloaked in shadow. It moves toward us. My head hurts, trying to assemble all of these pieces into a whole—I remember too late my glasses are on the table—but then, then, for just a moment, he's clear.

His face, as familiar as a graphite line.

It's Ben.

I jump to my feet. It's a mistake. The heat, the alcohol—the world goes static gray and the sound goes underwater and I slide downward, downward, and then I can't breathe at all.

CHAPTER ELEVEN

WATER ROARS IN MY ears. My heart is a monstrous thing, beating its heavy rhythm throughout my body. I try to inhale, and my throat starts to convulse. And then someone's got their arms under my shoulders, and they're pulling hard.

Air. First I'm just grateful to breathe it; then I'm shocked, almost angry, at how cold it is. My skin is bare and wet. I shudder and groan.

"She's okay. She's okay," says a girl's voice.

"Get back, give her some air. Can someone get a glass of water?"

"Ruth. Ruth, how many fingers?"

I look blearily up at the circle of faces above me. "Glasses," I croak.

"What'd she say?"

They all murmur at each other for a moment. Someone

wraps a towel around my shoulders. Tabitha thrusts a glass of water into my hands.

"Glasses," I say again. "My glasses. I can't see."

The world is still spinning wildly, but it comes into sharper focus when I feel someone slide my glasses onto my nose.

And that's when I realize I'm lying against Ben Peavy's leg.

I turn my head to the left, and I vomit.

"WHAT ARE *YOU* DOING here?"

I'm lying somewhere cool and bright. My eyes are closed, but the insides of my lids glow from the light, and for a moment I see blood, smeared across the field of my vision. The voice is Tabitha's, sloppy and slurring but indignant.

"I'm here to get my stepsister." That's a different voice— familiar, but I can't remember where I know it from. A girl's voice. The world tilts around me, topsy-turvy.

"Your sister? Wait. What?" I feel someone scuffling around next to me. "Ruthless. You didn't tell me you had a sister."

"I don't," I mumble. I try to say something else, but my tongue gives up before it even starts.

"Well, she's here to get you," Tabitha says.

I force my eyes open. I'm lying on the floor in the front foyer. I don't remember how I got down here, but my clothes are on over the wet swimsuit.

Tabitha's lying on the floor next to me. There's a moment where the pose feels like one of those innocent moments of childhood, lying next to someone in the grass, hair spread out behind you so it tangles with that of your friend. Then she lets out a hard giggle.

"Oh, man, we're fucked up," she slurs.

Ingrid's standing over both of us, her face unusually serious. She's wearing pajama pants, printed all over with galloping horses, and a winter coat. She kneels down next to me. "They said you passed out?"

"I just fainted," I say. "I'm okay."

She looks over at Tabitha, who's still in her swimsuit. I can hear music and voices from down the hall. It sounds like the party's still raging.

"Are *you* okay?" Ingrid asks Tabitha. Her voice is gentle, but there's an edge to it, too. Like she's a little angry she even has to ask.

Tabitha gives a light, almost mocking laugh. "Don't worry about me, Ingrid, I'm already burning in hell. A little intox . . . intox . . . intockation isn't going to make much difference."

Ingrid doesn't respond for a long moment. Then she takes off her coat and wraps it around Tabitha.

"Nice jammies," Tabitha says.

"Thank you," Ingrid says calmly. "Is there anyone else here who's sober? Anyone who's going to look out for you?"

"I'm here."

We all look up to see Ben in the doorway, holding two more glasses of water.

Ingrid gives him a weak little smile. "Hey, Ben. I'm sorry about Zahra. I hope we find her quickly."

His expression doesn't change. "Thanks," he says. "You're this girl's sister?"

"Yes," Ingrid says, just as I say, "Step."

"Do you need help getting to the car?" He moves like he's going to help me up, but I quickly push myself up onto hands and knees.

"No," I say. "I think I'm okay."

It's while I'm still down there that I see it.

A dark stain across the leather of his shoe.

Muddy red, like dried blood.

Bile rises again in my throat, but I choke it back down. I stay there for a long time, bracing myself against the glossy wood floor. Then, slowly, I climb to my feet.

"Okay," I say. "I'm ready."

"Bye, bitch," Tabitha sings out.

IN THE CAR I brace myself for a lecture. I'm sure I'm about to hear some scripture, about obeying your parents or about the evils of alcohol or whatever. But it doesn't come.

"Just let me know if you're going to yarf," she says. "I'll pull over."

"Yarf?" I say. I giggle stupidly. "Okay, Ingrid."

We're quiet for a few minutes. The clock on the dash says just after midnight. It surprises me—I don't know where the time slipped.

"So I guess you know Tabitha?" I say, glancing at her from the corner of my eyes.

She sighs. "Yes, I know Tabitha. We've been in school together since third grade."

"Not a fan, huh?" I say.

"Not so much. She used to call me 'thunder thighs.' Among other things." She gives a little shrug. "She's kind of a . . . you know, a B-I-T-C-H." Her voice drops to a whisper as she spells out the last word.

"Yeah, I can see that." I look out the window at the world sliding past. The street lights are all blinking rhythmically, the way they do after midnight. Everything's dark and silent.

"Your dad told me why you didn't drive me home," she says. "I'm sorry. Zahra's a really nice person. I didn't realize you guys were friends."

I barely hear anything but what she said about Zahra. "She's nice?" My voice sounds young and stupid, but I don't care. It's the first time someone has described Zahra in a way I recognize.

She glances at me, then looks back out the windshield.

"I mean, I don't know her very well. She's in Key Club with me. She's one of the only people there who seems like she really cares, instead of just using it to pad her college applications." She plays with a lock of hair, twisting it around one finger. "We did a service project at the domestic abuse shelter last year and she was the only person besides me that showed up every single weekend."

I rest my forehead against the cool passenger-side window. Outside, we're approaching the western edge of Russian Jack, which rises up from the road in a bristling black hump.

Kindness and service projects are good, but they don't bring Zahra any further into focus for me.

"Anyway. Why didn't you answer any of my texts?" Ingrid asks. "Or your dad's?"

I frown a little. "Oh, I was . . . I was in the hot tub. I didn't have my phone on me."

"Well, you're in for it tomorrow," she says. "I tried to cover for you. But he was pretty mad when you didn't get home by curfew."

That brings a knee-jerk scowl to my face. "Oh, like he has any right to judge me."

She looks at me with wide blue eyes.

"Ruthie, your best friend is missing. He was scared something happened to you, too."

I hadn't thought of it like that. I twist the edge of my shirt between my hands, chewing on the corner of my lip.

Then I look back at Ingrid, her fingers curled tight around the wheel. She's blinking a little too quickly. She looks freaked out.

"You don't have your license," I say, suddenly remembering.

She sets her jaw. "Yeah. Well, as long as I don't have to parallel park, we should be okay."

"You broke the rules to come for me." I don't know why, but there's something about it that strikes me as urgent to make clear. Scripture-quoting, clean-mouthed Ingrid sneaking out to steal our car. For me.

"Of course I did," she says, genuinely surprised that I'm surprised. And I don't know how to tell her all the things I'm thinking—that I'd written her off, that I'd assumed there was no way we'd be friends, that I don't actually know if I want to be a part of this family, that I don't understand religion or faith or any of it.

And I also don't know how to tell her that no one has ever come for me before—much less illegally and in pajamas and on a school night.

So instead, I just close my eyes, and tilt my head against the window.

"Thanks," I say.

CHAPTER TWELVE

INGRID'S RIGHT. AT THE breakfast table I'm treated to an awkward lecture on the curfew. "I know this is . . . a new situation, for both of us," Dad says, spreading jam on his toast. "But I expect you home by ten on a school night."

I nod mutely, hoping the smile I've pasted on my face does a good enough job of hiding my misery. My skull feels like it's hanging in splinters, jabbing into my brain every time I move.

He looks significantly across the table. "I'm sorry about your friend, Ruthie. Let us know if there's any way we can help."

You can stop talking, I think. *Immediately. And turn down the lights.* But I just give a little nod. "Thanks," I whisper.

It's a relief to step outside into the biting cold. The chill feels good against my clammy skin. I get why people drink now. It'd felt good to forget for a little while, to turn off my brain. Here in the hard sober light of day I feel trapped in my own thoughts, like they're a spiderweb holding me tight. I tug one strand, trying to untangle myself, but there are five others attached to it. All of them about Zahra.

Ingrid hands me a bottle of ibuprofen without a word. I pop two, then climb into the driver's seat. "Good thing I didn't yarf on the passenger side," I say weakly.

She just smiles.

I still haven't had a chance to talk to a counselor about my schedule, but I've decided to keep yearbook anyway. It's a chance to stick close to Zahra's friends, to Zahra herself, if she comes home safe.

But Merrill High has a rotating class schedule, so I don't have yearbook this morning. Instead I make my way through biology and English and economics. The mood is subdued. I feel like I keep hearing Zahra's name from all sides, but when I turn to look for who's talking I can't ever find the source.

By lunch, I'm starting to feel better. The roiling nausea has stabilized, but I'm still not very hungry. Ingrid and I head to the cafeteria after fourth period, and I buy an orange juice and turn to find a seat. But before I can move, my eyes lock with someone else's.

It's the boy from yesterday, the one that stared at me while I was at my locker. He's sitting alone, a crumpled lunch sack in front of him. His pants are frayed at the hems, pooling across the top of his worn-out work boots. He's got his hoodie sleeves pulled down over his wrists.

I glance around to make sure it's me he's looking at.

"Hey, hang on just a second," I tell Ingrid. "I've got to talk to someone."

I walk purposefully through the cafeteria and sit down across from the boy. He looks startled by that, green eyes going narrow.

"What do you want, Ruthie?" he asks.

I blink. Then I look him over again. I notice that his eyes are oddly swollen, almost purple. He's either exhausted or sick. "Do I know you?"

His mouth falls open. Then he gives a short bark of laughter.

"For real?" He scans my face, then shakes his head. "You really don't remember me."

"Sorry," I say. I search for something familiar in his eyes, in the curve of his mouth. "I've been gone a long time, and . . ."

"I used to live down the street from you. At Walker Court," he says.

"Oh!" I force a smile, even though I'm still drawing a blank. "Okay. What was your name again?"

"Seb," he says. "Seb Collins."

"Oh, yeah! Didn't you live in the trailer with the . . . the blue trim?" I ask. I'm improvising wildly and he seems to know it.

"No," he says shortly.

A memory springs up, one I didn't know I had. Walking home from the bus toward the end of eighth grade, my guitar in hand. A small, hunched-looking boy walking a few paces behind me. We always got off at the same stop, and we never said a word to each other, but our trailers were close together.

Then one day, I heard his voice, creaky in the midst of dropping. "Can I look at your guitar?"

I remember pulling it out on my front steps and handing it to him. I remember how he inexpertly brushed his hands over the frets. He had a bruise over one eye.

"I got one at a garage sale but it's missing its strings," he said. "Once I fix it up I'm going to learn how to play."

It was just a week or two after we left my dad, and I was a robot girl, a wind-up doll, going through the motions. I didn't know how to talk to people. So I don't remember what I said to him then. Was it something noncommittal, like *neat, cool, nice*? Something friendly, inviting? *I've got some extra strings, let me get them for you*? Or, *You should come over when you fix it up, I'll show you what I know*? Or something haughty and dismissive? *Good luck with that. It's actually not as easy as it looks.*

I don't remember. I feel like it could have been any one.

Now, I examine Seb's face, trying to see some hint of that little boy in his features. I don't even know for sure if it's him. But something in his hard green eyes makes me think I'm right.

"Do you still live in Walker Court?" I ask, my attention going sharp. I suddenly realize—if he does, he could know Zahra.

But he recoils a little, his lips curling in a grimace.

"Nope," he says flatly. He picks up his lunch sack. "Not since ninth grade." He stands up. "Any other questions, or can I go eat my lunch in peace?"

"In peace? Wait a minute, you're the one . . ." I sputter. But he's already walking away. On his way out the door he throws his lunch bag violently into the trash.

I sit motionless, watching after him. Was that all just about a guitar? Or is there something else, something I don't remember? It occurs to me that I've only ever seen the guy alone. Maybe he's just . . . pissed at the world.

Thoughts of Seb Collins disappear, though, when I get up to find Ingrid. Because she's sitting at a small round table, right in between Tabitha and Marcus.

"How do you know Seb?" Ingrid asks as I slide in next to her.

"I used to live next door to him," I say, swallowing my own question about why she's sitting here with Zahra's friends instead of with her own. She made no bones about the fact that she didn't much care for Tabitha last night.

Tabitha's wearing oversize black shades and is picking at the corner of an energy bar. When I lean toward her I catch a faint whiff of alcohol, and I'm not sure if it's coming from her water bottle or if it's just last night's excess leaving her pores. On the other side of Ingrid, Marcus is busy looking at his phone.

The pained silence speaks volumes about how welcome Ingrid and I are at this table.

God, this lunch period is nothing if not proof that I'm not the only awkward person in the world.

"How're you feeling today, Tabitha?" I ask politely.

She takes a swig from her water bottle. "Never better," she says. "But I'm sorry *you* got so fucked up, Ruthless. I didn't know your tolerance was that low."

Ah. We're back to passive-aggressive digs, in the cold sober light of day.

"You were pretty out of it yourself last night," Ingrid says cheerfully. "I'm glad to see you're hydrating, though. Binge drinking can be so hard on the skin. You want to get that moisture back in there."

Marcus mouths *holy shit* in my direction. Neither Tabitha nor Ingrid seem to notice.

"Anyway," I say loudly. "I still have your suit. I'll bring it back tomorrow."

"Sure." She might be looking at me, but I can't tell; the shades are so dark.

I think about the night before—the sketchbook in Tabitha's bedroom, filled with studies of Ben. Think about the casual way she hopped from guy to guy in the hot tub, like they were interchangeable. Had she hooked up with Ben the same way? Or had it been a crush, unrequited and unfulfilled? I look down at the table and pretend to study my fingers, but I let my eyes flick toward her.

"Have you heard anything new about Zahra?" Ingrid asks.

Tabitha just gives a sullen shrug, but Marcus shakes his head. "No. But at least they got the story up on the news. I was kind of worried they wouldn't. Black girls don't always get good press."

An awkward silence falls over the table. Ingrid and I look at each other, our eyes round. Tabitha just smirks and sips from her Gatorade.

He's right. I'd never thought of it like that, but he's right.

"I'm glad someone in the newsroom gives a shit, I guess," I finally say. Ingrid nods fervently.

"So what did Ben say last night?" I ask. "About Zahra, I mean?"

"We didn't talk about it," Tabitha says. She takes off her shades and squints blearily across the table. "Her, I mean. We didn't talk about her. I was a little indisposed. Ben just hung out and made sure I didn't die of alcohol poisoning."

"We talked a little," Marcus says. "He's pretty pissed. The cops had him in the station for, like, nine hours yesterday. But I guess he's got a really good lawyer, so . . ."

I blink with surprise. "That was fast."

"Well, yeah." Tabitha takes another sip from her drink. "He's not a moron. You don't talk to the cops without a lawyer."

I nod slowly, but I can't help but wonder about that. I get being calm in a crisis—I'm sure there are people creeped out by my calm in the wake of Mom's death. But it feels like another level entirely to think immediately about hiring a lawyer before you're technically even a suspect. And what does Marcus mean, Ben was "pissed"? That's not how I'd expect someone worried about their ex to react.

"I heard they were fighting about another boy," Ingrid says suddenly.

A flush spreads across Tabitha's forehead.

"Hi, do you even *know* Ben?" she asks. "What do you even care?"

I hold my breath for a moment, cutting my eyes back at Ingrid. She doesn't seem fazed.

"I don't know him *well*," she says. "I mean, I know who he is. But Sophie Advincula told me Ben accused her of cheating."

Now we're all looking at Ingrid. Tabitha's expression hasn't changed, but her cheeks are steadily darkening. It gives the impression of a soda bottle being shaken, the fizz mounting but the cap still firmly on.

"I don't even know who that is," Tabitha says with forced calm. "So I don't know how she's supposed to know something I don't."

"She was at the party last Friday," Ingrid says. I'm starting to see something beneath the veneer of sweetness and light. She may be sincere, but she's also relentless. "Anyway, she also said Ben called Zahra some really bad names."

Tabitha's lip coils like a rearing snake. That's when I know it's true. Ben broke up with Zahra because he thought she was cheating—and Tabitha knows it.

"Oh, bad names? God forbid," she sneers. "Grow the fuck up, Ingrid."

Ingrid just gives a little shrug. "I'm just saying, it's probably good he got a lawyer."

Before Tabitha has a chance to answer, someone slides in next to me on the bench. It's Jeremy, a paper McDonald's bag clenched in his fist.

And with him is Ben, squeezing in on the other side, right between Tabitha and Jeremy.

My lungs clench, the air suddenly too heavy to breathe. I squeeze over as far as I can, dizzy with nerves. Neither Jeremy nor Ben seems to notice the tension at the table.

Jeremy looks around at us all. "I know, I know, fast food at peak running season. But French fries are God's own hangover cure."

No one answers. Next to him Ben's in the process of unwrapping a Big Mac, silent and efficient.

"And no, I didn't invite you, Tabitha, because you always nag," Jeremy goes on. "Not all of us can live off PowerBars and . . ."

He trails off, looking around the table. "Uh. What's up? Was there some kind of news?"

"No," Marcus says quickly, glancing at Ben. "Nope. No news."

I glance at Ingrid. Is she ballsy enough to say anything to Ben's face? But she just smiles.

"Hey, Ben," she says. "Thanks again for looking out for Ruthie last night."

Ben glances up at Ingrid, then looks at me. "Sure," he says. His voice is low and quiet, but not unfriendly.

I expect him to say something more, to acknowledge the tension at the table. To ask a question. But he doesn't. He just smears some ketchup on his burger, puts the bun back, and takes a large and eager bite, as if everything were completely normal.

What happened that night? And how many people know about it? I pick at the rest of my food, listening as the conversation dies out and the rest of the table eats in silence. It's clear that I'm not going to get the truth from Ben's friends. Which means I'm going to have to find out for myself.

CHAPTER THIRTEEN

WEDNESDAY AFTERNOON I DRIVE back to school just before five. The building is mostly dark, but the athletic center—the wing of the school with the gyms, the pool, the locker rooms, and all the equipment—still blazes bright. I find a parking spot near the glass entryway, and wait.

All the fall sports teams are wrapping up for the night. From where I'm parked I can see the football team heading toward the glass doors, lugging tackling dummies and other equipment behind them. Kids in swim team letter jackets come out, hair slicked and wet. The lights over the courts are still bright as the tennis team's coach delivers a final lecture before dismissing them for the night.

And there, stepping out of the darkness, come the runners.

They practice on the trails. On that same arterial network where I rode my bike last night—on the same network that swallowed Zahra up into its darkness a little less than a week ago. The cross-country team emerges from the woods like ghosts springing out of the ether, invisible one moment and there the next. I recognize most of them by now—the girl with the hoops, a few boys from the hot tub, their bodies slumped with exhaustion. Their breath billows and steams away from them. I watch as some of them make their way to the school— to shower, probably—while others go directly to their cars.

The four of them come last. Tabitha, Jeremy, Marcus, and Ben. Ben has an arm around Tabitha's shoulders. I can't quite make out their expressions. But they wouldn't be hooking up just days after Zahra's disappearance, even if Ben and Zahra did break up.

Right?

They stand in front of the door for a few minutes, talking. Marcus and Jeremy break away first, heading into the school with a wave. Tabitha and Ben stand another moment, his arm still around her shoulder. Then they hug—a long, lingering hug.

The light appears between them again as their bodies separate. And then he turns and walks out into the parking lot. I sink down low in my seat as he passes near my car and watch his progress in my rearview mirror. He stops and talks to a football player for a second. A little further on, a few girls in cheerleader's uniforms run toward him, one throwing her arms around him. I'm sure they're all talking about Zahra. I'd bet anything some of these kids are the same ones spreading rumors, talking about the fight he had with Zahra, all but accusing him behind his back. But to his face, they're all camaraderie and fist bumps.

Finally, he makes it to a truck parked back near the entrance. I watch as he climbs in and starts it up. I wait until he's already pulled out of the lot before I follow.

I look around one more time, and am not surprised to see Tabitha, still standing in the doorway, still watching him.

THE STREETS ARE CHOKED with rush hour traffic, a smear of red brake lights across my windshield. Ben is easy to tail. The truck sits tall in traffic, and his muffler desperately needs a tune-up. I'm so busy watching him I almost drift into the other lane. Someone lays on their horn and I correct, my heart beating out a frantic tattoo. Crap. I duck down as low as I can in the driver's seat, praying he doesn't see me.

If he does, he doesn't let on. Maybe a quarter mile down the road from the school, he turns left at a light.

The subdivision is full of tidy little houses, most of them older. In the dark I can mostly only see the bright lights in the windows—kitchens framed with eyelet lace, living rooms with the news flickering on the TV. I trail a few blocks behind Ben's truck, marking his turns. It's not even a full minute before I see him pull into a driveway. I park a few houses down against the curb and watch.

It's a boxy red house with a wheelchair ramp at the front door and hanging baskets of flowers under the eaves. A yellow porch light illuminates a handmade wooden sign that says

PEAVY. Ben gets out of his truck and heads up to the front door, letting himself in.

I sit there for maybe ten minutes. My fingers start to seize up in the cold; I huddle further into my coat, pull my hood up over my ears. I'm not sure what I think I'm going to discover, watching the exterior of his house. For a second I think about giving up and going home. Ben's probably in for the night anyway—taking a shower and eating dinner and starting homework and texting friends, doing all the normal after-school stuff.

Then I think about the blood on his shoe, and my jaw tightens.

I have to learn more about him, and I'm not going to get answers from his friends. This might be the only way to find out who Ben Peavy really is.

Then his front door opens again, and I duck low in my seat.

He steps out, carrying an armful of uneven packages, wrapped up in white paper. He throws them into the back of his truck. Then he climbs in the driver's seat and turns the engine.

My eyes dart down the street after him. Then, too curious to stop myself, I follow.

He steers past the small-craft airport, past the hospital. Down a dingy commercial street and into a neighborhood of cheap apartments and boxy, vinyl-sided houses. He finally pulls up to one; in the dark I can't make out much besides a metal mailbox at the gate, painted to look like a leaping salmon.

I watch as Ben gets one of the packages out of the truck. He knocks on the door in a rhythmic pattern. Knock-knock, pause, knock-knock. The door swings inward and I catch a glimpse of a woman, bundled up in an oversize sweater. From here she looks Native, her complexion almost the same as Ben's, but I'm too far away to be sure. Ben talks to her for a moment. She nods, says something back. They both laugh. Then she goes inside and shuts the door.

He gets back in the truck, and he's off again. He drops off two more packages in the same neighborhood, always knocking the same way. Alarm bells are going off in my mind. What the hell kind of door-to-door delivery requires a secret knock?

The fourth stop is a duplex with peeling gray paint. Knock-knock, pause, knock-knock. The door opens. It's a man covered in tattoos, maybe just a few years older than we are. Ben tucks the package under his arm to fist-bump him. Then, instead of handing it over, he goes inside, still holding the package. The door shuts behind them.

I don't know how long I sit there, watching the door. Finally I get out of the car. I walk calmly, quietly across the street to the duplex, as if I belong there.

The windows are covered with foil. My mom used to do the same thing—it's the cheapest way to keep the sun out in the middle of summer so you can get some sleep. It was always kind of a ritual to take the foil down in the fall. Here, no one's bothered, even though the days are getting shorter all the time. Broken appliances line the side of the

J174house—an ancient washing machine, a stained toilet. I walk cautiously around the edge of the house, looking for a crack in a window.

In the back, I find one, looking into a cramped kitchen. I stand on tiptoes, trying to see some sign of Ben and the man inside.

Something clicks behind me. I straighten and turn. The barrel of a rifle stares back at me.

CHAPTER FOURTEEN

"Who the fuck are you?"

It's the tattooed man, the one Ben went inside with. He keeps the gun trained on me.

I can't take my eyes off it. Its long black muzzle, the glossy wooden stock. Distantly I'm aware I should be doing something—putting my hands up, maybe, or trying to back away, but I stand frozen and stare.

"Hey. Hey!" Ben comes rushing around the corner then, panic pulling his eyes wide. "Solomon, man, calm down. Put that thing down, okay?"

"The fuck you doing looking in my windows?" The guy doesn't lower the gun at all, but he does look up at me, nostrils flaring.

"I . . . I wasn't. I mean, I didn't mean to. I mean . . ." I trail off. I don't know what to say. My body feels too heavy and awkward to move, so I don't bother.

"She's not spying on you," Ben says. "She's spying on me."

His voice is quiet and calm, but there's something chilling about that. I can feel the hair on my neck arching upward. Suppressed anger is always scarier, somehow. Maybe it's just because you're holding your breath, waiting for it to erupt.

"That's right, isn't it?" he asks. "I had a feeling about that car but I thought it was my imagination." He jerks his head toward my car. "She thinks I did something to Zahra."

The guy with the gun looks confused. He looks at Ben like he's waiting for instructions.

Ben takes a step toward me, so our faces are just a few inches apart.

"Just what do you think I did, anyway?" he asks softly. "What do you think you're gonna learn, following me? What, you think I . . . I killed her and I'll go back to the scene of the crime, or something?"

I shake my head. My throat is tight, and I can't seem to make myself speak. His eyes flash.

"I loved her." The words rip out of his throat, sudden and ragged and loud. "Okay? I fucking loved her more than I've ever loved anyone. I'd never hurt her. God, I can't believe I feel like I have to explain myself to you. I. Loved. Her."

My lips tremble. *Don't say it, don't say it, don't say it,* I think, but I can't help myself. "Why are you using the past tense?" I ask.

He gives a frustrated snarl, turning away to slam his fist against the side of the house. I jump back, startled.

"You see?" he asks the other guy. "See how quick I go

from being a, quote, 'credit to my people' to being just another fucking dirtbag Native criminal? Man, I told you." He turns back to me. "Whatever, think what you want. You're not the only one."

I swallow hard. Suddenly I feel like I've made a mistake. A big one—and it's not just because I have a gun trained on me.

"Get the fuck out of here," he says. "Stay away from me and my family, or I really will hurt someone."

He turns and storms back around the side of the house, leaving the man with the gun behind, looking uncertain.

He lowers the muzzle a little, trying to save face. "You heard him," he says. "Get gone."

I summon all my strength, straightening my spine. Then slowly, deliberately, I walk back to my car.

I don't realize how shallowly I'm breathing until I'm half a mile away, heading back to my house. I roll down the window, gulp at the fresh air. The image of that muzzle—its round darkness, its unblinking eye—is seared into my mind. I blink hard, trying to clear it out.

Now I've seen Ben's temper—seen the rage that was hard to imagine before. But I also feel a creeping sense of guilt. I hadn't stopped to think about how scrutinized he must feel. About how unfair it is that he's probably had to work doubly hard to get the attention a white boy would get. And how unfair it is for that admiration to be gone the moment he's suspected of doing something wrong.

Tears suddenly spring to my eyes. I pull over to the side of the road. I cover my face with my icy fingers.

"I don't know what else to do," I whisper into the darkness. "Help me, Starmaiden. Send me some kind of . . . some kind of sign. Help me find you."

If this were our book, there'd be a glimmer of stardust before me. A rune or a compass or some kind of pathway would open up in brilliant light.

But it's not. It's the real world. It's the same ugly stupid place I've always lived, where people vanish, where sick sad things happen, and where I am completely powerless to do anything about it.

CHAPTER FIFTEEN

"WE SEE, BROTHERS AND sisters, that blood is connected to sin from the beginning of time."

It's Sunday—a week since I got back home. If you'd told me then that I'd be sitting in church today, in the middle row of the biggest fundamentalist congregation in Anchorage, I would have laughed in your face. But here I am, perched on the end of the pew next to Ingrid. Dad and Brandy are on the other side of her, sitting ramrod straight and looking attentively at the lectern, where a middle-aged white man stands with a carnation in his lapel. His face is flushed with excitement.

"We see it in Genesis three twenty-one, after Adam and Eve become aware of their nakedness. 'Unto Adam also and to his wife did the Lord God make coats of skins, and clothed them.'" He slaps the podium with a bare hand. "Can you imagine, brothers and sisters, the smell of that first slaughter?

Can you imagine the blood, red and hot and stinking of sin, when that first creature was killed for its hide?"

My best friend's grandfather. It still boggles the mind.

"Eve, in particular, is punished with blood. Her blood, like her sin, is unclean. Leviticus fifteen makes that abundantly clear. 'And if a woman have an issue, and her issue in her flesh be blood, she shall be put apart seven days: and whosoever toucheth her shall be unclean until the even. And everything that she lieth upon in her separation shall be unclean: everything also that she sitteth upon shall be unclean . . .'" He draws out the word *unclean* every time he says it. "When we fell from innocence, brothers and sisters, when we ate of the apple, we learned of birth and death. We learned of suffering. It was a high price to pay. A very high price."

It's hard to picture easy-going, quick-to-laugh Charity coming from a background like this. It's even harder to picture Zahra taking an interest in it. I think about what Ron said—how, suddenly, in the middle of her freshman year, Zahra went to live with her grandparents. With this man, currently waxing eloquent about the menstrual cycle and its relation to sin. I imagine her sitting through this sermon, stifling her giggles. She couldn't have stayed here long—no matter how much she's changed, that much is still true.

"And yet it is through blood that we are purified and given our path to eternal life!" The pastor slaps the podium again for emphasis. There's a quick squawk of feedback on the mike. "It is through the blood of the Lamb, pouring hot and red from His living body."

I glance at my dad from the corner of my eye. He's on the other side of Ingrid from me, his expression earnestly rapt. I know a lot of people find religion when they get clean, but I wonder how he landed here, with this particular church. I get the appeal of a higher power—but you'd think he'd be more in line for a message of hope, or forgiveness. Not whatever the hell this is about.

But then, he's not alone. The church is packed. The congregation is mostly white—though there are a few very large families of interracial adoptions, children from around the world squirming in their seats. In front of us there's an impossibly young mother with a duckling row of toddlers she keeps shushing. There's a bunch of teenagers, too—I met them all in the youth group meeting before church proper, when Devon, the "hip" young youth pastor in chinos, introduced me around. They're all clean-scrubbed and earnest and at least superficially nice.

My thoughts wander as he drones on, turning in anxious circles, fidgeting over every scrap of information I have. I avoided Ben for the rest of the week, eating lunch with Ingrid and her friends in the choir room. I wonder if he's told Tabitha or the others about me following him. My guess is no. Tabitha's taken to texting me pretty regularly since lunch that day, and she hasn't mentioned it.

I can still remember how it felt to have that gun trained on me. Can still feel the strange, flat calm that suffused my body. But it hadn't been Ben holding the gun. He'd come out to save me. To be honest, he'd seemed almost as freaked out as me at the rifle. That doesn't necessarily mean anything. But it does sort of complicate the idea of him as a cold-blooded murderer.

Ingrid nudges me, and I open my eyes. The congregation is getting to its feet. I stand up, too, blinking to clear my head a little. Does this mean we get to go home? Church is over?

No. Ingrid's picking up one of the heavy red hymnals, flipping it open as the music starts. I glance down at the lyrics and sigh. Would you look at that? They're about blood.

"What can wash away my sin?" Ingrid croons. She's got a sweet, bright voice. "Nothing but the blood of Jesus!"

There *are* other parts to the Bible, right? I seem to remember something about loaves and fishes. Or maybe a nice story about a rainbow-colored coat. I've seen the musical and it definitely focuses less on carnage. But even though nineteenth-century American religious music isn't quite my scene, I can't help but sing along, finding the alto harmony to complement Ingrid's soprano. I've always loved singing duets. Something about the movement of two voices together, the way they make space for each other, the way they hoist each other up and strengthen each other. Our eyes meet for a moment, and we smile.

The organ gives a few wobbly final chords. Everyone's still as the echoes die away. And then, by some unspoken consensus, the spell is broken. It's all over. People begin to stretch and move, turning to talk to their neighbors, giving awkward side-hugs. Dad and Brandy get caught up in a conversation with an older couple in front of us. Ingrid turns to look at me.

I frown, looking up at the pulpit.

"What's the matter?" she asks.

"I just think it's odd that he didn't say anything about Zahra," I say. "His own granddaughter's missing, and he doesn't say anything about it? Doesn't pray for her?"

"I mean, I'm sure he prays for her privately," Ingrid says. "Maybe he just doesn't want to talk about his personal life."

Maybe. But it's still weird to me.

"Does he come out to, like, mingle after a performance?" I ask suddenly.

Ingrid turns to look me fully in the face, her brow furrowed. "You mean a sermon? Not usually. I think he usually heads to one of the offices after."

"I kind of need to talk to him," I say. "Is there some way to . . . you know, go find him? Could you introduce me to him?"

She gives a short laugh.

"I mean, it's not like I know him personally." She gestures around. "It's a big congregation."

"Yeah, but what if I have questions?" I say. "About . . . my *unclean* menstrual issue? Or something spiritual?"

She purses her lips. "Well, you could talk to Devon. That's who you'd usually go to."

I try not to make a face imagining Devon answering questions about any part of my body. Ingrid glances around the room, then seems to give in.

"But if you really want to talk to Pastor Worthen, I can show you where his offices are."

THE OFFICES ARE DOWN a narrow, indirectly lit hallway lined with carpet so thick our feet make no sound. Most of the art is predictable: white, blond Jesus knocking at the door; white, blond Jesus sitting with the white, blond children. I wonder if it bothered Pastor Worthen to have a black grandchild. But maybe that's not fair—blond Jesus is a staple with people like this. That doesn't mean he's racist. Necessarily.

The door to his office is rather grand, with molding around the edges and a brass nameplate. DALE WORTHEN, D.MIN. Without hesitating I knock, three quick raps. Ingrid gives me a nervous look.

Behind the door, a murmur so faint I didn't even register it at first suddenly goes quiet. A moment later, the door swings open.

The woman who stands there is middle-aged, as bony-thin as Dale Worthen is stocky. Her ash-blonde hair is twisted at the nape of her neck, and she's dressed in pale cashmere. It gives her the impression of being strangely washed-out, almost ghostly. But then I meet her eyes—and I can see the faintest flicker of Zahra, there in her deep-set hazel irises.

"Hello there," she says, and her tone is softer than I expected. She gives a fleeting little smile. "How can I help you girls?"

Behind her, I can see Worthen at his desk.

Ingrid fidgets with the hem of her cardigan. "Hi, Mrs. Worthen. I . . . I'm Ingrid Bell, and this is my stepsister, Ruth Hayden. She's new to the church, and she wanted to . . ."

"I wanted to talk to Pastor Worthen. About . . . about Zahra. I'm a friend of hers," I say.

"Ah." Her lips press together tightly enough to go pale. She shifts her weight, almost as if she's trying to shield her husband from our view. "Girls, that's very kind, but I'm afraid . . ."

"Let them in."

Pastor Worthen's voice comes from behind her, not loud, but firm. It's almost strange to hear his normal tone of voice after hearing his sermon boom and echo around the chapel.

The woman's eye twitches, ever so slightly. She opens the door wide and gestures for us to step in.

The room is covered from floor to ceiling with theological books. *A Quiverfull of Blessings. A Woman's Place. Spare the Rod, Ruin the Child.* The walls have rich wood paneling, and fresh flowers stand in a tall vase on an end table. The sofa and chairs are all brown leather. Pastor Worthen is sitting behind a large oak desk, hands clasped in front of him.

His eyes are blue, almost flat in color, as they flicker between me and Ingrid. Just behind us, his wife smooths her skirt with quick, nervous movements.

All at once, he breaks into a grim, toothy smile. It reminds me of a shark. Or maybe I'm projecting, after the gory sermon.

"Welcome to Victory Evangelical," he says to me. "Ruth,

you said? And Ingrid. I remember you. You were the angel of the Annunciation last Christmas, weren't you?"

Her cheeks flush pink. "Yes, thank you, pastor."

He nods toward the chairs across the desk from him. "Take a seat, girls, take a seat."

We both sit down. I sense rather than see Mrs. Worthen, still standing off to one side, making small rustling movements like a bird beneath a hedge. She's all nerves.

"I'm sorry if I'm interrupting," I start, but he shakes his head impatiently.

"No, no. We were, in fact, just talking about our granddaughter. Weren't we, Grace?"

His voice is calm, but there's a note in it I can't quite place. Something hard and sharp. I glance back at Mrs. Worthen and see her drop her eyes to the carpet.

"I'm . . . I'm very sorry," I say. "That she's missing. I just wanted to find out if there's anything I could do to help."

Here comes the smile again, quick and almost aggressively white.

"Thank you, Ruth. I thank you." He clasps his hands together on his desk. "Please just keep us in your prayers for the time being."

I nod. "I will." I pause for a moment, to see if he has anything else to say. "Are you—either of you—going to be at the search party later?"

"No," he says bluntly. And then, seeing my surprised expression, he shakes his head a little. "No, I find it's better to keep my distance from my daughter and her family," he says.

"They have chosen to live their lives outside the biblical values I tried so hard to instill."

I don't know why that means he can't go look for his own granddaughter. But it does make me remember something else.

"That's not always been the case, though, right?" I ask. "Mr. Gaines said Zahra lived with you for a little while. That she wanted to be saved."

There's a soft gasp from off to the side, but when I look at her, Mrs. Worthen is still studying the carpet. Next to me, Ingrid's gone very still. I think she's even holding her breath.

God, have none of these women ever asked a man a direct question before? I turn back to face the pastor. A ruddy patch has swept up his neck, across his cheeks. There's a large picture window behind his desk, with a view of the school grounds below—the playground, the sports field—and beyond that, a line of trees. He swivels to one side in his chair and looks out.

"My granddaughter wasn't ready for what the Lord required of her," he says.

His voice is so even that it takes me a moment to really understand what he's saying. To hear the anger, missing from his tone, but implicit in the words. The ownership: not *Zahra*, but *my granddaughter*. What, exactly, had the Lord required?

What had Worthen?

But before I can frame the question in my mind, he bows his head. "Let us pray."

Next to me, Ingrid drops her gaze. It takes me a moment to follow suit.

"Heavenly Father, we ask that You aid our sister in Christ, Zahra Gaines, in this hour of greatest need. We ask that You open her heart to Your Word so that she can be saved. We ask that she be given Your Spirit so that she can live forever at Your side. In Jesus's name, amen."

"Amen," murmurs Ingrid.

I echo it a half second too late.

He stands abruptly. "I'm sorry to say I have a meeting with the church officers that I need to prepare for," he says. "But please, come by any time if you have any spiritual concerns," he says, shaking my hand with both of his. There's a subtle stress to the word *spiritual*.

"Thank you for making the time to speak with us," Ingrid says. She turns and starts toward the door.

I turn to follow her, my brows knit in frustration. As I pass, I meet Grace Worthen's eyes. For a second I feel like she's trying to tell me something, urgently and silently, with her gaze. But then she smiles that same tight smile and opens the door for us without another word.

Back in the hallway, the potpourri smell is almost stifling. "Come on," I say. "Let's go out front and wait for the parents."

We make our way down the hall, back to the chapel. "What a lovely man," I mutter. "I can see why you guys come here."

"It's complicated," Ingrid says softly.

I just shrug. I can't stop thinking about that prayer . . .

about the fact that he'll pray for her soul, but not her safety. If God's real, he should just bring Zahra home safe and sound . . . not play some cat-and-mouse game with her salvation. Maybe that's why Charity doesn't want anything to do with him. He's the kind of person who'd rather have a granddaughter who's saved than safe.

Back in the chapel, the crowds are starting to dissipate. I wonder what it's like to stand at that pulpit, to have so much attention directed your way. Not just attention—faith. Belief. It must feel so powerful, to wield that kind of influence.

So why wouldn't he want to use that power to help find Zahra? Is it just a petty family grudge?

Or some rift deeper, and darker, still?

CHAPTER SIXTEEN

By Sunday afternoon the sky is chalk white. Everything looks stark underneath, the bare trees gnarled like claws, the undergrowth dying in thick brown tufts. There's a muted hush over everything, even though the parking lot is packed with people.

There have been a few other, less official search parties earlier in the week—people out combing the trails for her. But this is the first big organized search. It seems absurd that it's taken over a week for them to organize it, but everything about Zahra's disappearance has been murky. There's no clear timeline, no real sense of when she vanished or who last saw her. So I guess it makes sense for the search process to be a mess, too.

Ingrid and I walk through the Goose Lake parking lot, the meet-up spot for the search party. Half the school's here, and the trailer park, too. There are news vans lined up on one side of the lot, reporters in windbreakers smoothing their hair and talking into microphones. I see a girl whose name I don't know weeping for a camera.

"Everyone's got to have their fifteen minutes of attention," Ingrid says under her breath.

"Yeah." But I don't mind. I've never been so glad that Zahra's popular—it means she's getting coverage. It's like Marcus said. Not all girls get this kind of press—especially black girls.

Ron stands at center of a shifting mass, people moving in and out of orbit. There are faces I recognize from the trailer park, and other people who must be friends or family. There's a stocky man with a low fade who has to be a brother or a cousin or something—his features are so like Ron's.

When Ron sees me, he smiles and opens his arms for a hug. Ingrid hangs back a little, giving us some space.

"Ruthie," he says. I can feel his arms tremble around me. "Thanks for coming."

I can only nod as I pull back to look at him. He looks awful—like he hasn't slept all week.

"Where's Charity?" I ask. "And Malik?"

He gestures across the lot. "Malik's over there with his cousins. Some of my family's up from Texas, to help out. Charity . . ." He hesitates. "She's in bad shape. I made her take a Xanax and she's finally getting some sleep."

"Good," I say. "I bet she needs it." I bite the corner of my lip, wondering if I should say anything, and then I plunge on. "Went to church with my family today."

His mouth gives a sudden downward twist. "You met the good pastor, huh? He give you a load of fire and brimstone?"

I glance at Ingrid. She's a few feet away, hands in her pockets. "Blood and guts, more like," I say softly. "But they're praying for Zahra."

"Isn't that nice of them," he says. "Don't see many of his church folk here right now, though. Do you?"

"No," I say.

"Yeah." He shakes his head. "That old man is a piece of work. Charity hasn't talked to him in years. He didn't have much use for me, I'll tell you that much. If he really wanted to help out, there are ways he could."

"I still can't believe Zahra tried to live with him," I say.

He hesitates for a moment. "Yeah. I don't know what that was all about. When they were little Charity used to take the kids over for visits. But she never trusted her parents with them alone. Not after the way she was raised." He shakes his head. "I grew up Baptist and my grandma never spared the rod, but from what she told me, her parents really took it to a whole new level."

"But then her freshman year . . . ?" I start to ask and he gives a hard chuckle.

"Yeah. Not long after you left, actually." He purses his lips in thought. "She was going on about salvation and sin and all that crap. I always thought maybe someone at school got into her head about it."

I nod. It sounds out of character for Zahra—especially out of character for the Zahra I knew back then. But you have to learn to deal with a whole new social ecosystem when you start high school. Maybe she'd been feeling particularly vulnerable, and her grandparents' religion had seemed like a welcome bit of structure.

Or maybe whatever had happened to her—whatever Tabitha keeps alluding to, whatever apparently made Zahra so anxious and unstable—had left her looking for some kind of meaning.

"Anyway," Ron says. "She came back home after a couple weeks. Refused to talk about it. But she hasn't talked to them since." He shakes his head again. It looks like he's about to say something else, but someone calls his name from another cluster of people, and he glances up. "Sorry, Ruthie, I've got to make the rounds. You come by the house sometime soon. I know it'd mean a lot to Charity."

"Okay," I say. "Thanks, Ron."

I look around again for Ingrid. I'm a little startled when I find her with the cross-country team near one of the trailheads. She stands out in her purple swing coat and wool beret in the middle of all that sleek winter workout gear. Tabitha's watching her with mild irritation.

And there's Ben.

His eyes meet mine, and I see the faintest hint of a smirk flit across his face. I steel myself and walk over to them.

"Hey," I say to the group at large, fidgeting with the fringe on the end of my scarf.

"There you are," Tabitha says. "What's up, Ruthless?"

"Hey," I say. "Just hoping we find Zahra today."

I can feel Ben's eyes on me, but I force myself not to look at him.

"So the cops been all over you, or what, man?" Marcus asks Ben.

Ben nods. "Yeah. Nothing formal yet. But they're not subtle. I spent nine hours on Friday at the station making a statement, and they've come to the house almost every day since with follow-up questions."

"Your mom must be freaked, huh?" says Marcus.

"Mom, Grandma, the kids." He pushes his hands through his hair. The top is growing out, a long, thick pompadour that flops over one eye. "Yeah, they're all scared. Mom's spending I don't know how much on this lawyer."

"Lawyer?" The girl from the party—Annika, the cross-country co-captain—does a double take. "Why do you need a lawyer? Doesn't that just make you look guilty?"

There's an awkward silence, and then Marcus smiles at her, not unkindly.

"You know what else makes you look guilty?" Marcus says. "False confessions and planted evidence. It doesn't just happen on, like, podcasts and shit. Some of us get to worry about that in real life, too. Especially if we have a little . . . what's the word?"

"Melanin," Ben says bluntly. They're both smiling faintly, but there's something almost weary about their expressions.

I feel my cheeks go warm. I'd reacted the same way as Annika to the news that Ben had a lawyer. I suddenly feel like an asshole.

Annika's eyes go very round. "Don't you think that's a little paranoid?" she says. "I mean . . . the cops just want to find Zahra. They're not going to *frame* you or something."

Ben just looks at her, brows furrowed, like he almost feels sorry for her. "Sure. Let's see how hard they try to find out what really happened to a *black* girl whose *Native* boyfriend doesn't really have a decent alibi. Let's see just how many resources they put into that particular search."

"I didn't mean . . ." She recoils a little. "The cops aren't going to just . . ."

"Oh my God, Annika, just shut up while you're ahead." Tabitha rolls her eyes skyward. "Your ignorance is giving me a headache."

I'm extremely relieved when an older white woman with a megaphone suddenly climbs onto the bed of a truck, and we all go silent.

"Okay, gather up, everyone, gather up." She's grizzled, with a smoker's hoarse voice and hair that washed-out color in the limbo between blonde and gray. "I'm Becks. I'm a friend of the Gaines family. Thanks for coming to help look for our girl."

"God, she knows the weirdest people," Tabitha mutters. I ignore her. I'm pretty sure for Tabitha "weird" just translates to "poor," at least in this instance.

"Couple ground rules before we really get going." Becks adjusts the volume a little. "No solo acts. Go in groups, or at least find a partner. There've been bears around here this summer so make some noise while you walk. Talk, or sing, or whatever. They don't want to mess with humans. If you let them know you're coming they'll leave you alone."

The thought makes the small hairs on the back of my neck arch up. Every kid in Alaska has grown up on stories of bear maulings. There was a girl a few years ago who got attacked right on the bike track. I remember seeing the pictures—the long ragged tears in her face and across her scalp, stapled together after the bear chewed on her head.

"Also, if you find anything—*anything*—that might have belonged to Zahra, that might be important to the investigation . . . do not touch it. The police have asked us to be very careful about that. Don't mess with anything that might be evidence. Drop a pin on your phone and message me. My number's on that whiteboard—go ahead and get it in your phones."

From the expressions around me it's clear that everyone's picked up on what she hasn't said: that "evidence" could be Zahra herself. Could be Zahra's body. Most everyone is all tight-jawed and steely, but there are a few little breathy gasps, a few soft sobs from the crowd.

I turn to look around. The Key Club kids are pairing off. I see Ms. Yi from school, and a few other teachers, heading west on some trails.

Behind me, Tabitha starts to give directions.

"Okay, I think we should take some of the unpaved trails, since we're more equipped for it. Marcus and Jeremy, you guys head north. Preston, Maggie, April, Tor, you can manage the university grounds, yeah?" She glances around. "Ruthless, how about you go with . . ."

"Me," says Ben.

Tabitha and I both turn to stare at him. I open my mouth to say something, but before I can, he steps up to my side and winds an arm firmly through mine.

"Ruthie's going with me," he says again.

CHAPTER SEVENTEEN

FOR A MOMENT, I think about refusing to move. Just standing there in the parking lot, daring him to try to pull me after him. *Really? You think I'm going to wander into the woods with you, when just four days ago your friend had me at gunpoint? You think I'm going to trot obediently along when you screamed at me?*

But then I do something else.

I squeeze his arm back. Hard, sudden, forceful. I make sure he knows that I'm there, and that I'm not afraid.

"Okay, whatever," Tabitha says. She doesn't look happy, but she just turns back to the others. They're already breaking off in small groups, heading in their different directions. Her eyes fall on Ingrid as she realizes everyone else has a partner. "Oh, great, I guess *I'll* be with the American Girl doll."

I can't make out Ingrid's rejoinder. Ben's already steering me sharply toward a fork in the trail.

There are dead leaves along the path, brown and gold, and the air is damp. It feels like it's going to rain. Somewhere in the woods I can hear the croak of a raven, and then the answer of another. Probably alerting one another that there are humans coming. Ravens are smart, and work well together. More than you can say for us.

"So," he finally says. Then he falls silent. I look at him out of the corner of my eye. His lower lip juts out, a thoughtful pout. I feel odd noticing it—the second I even register that fact I think about how many times Zahra must have kissed those lips, about how much she must have loved that full, expressive mouth.

So I'm already flustered and embarrassed when he speaks again.

"You could've been killed the other day," he says.

I blink. I can't tell if his tone is an accusation, or an apology. So I just nod.

"I mean, what were you thinking?" He kicks at a rock. It rolls down the path ahead of us. "Do you realize how crazy it is to just . . . follow someone around, when you don't even know them?"

That word's always rankled me. "I'm not crazy. Don't call me crazy."

He winces a little at that. "That isn't what I meant . . . Look, I'm trying to apologize. I know, I suck at it, but cut me some slack here, things are kind of fucked up." He runs a hand through his hair. "I'm sorry I freaked out at you. And I'm sorry about . . . you know, the gun. That was my cousin. I didn't realize he was going to charge out there like that. He's kind of . . . paranoid."

"You think?" I ask.

"Well, you were sneaking around his yard," he says. "His place has been broken into three times this year. He's gotten twitchy."

I look down. "We're all a little twitchy right now, I guess."

We're quiet for a moment. I realize suddenly the ambient traffic sound has disappeared. We're fully in the woods now.

"I didn't hurt her," he says, suddenly, softly. I wonder how many times he's had to repeat that in the last few days. To how many people. "I wouldn't ever hurt her."

I can't say "I know," because I don't. Not really. But I nod.

"What were you delivering that day I followed you, anyway?" I ask.

"Caribou," he says. "I got a few of them, so I share the extra out."

For a moment I think about that—about the kind of guy who goes out and guns down an animal when he's angry at his girlfriend. That explains the blood on his shoe, anyway.

"Oh," I say. "That's . . . nice."

He gives me a sideways look. "Glad you approve," he says, his voice mild. "It's important to me that white girls are comfortable with me exercising my ancestral rights."

Blood rushes to my cheek. "Oh. I . . . I'm sorry, I didn't mean to . . ."

"Relax, colonizer, I'm teasing." He shoves his hands in his pockets. "Zahra hates it, too. She addresses my jerky as 'Bambi' if she ever sees me eating it."

I can't help it. I grin. "I can hear her saying that so clearly."

I think about the stacks of books in my room; I think about Ingrid's Bible verses. We all try to find something stable to hold on to. And for Ben, coming from a people rooted in a subsistence lifestyle, it probably goes even deeper than that.

"I'm sorry, too," I say. "I . . . honestly don't know what I was thinking. I'm just so desperate." I fidget with the ends of my scarf, bright red against the black wool of my coat. "When I left here, Zahra and I were inseparable. I didn't expect things to be exactly the same, but . . . so much has changed. I feel so helpless. Like I'm fumbling around in the dark. Or like . . . it's a stranger that I'm trying to find, and I have to do it by sneaking and spying and, like, tricking people into telling me things. It's so screwed up. But I have to do *something*."

I stop abruptly, suddenly afraid that I sound like a creeper, a stalker, a *crazy* person. But he just nods slowly.

"Yeah. Yeah, I can see that. Zahra . . . I love her so much. But she keeps everything so close to her chest. Like, I've never heard her mention you, but that's no surprise. She just doesn't talk about herself. Not her past, not her present. Not whatever she's feeling. So when something upsets her you just have to hold fast and make it through the storm, because she's not going to tell you what's going on." He stops in his tracks. We're in a small clearing, bright with fallen leaves. "I think that's been the problem between us all along. That's why we broke up. I mean, that's not what we fought about. We fought about . . ." He trails off for a moment, his cheeks suddenly getting ruddy.

"Cheating," I say softly. "Right?"

He nods. "Some guy at work, I guess. She kept saying they were only friends, and it wasn't anything I had to be worried about, and I wanted to believe her. But . . . I couldn't. I couldn't believe her, because she doesn't let me see inside. We've been together over a year now and I don't know if she's ever been open with me, about anything."

He sits down on the side of a fallen tree. I pause for a moment, then sit there, too, a foot or so away from him. The bark is rough with some kind of scaly fungus that's growing across it. Nothing goes to waste out here, as long as humans don't interfere.

"It's so stupid," Ben says. He's not looking at me; I wonder if he's talking to me, specifically, or if he'd tell anyone willing to listen right now. "She's always there for other people. When we first met, it was just a few months after my dad died. It was a car crash—but he lingered a long time, and we had to decide to . . . you know, to remove life support. And I was just wrecked. And there's this girl in my life who somehow just knows when I need to be distracted and when I need to be held and when I just need to . . . to be sad." He looks a little embarrassed. "But she won't let me do the same."

"I'm sorry about your dad," I say softly. "My mom died just a few weeks ago."

He looks startled. "I didn't know."

"Yeah. I haven't exactly advertised it. And Zahra's kind of eclipsed it." I look down. "It's okay. I mean, it's not, but . . . I'm okay. I'm getting through it. But I don't know if I can stand losing anyone else right now."

I look around us. The temperature's dropped since we arrived, and I shiver a little inside my coat.

"Do you think she's out here?" I ask.

He opens his mouth to answer. But before he can, there's a rustling in the trees, just behind us.

I jump to my feet, images of what it could be flashing through my mind—a moose, browsing for fall berries, or a bear, ambling blindly though the trees. Or a killer. A shadow-faced man with a knife, a gun, a garrote. But then I turn and I see Ingrid, coming through a narrow gap in the trees.

"Holy shit, you scared me," I say.

"Hi to you too," Ingrid says. Her cheeks are flushed apple red from the cold, and there are twigs in her hair. "Sorry. We got a little turned around on one of the side trails. We've been quiet so we could follow your voices."

"Ingrid, right?" Ben asks. She smiles, obviously pleased that he remembers.

"Hi, Ben. How are you holding up?"

Before he can answer, Tabitha stumbles out from behind her. "Slow down, will you?"

Ingrid turns a smug look back toward her. "I thought you were so worried about me keeping up with your amazing athletic stride."

Tabitha's voice drips venom. "I just mean you can't crash around the trails like an elephant. You're going to ruin any evidence."

"You're such a . . ."

Their voices fade abruptly, as if someone's turned the volume down on a stereo. My gaze has snagged on something, some spot on the far side of the clearing. For a moment I don't know what I'm looking at. My mind can't quite put the pieces together: there are trees and bushes, dirt and rocks, and something else, something small and plastic and black.

Probably just trash, I think. But I'm already on my feet, moving across the clearing. Stooping down to look.

It's an Android, a recent model, with a cracked screen. It's covered in dried mud, but even still I can see how the black plastic case has been decorated. Someone's drawn delicate, unfurling vines all along the sides and back in silver Sharpie.

"Ruthie?" Ingrid asks. I realize they've gone quiet behind me. I don't turn around.

I know those vines as well as I know her handwriting. As well as I know anything about her.

"Zahra," I say.

CHAPTER EIGHTEEN

LATER THAT NIGHT I creep up the stairs, the wood creaking softly under my feet. It's almost three in the morning. I've been trying to sleep for two hours, but I give up. It's not happening.

I don't know why I would've expected it to. Do you really get to go home from a crime scene and resume life as usual? Do you find your best friend's phone, cracked and broken in the middle of the woods, and then go to bed for a restful night's sleep?

Within minutes of my reporting the phone to Becks, the place was swarming with cops. Cordoned off with police tape, perimeter established. All civilians instructed to clear the area and go home. They didn't want us trampling evidence.

Tabitha was wild with grief. "It's her phone," she kept saying. "She never goes anywhere without it." And for his part, Ben looked stricken, his Adam's apple bobbing wildly, like he was trying and failing to swallow something. It was like the sight of Zahra's phone had finally made it all real to them. Wherever she was, she didn't have the one thing you could use to communicate with someone, to find your way back home, to summon help. She was truly out of our reach.

I barely remember walking out of the woods. I remember a cold hand in mine—Ingrid's, I suppose, because she was the one whose voice I kept hearing. "Just keep walking. That's it. One step and another . . . oh, be careful, there's a root sticking up right over here." It was just like the moments after my mom died. Just like the times I went on autopilot as a kid, when my dad was particularly messed up. I followed Ingrid obediently until we made our way back to the parking lot.

There's been no word—and who knows when there will be? According to the local news site I keep refreshing on my phone, the trail is closed and there are search and rescue teams combing the area. But it's a big park, and there's a lot of ground to cover. It might be a while before they make an official statement.

Upstairs I pad across the dark kitchen and open the fridge. I'm the furthest thing from hungry, but my throat is parched. I grab a lemonade and have the door half shut when someone in the living room clears their throat, and I drop the bottle on the floor.

I stoop to pick it up, and then go to the doorway.

The lights are off, but the TV is on, the sound down low. It's tuned to some kind of cooking competition. Brandy's sitting in the easy chair in her pajamas, a mug of tea next to her.

"Sorry," she says softly. "I didn't mean to startle you."

"It's okay." I watch the screen so I don't have to look at her. The chefs are running around the kitchen, scooping up ingredients in their arms for whatever it is they're hell-bent on making.

"Can't sleep either, huh? Want me to make some tea? Or hot cocoa?" She makes a movement like she's going to get up, but I shake my head quickly.

"No, that's okay. I've got a drink."

She nods. Then she glances at the empty couch. "Want to sit? I'll let you have the remote."

I crack open my lemonade and curl up on the sofa. On the TV a guy with tattoos is trying to melt gummy bears in a pan while a woman in a bandanna juices a few dozen key limes as fast as she can. It's very dramatic.

"No new information?" Brandy asks. Her face is ashen in the flickering light, all the old scars puckering her skin thrown into ugly relief. I was surprised when I found out she was only thirty-five; she looks so much older.

"No." Ingrid had told Dad and Brandy about what we'd seen over the dinner table. I didn't have the energy to go through it all again, and then they didn't say anything about me heading down to my room to hide for the rest of the evening.

"Lots of people use that kind of phone," she says tentatively. "Right?"

"Tabitha was sure it was hers." I take a sip of lemonade. "There were drawings on the cover. In silver Sharpie. That was always Zahra's trademark."

"Shit," she says softly.

I must look at her strangely, because her cheeks darken a little. "Pardon my French," she adds.

"*Bien sûr*," I say. She gives a little smile.

"I don't get the feeling you were too jazzed about church, so maybe this is the wrong thing to say, but . . . I've been praying for her."

For some reason it doesn't annoy me as much as it should. Maybe it's just because she says it so simply.

We watch the TV in silence for a few minutes. My eyes track the contestants as they plate their food, but my mind is spinning in circles, trying to lay out the possibilities and argue for or against their likelihood. Anything could have happened. Someone could've snatched her from the path. A stranger. Or even Ben. He could've steered me to that particular clearing so I'd find the phone—though that line of thinking doesn't feel quite right, anymore. Or she could have dropped it in the middle of a panic attack. Or she could have dropped it while running from an animal. Other than telling us she was there, in the woods, and that she lost her phone, the discovery hasn't given us a damn thing to go on.

"You don't have to go, by the way."

Brandy's voice startles me. I look up at her.

"To church. Your dad . . . will argue. But I'll make him understand." She gives a small smile. "Pastor Worthen can be intense. And I don't think anyone benefits from forced ministry."

I open my mouth to say something—like, "Thank you for understanding," or "Don't worry, I'll keep going because he's Zahra's granddad and I'm desperate for any connection I can make." But those aren't the words that come out.

"Do you believe in all that stuff?" I ask.

She looks away from the TV screen. The show's gone to commercial, and as is traditional for a three a.m. promotional spot, there's a negligee-clad woman talking on the phone in an embarrassingly sensual voice, urging the viewer to Call Now. "I believe in God," she says slowly. "And I believe in prayer."

"Yeah, but . . . all the other stuff. About sin, and obedience, and . . . like . . ." I shrug a little. "Do you think women are supposed to listen to their husbands?"

"Nah." She leans back in the chair. "I'm pretty sure Jesus is the only man ever born who's worth obeying."

"Then why do you guys go to Victory Evangelical?" I ask. "There are other churches. Some might be . . ."

"Nicer?" she says with a small smile.

"I mean . . . yeah."

The light flickers along her skin. She doesn't look beautiful, exactly, but there's an eerie, almost ghostly magnificence to her. If I were putting her in *The Precipice*, I'd make her an oracle. A sacred priestess, chewing laurels and channeling the voice of a god.

"Has Ingrid told you much about her childhood?" she asks.

I shake my head a little. "I mean, I know you were . . . you know."

"A meth-head, yeah," she says. She takes a sip of her tea, and I'm impressed by how calmly she can say it. "I don't want to say too much, because some of it is Ingrid's story to tell, whenever she's ready. But if you've ever met a tweaker you can probably imagine some of it. I've sold her shit for drug money. I've sold myself for drug money. Yeah, I mean what you think I mean," she says at my shocked look. "I've been homeless, I've been in prison. Ingrid's been in foster homes on and off for years."

I realize I'm holding my breath. I unclench my fist, roll my shoulders.

"Anyway, Grace Worthen caught me living out of my car in the church parking lot when Ingrid was about nine years old. I usually moved the car every night so it wouldn't be too obvious, but that morning I slept in, and she came and knocked on the window. I pretty much freaked out. I was sure she'd call the cops on me."

Her voice is calm and even. I wonder if, someday, my dad will be able to talk about his mistakes like this. Because so far, he's seemed to want to shrug them off. Brandy is five years into her sobriety, and her tone is different; there's a matter-of-factness to it that makes me trust the tale. That makes me trust her, a little.

"Anyway, I was scrambling to gather up our stuff and get out of there, and Ingrid was in the back seat sleeping, and this lady in a pastel suit is looking in and I'm freaking out. I'm like, I can't lose my baby, not again, not even if it's the best thing for her. That's addiction, man. When you're willing to make your kid sleep in the car in the middle of winter because you're too selfish to do better. But Grace invited me in. There's a locker room in the church, and she let me clean up and she gave me something to eat. Not a word about cops or social services.

"It's not a Hallmark movie of the week," she says softly. "It's not one of those big moments that, you know, swoop in to change someone for good. I had a little more fucking up to do before I hit my bottom. But when I was ready, I knew I could go back to her. I knew I could trust her. She—well, the Women's Ministry Group that she leads—they helped me find a job. They helped me find an apartment. They helped me keep my daughter. So yes . . . Pastor Worthen's ministry is a little on the intense side for my tastes. I won't lie. But the community in that church—they're legit. They're doing God's work. I'm only here because of them."

She goes quiet. I don't really know what to say. Honestly, until now Brandy's seemed on the bland side to me. No, that's not quite right; the truth is, I haven't thought enough about her to decide if she's bland. I haven't thought about who she is or what she's been through, or what kind of relationship she might have with Ingrid or my father.

"I'm glad you are," I say, finally.

She smiles. Then she looks at the screen again. "Oh, it's back on."

The girl with the bandanna unveils her tilapia-lime faji-tas. One of the judges makes a pained grimace.

My text alert goes off. It's Tabitha.

> **There's blood spatter on the phone.**

The screen seems to sear my eyes in the darkness, but I can't tear them away. I hold the phone so tight my fingers start to cramp.

I open up the news on my phone's browser. MISSING GIRL'S BLOODY PHONE FOUND NEAR CHESTER CREEK TRAIL, says the headline.

Anchorage police confirmed that the cell phone found in today's search belonged to Zahra Gaines, 17. Blood evidence collected from the scene will be sent to the lab to determine its origin.

For a second I see it, as if it's right in front of me. Blood, spattered across the phone. Blood, flecked across the leaves, the stones. Blood, pooling around a body.

But no. Because they didn't find a body. We didn't find a body.

There's still hope. There has to be.

I look back at Brandy. This dowdy, ravaged woman who, even after all this time sober, still can't sleep at night. For once I wish I had some kind of faith, too, some religion or belief that might see me through. All I've ever really had is the Precipice, and Zahra.

The old oaths come easily to my mind.

By the light of the midnight sun, by the gods of the fen and those of the dale, by the mountaintop guardians and those

*that keep the ocean's tides, I will find you. I will not rest until
I do.*

It was the way the Starmaiden and Lyr swore their fealty
to one another. Even though I know the gods invoked are not
in the fen or dale or mountains or oceans but are in a series
of battered, sticker-encrusted wide-ruled notebooks, repaired
with tape, stashed downstairs in my room.

I will find you, I think again. *I'll do anything I have to along
the way.*

CHAPTER NINETEEN

THE CUP AND SAUCER is inside a tired little seventies-era mall, tucked between a wig shop and a country-and-western clothing store. The first thing I notice is Zahra's picture, featured prominently on every surface; her coworkers have posted her flyers all over the store. Her chiseled face, her stark hair and full lips and long-lashed eyes peer out dozens of times over.

"She really is pretty," Ingrid says softly, looking at one of them.

It's Monday morning—a half hour before school is scheduled to start. The coffee shop is the only thing in the mall open this early. All the other shops are still locked up tight, and the only people roaming the halls are senior citizens in track suits, walking their laps in the safe, warm mall air.

The coffee shop decor is a mix of frumpy and twee. The chalkboard menu is written up in pink and green, with vines and flowers that I recognize as more of Zahra's etched around the edges. The merchandise shelf is stocked with tea sets and coffee pots; the girls behind the counter wear aprons in a pattern that can only be called "Grandma's curtains."

It's hard to imagine Zahra here. But it's increasingly hard to imagine her at all.

There are two baristas on duty this morning. One is wiping down the espresso machine with a rag; the other's restocking muffins in the pastry case. The place is otherwise empty. I step up to the counter, Ingrid just a half step behind, and clear my throat.

The one at the espresso machine looks up. She's a few years older than us, maybe, her hair black with bright green sections, her arms covered in tattoos. I recognize her from the Walk and Roll for Hope photo I found online. "Hey, what can I get you?"

"Just a drip coffee with room," I say.

"Mocha for me," Ingrid puts in. "Double shot."

"Margo, will you ring them up?" asks the green-haired girl.

Margo's closer to our age, with blunt-cut bangs and a freckled, snub nose. She makes change, and I drop it into the tip jar with a conspicuous jingle.

"Um . . . can I ask a kind of weird question?" I say.

She cocks her head to one side. "What's up?"

"What's the name of the guy who works here?" I feel myself blushing. They are going to think I'm a creeper. But Ben said the guy Zahra was messing around with—or at least supposedly messing around with—was someone from work.

Margo glances over her shoulder at the other woman. "Do you know what she's talking about, Soo-Jin?"

The green-haired barista puts our drinks down on the counter in front of us. "Sorry, babe, there aren't any boys around these parts."

"No boys? But . . ." I trail off. My eyes fall to the picture of Zahra taped to the countertop. Nothing for it but to be straightforward, I guess. "Zahra's a friend of mine. I heard a rumor that she was flirting with some guy at work. You're sure there's no one here?"

The green-haired barista's expression changes, her lips turning downward. "You know Zahra? Hey, are there any updates? No one's telling us anything. The news said they found her phone."

I nod. "We were the ones that found it."

"Shit," she says. She brushes a lock of hair behind her ear. "We were both working yesterday or we would've been there, too."

"We still don't know much," I say. "The phone was broken. And I guess there's . . . you know, trace amounts of blood on it."

Margo's hands fly up to cover her mouth. Soo-Jin looks faintly nauseated.

"I knew something was wrong when she didn't show up for her shifts. I called her parents, but they said she'd just gone off with her boyfriend," she says, resting her hands on the counter.

"Weird that they weren't worried, don't you think?" Ingrid asks, glancing at me. I just shrug.

"They're kind of like that. Hippie types, you know?" I say. "Anyway . . . so there aren't any guys who work here? Not even, like, stocking or delivering?"

Margo and Soo-Jin exchange a meaningful glance.

"No one that works here," Soo-Jin says. "But there was a guy around all the time this summer. He used to come in for lunch and she'd take her break with him."

"Specifically *not* her boyfriend," Margo says.

Ingrid's eyes go very round. "You don't know his name?"

"Nope. I snooped as much as I could but I never managed to find out," says Margo, without shame. "He always paid in cash."

"Crumpled ones," Soo-Jin giggles. "Remember, we used to tease Zahra about it? We kept asking if he was a stripper."

Margo snorts. "Oh my God, she turned so red."

"But as far as you know, they only ate together?" I ask. "They weren't hooking up?"

Margo twists her mouth to one side like she's thinking about it. But Soo-Jin is the one that answers.

"Zahra's an odd bird," she says. "She gives off this aura of being super warm and nice and easy to talk to, and it's not until you stop to think about it later that you realize she didn't really tell you anything about herself. You can feel really close to her, and at the end of the day be asking why."

The words hit me with a dull, sickly thud. *It isn't just me*, whispers one voice, exultant. Somewhere else, another answers mournfully: *It isn't just me?*

Am I the one that doesn't know Zahra? Or is Zahra the one that refuses to be known?

"So the whole thing was hard to read." Soo-Jin's still talking. I force myself to focus back on what she's saying. "Maybe they were just friends, but it felt like they were sneaking around. She'd eat with him back on the loading dock every day, out of sight of customers and stuff. And a few times when Ben came to surprise her around lunch time she'd get really nervous."

"Who knows, with that girl," Margo says.

All this time I've been half-assuming that the rumors of Zahra cheating are just that. Rumors. I realize now I've only thought that because it seemed so out of character, even with all the evidence that my best friend has changed. But there is, at least, another boy in her life—one no one really seems to know.

"Did you ever find out anything else about him?" I plead. "Where'd she know him from? What'd he look like?"

"He looked like half the guys in Anchorage," Margo says dismissively. "Scruffy and boring."

"Margo's got a rare case of white-dude face blindness," Soo-Jin says. "Or maybe she's just a lesbian."

"Really?" Ingrid gives a little jerk of surprise, looking at Margo again. I grit my teeth a little. Now is not the time to have to find out my stepsister is a homophobe.

"Well, I'm bi," Margo says. "But I'm waiting to experiment with dudes until I get to college."

"Anyways," I say, trying to steer the conversation away

from anything that might lead to a Bible study session or get us kicked out of the mall. "He was scruffy, you said?"

"Yeah, he was a little unkempt," Soo-Jin says, thinking. "Cute, though. Brown hair. Really skinny."

"Too skinny," Margo puts in.

"That's how some of us like 'em," Soo-Jin says. "If he were my boyfriend I'd slap some skinny jeans on him and he'd be perfectly presentable. But you know the type—cargo pants and wrinkly flannel shirts. Work boots. A little stubble."

Margo's right; that could describe half the guys in town. I try not to show my frustration on my face.

"I know he goes to your school, though," Margo says suddenly. "Last time we saw him was mid-August, and he came in with his class schedule to show her. I got a glimpse. Didn't see any of the particulars, but it said MERRILL HIGH right across the top."

"That's something, anyway," I say. I'm already running through images in my head, trying to match someone I've seen in class or in the halls to their description. Nothing's ringing a bell. "Could I get your numbers? You can text me if you think of something else, and I can let you know if I hear anything that's not on the news yet."

"Yeah, that'd be great." Soo-Jin takes my outstretched phone and types her info in, then hands it to Margo, who does the same. When I take it back, I message both of them so they have mine.

"Thanks, guys." I slide my phone into my pocket and pick up the coffee. Its heat is comforting against my chilled fingers.

"We've gotta get to school, but I'll let you know if I hear anything at all, okay?"

"Yeah. Thanks." Soo-Jin looks at us a moment, then pulls a couple of muffins out of the case and pushes them across the table. "On me, okay? Let us know if there's anything else we can do."

"Yeah, be careful out there," Margo says. She gives a little wave as we head down the hall.

I don't register how quiet Ingrid's being until we're back in the parking lot, unlocking the car. She's got the cellophane-wrapped muffin in one hand and keeps looking down at it with an odd expression on her face.

"Are you okay?" I ask.

"Huh?" She looks up at me over the top of the car, her face strangely blank. I'm about to repeat my question when I hear a text from my phone.

It's from Margo.

> Just remembered the guy had a metal cuff bracelet. Silver tone. Something engraved across the top. Never got a good glimpse of what it said.

I slide the phone back in my pocket. When I look up, Ingrid's in the car, seat belt buckled, searching through the radio stations. I climb in and start the car, my mind already running over all the boys I've met, all the guys I've passed in the hall, trying to remember if I've seen a glint of silver on their wrists.

It's not much . . . but it's something.

CHAPTER TWENTY

I SLIDE INTO YEARBOOK just as the bell rings. On the chalk-board Ms. Yi has scrawled *Independent work period.* She's in the back of the room, talking quietly with some kids about the different parts of a camera. Other kids sit at the computers, working through tutorials or just messing around on social media.

Tabitha's lying with her head in her arms on the table in front of her. Marcus looks like he's been up half the night, too, and Jeremy's not even there. I set my muffin on the table and lean in toward them.

"Do either of you know a guy who wears a metal brace-let?" I whisper.

Marcus frowns a little and shakes his head. Tabitha lifts her head up a little, looking blearily through stray locks of hair. There's a smear of unwashed mascara under her eyes, and there's still a faint whiff of alcohol coming off her.

"What are you talking about?" she croaks.

"I just went to the Cup and Saucer."

"Ugh, I hate those bitches," she says. "They talk shit about everyone."

I ignore the irony. "They seemed nice enough to me."

She just presses her lips into a smirk. "They used to try to get Zahra to stop hanging out with me. They always acted like *I* was the stuck-up one, but they've been nasty to me every time I hang out with them. They have all these little in-jokes and they act like I'm too stupid to get them."

I just nod. I can only imagine how those meet-ups would've gone. Tabitha getting territorial, jealous, hating that she had to share Zahra with these other girls with their inside jokes and easy rapport; Margo and Soo-Jin baffled by Tabitha's resentment and laughing off her attempts to pull rank.

"Well, they said there was some guy who used to come hang out with Zahra on her lunch break," I say.

She raises one narrow brow. "That's not exactly breaking news, Ruthless," she says. "Everyone knows about that by now."

"Yeah, but they actually saw the guy," I say. "They gave me a description. White guy, skinny, brown hair. It might help lead us to—"

"Jesus, would you knock it off with the Nancy Drew shit for, like, five minutes?" She slaps the table with both palms. Then she closes her eyes and rubs her face. "You're so fucking relentless."

I recoil a little.

"Yeah," I say shortly. "I am. I want to find Zahra. I want to bring her home."

She doesn't say anything for a minute. Her eyes dart down and to the left, a twitchy motion like a scurrying animal. She's scared, I think. She's scared to talk about this.

But when she speaks, her tone's belligerent.

"You really think you're going to find something the cops missed?" she asks.

"I don't know. But they're so focused on Ben—what if this other guy is the one they should be looking for?"

Marcus's eyes widen. He looks from me to Tabitha. "That could help clear Ben's name," he says. "If we could find him."

Tabitha slouches back over the table, bracing up her forehead with her hands. "If there is some other guy, they'll find him, okay? They've got her phone now. They'll be able to see whoever she's been texting."

"That could take forever," I say. "Forensic stuff like that takes time. Time Zahra might not have."

She stands up and gives an exaggerated shrug.

"Do whatever it is you're going to do, all right? But Zahra's the one who walked away that night. She was the one that left us." She strides over to Ms. Yi. "Can I go to the nurse? I have a headache."

I sit dumbly while Ms. Yi fills out a hall pass for her, then gives her a quick hug. Tabitha shoots us one more angry look, and then she's gone.

What the hell was that about?

"Don't mind her," Marcus says softly. "She's . . ."

"Drunk," I say bluntly.

"Well, yeah," he admits. "But she's also really freaked out."

There are a hundred things I could say to that. I could tell him that I'm scared, too, that I'm struggling to keep hope alive, that I have been alone so many times in my life—as alone as Tabitha, rattling around in that big empty house. I could describe the way my fears work—the strange automaton I become, the way I go small and silent inside, the way it cuts me off from everyone around me. I could point out that Zahra's life is on the line, and Ben's, too, and that we have to be strong for the people we care about. But I don't say anything. I just shrug.

"But I think you're right," he says. "We should be looking for that dude. And I've got an idea."

He pushes off from the table, rolling his chair over to one of the computer stations. I follow, scooting behind him more slowly. He's already logging on.

"We take pictures all throughout the year," he says. "We upload them to this program that sorts and lets us tag them. See, if I put in Zahra's name . . ." He types her name into a search field, and about forty thumbnails spring up, her face small and lovely in the preview. "It looks for everything that's been tagged with that word."

There are a bunch of candid shots of her—in the classroom, listening attentively; in the crowd at a football game, red and black face paint on her cheeks. One of her sitting out on the lawn during lunch. In one she leans over to Ben and whispers something in his ear while he grins mischievously. In another, Tabitha sprawls across her lap and Zahra pretends to look annoyed. Somehow that one, in particular, hurts.

"We try to index as we go, but it always depends on who's uploading stuff. Some people get lazy, so there might be pictures without labels. So it's not the most efficient way to look. But . . ." He shrugs. "What else have we got?"

"No, it's a good idea." I clear the search field, and just open the folder for September. There are 903 photos in that month alone. This could take a while, and yield nothing.

He gets on the computer next to me. "I'll start looking through last year's pictures, see if there's anything there."

We work in silence for a while. All around us, kids are talking, working, messing around. Ms. Yi doesn't seem to have it in her to crack the whip today. She moves gently around the room, checking in with people, asking how everyone's holding up. I scroll through image after image, past swim meets and concerts and lectures, past shots of people horsing around in the hallway or sitting on the tailgate of a truck with a cup of hot cocoa in both hands. Every time I see something on a guy's wrist I zoom in. It's almost always a watch.

"What about this guy?" Marcus asks. I look over his shoulder, shake my head. It's a silver bracelet—looks like a MedicAlert band—but the wearer is heavy-set and wearing a crisp button-down shirt.

"Our guy's skinny," I remind him. "And kinda scruffy."

We keep looking, the second hand sweeping across the clock. I wonder if Tabitha really did go to the nurse, or if she just decided to skip. I wonder if she's in the bathroom, curled up and crying, or if she's on her way back to that big empty house.

And then I see it.

It's a picture from a chemistry lab. In the mid-background, there's a girl watching the procedure. Foregrounded is an Erlenmeyer flask set up under a long glass burette. A hand rests on the table next to it, a silver cuff around the wrist. This close I can clearly make out the inscription.

EVEN DRAGONS HAVE THEIR ENDING.

There's no image of his face. But there is a caption:

LIZ CHRISTIANSEN AND SEB COLLINS CONCENTRATE IN MR. VILLAFUERTE'S FIFTH PERIOD.

CHAPTER TWENTY-ONE

HE'S ALREADY AT HIS locker when I get there after class, shoving a textbook onto the narrow shelf. I watch him for a moment before I approach. His locker is almost bare—there are no pictures inside, no stickers, no notes. Nothing but a small stack of books and a lunch bag. He's wearing that same ratty hoodie I saw him in the other day, the sleeves pulled down over his wrists, so I can't see the cuff.

But as he swings the door shut I see a flash of silver.

He jumps as he turns and sees me there. I give him a tiny smile.

"Seb, right?" I ask.

"What do you want?" he asks.

"I want to talk about Zahra Gaines," I say. My voice rings out loudly over the hallway. No one seems to notice, but his eyes dart around wildly.

"Don't even know her," he says, walking around me. But I stick to his side, double-stepping to keep up.

"You know what her favorite book used to be?" I ask. "Actually, her favorite book used to be *Akata Witch*. But a book she also used to love is *The Hobbit*."

He doesn't say anything, but a patch of red springs up across his cheeks. That's all the proof I need.

"What's the line she used to quote?" I say, tapping my lip with my fingertip. "'Even dragons have their . . .'"

He grabs my wrist, hard, and pivots to the left, into a stairwell. I let him pull me along, then jerk my hand away as soon as we're alone.

"What do you *want*, Ruthie?" he asks again. His eyes are pale green flames, somehow both burning and cold. I force myself to stand up to my full height.

"I want to know the last time you saw her," I ask.

"It's none of your business," he spits.

"Yes. It is." I cross my arms across my chest and stare up at him. We're only a few inches apart. "But maybe you'd rather talk to the cops."

He walks two steps away, then pivots and walks back, clutching his hair. I don't move. My muscles sing with tension, but a familiar calm takes hold of me. I have control of my body and my feelings and my fear, and I won't flinch.

The curve of his mouth is tight and bitter. He gives a short, sharp exhale.

"It doesn't matter, anyway," he says. "The police have her

phone. So they'll see every single thing we've ever said to each other. That'll be a lot of fun to have made public."

"So you *were* texting her," I say.

"We were *friends*." He sits down on the bottom step of the stairs. "We used to text a lot."

"But you don't anymore?" I ask.

He's quiet for a long time. He picks at a hole in the knee of his pants.

"Last year . . . my mom left my piece-of-shit stepdad," he says. "I don't know what finally did it, because she didn't leave him when he broke my arm, and she didn't leave him when he smashed a broomstick over my head, and she didn't leave him when . . . well, you get the idea." He leans forward with his forearms on his knees. "Whatever, she finally figured it out. We were staying at the shelter."

I give a little "ah" of realization. The domestic violence shelter—where Ingrid and Zahra did their Key Club project together.

"I hadn't seen Zahra in a long time. We've moved a couple times. So when I kept seeing her around the place I almost didn't recognize her," he says. "I mean, she looked the same, but . . . she acted so different, I just, I wasn't sure."

"How so?"

He looks up at me sharply, and I realize I must sound eager. I swallow, tamp down the excitement.

"Serious," he says. "Sad."

I nod. He looks down again.

"When I recognized her I just kinda, like, ignored her.

Pretended I didn't know who she was. But one day she . . . she cornered me. She wanted to know what'd happened to me and my family. And . . . she wanted to apologize. For what you two did."

I grit my teeth. I'm tired of the hints and insinuations, the conversation always so elliptical. "Seb, will you just tell me what you're talking about? I'm sorry I don't remember, okay? But what did I supposedly do that was so awful?"

"You really don't remember?" The tone isn't passive-aggressive anymore; it's just sad. "God, what a joke. You two destroyed my whole fucking summer, and one of you doesn't remember, and the other . . ." He trails off. "The dog? Mrs. Pigeon's dog?"

The phrase stirs something at the back of my mind. I frown. Mrs. Pigeon had been an older lady a few streets down. I remember her in flowing caftans, hobbling around her garden. Mom used to go over to visit, and they'd sit on ancient plastic lawn chairs sipping sweet tea, Mrs. Pigeon smoking a Benson & Hedges and blowing the smoke toward the sky. Her dog was one of the littler breeds—a Shih Tzu maybe? But I still don't know what he's talking about.

He shakes his head. "Her dumb little dog went missing, and you told everyone in the neighborhood you'd seen me torturing it. You told all the other kids. They already thought I was weird. They were just looking for an excuse. I got the shit beat out of me every day that summer. And my little sisters— they heard the rumor and were hysterical. They believed it." He runs his hands over his face. "I don't know what it says about me that everyone believed it so quick. But whatever, I'm a freak, I already knew that. You guys just put the target on my back."

His words trickle down my spine like ice water seeping through my shirt—soaking slowly in, the memory drifting up to the surface. I suddenly remember the dog's name: Pepper. It was always getting out of the yard, trotting off to find the nearest garbage can to knock over. But one day it vanished. Didn't come back. A posse of neighborhood kids went looking for it. Everyone liked Mrs. Pigeon.

But the rest? I don't remember that.

"Why would we do that?" I ask softly. I don't really intend the question for him, but he laughs.

"I asked Zahra that. She said I'd been staring at you both." He blushes suddenly. "I used to come by her house and you'd be out sunning yourselves on the trampoline. I just wanted to talk to you, but I guess it came off like I was . . . you know. Gawking, or whatever."

I remember lying out on the trampoline in the early summer, before we started fixing up the playground. We'd pull up our shirts to the bottom of our bras so our bellies would get some sun, flipping through pages of whatever book we were reading. I remember a couple of neighborhood kids swinging by to harass us. Teasing us for reading so much. Most of it was probably just lighthearted, but at the time I didn't react well. I remember getting so upset about it. Zahra always laughed it off. Did I start to go on the offensive? Or to overreact, if I thought I was being made fun of?

I stare at his face, trying to call up some image of him as a kid. The memory that stirs is vague and once again, I don't know if it's even the right one. A boy—short and bone-thin, one of those scrappy-looking kids that jeers and postures for some kind of attention. *What's that, another dragon book?* he'd asked. *Sounds awesome.* Only the mildest tone of sarcasm. Hell, the kid hadn't even had enough emotional juice to come up with a decent insult. But I remember my whole body going rigid, all fight and no flight. I remember sitting up and throwing down the book, taking him in, my lips forming insults before I could think twice. *Why do you always comment on the cover art? Is that the only part you can read?*

Seb's still picking at the hole in his pants. It's not one of those "distressed" holes that make jeans look cool. It's the ragged-edged, uneven tear of clothes that have been worn all the way out. It's the look of pants he can't afford to replace.

"I didn't help my own case," he says. "I was a little bitch about it. Used to go home crying. Which then got me my ass kicked, because Steve didn't like crybabies. But yeah. It stayed with me a while. Obviously."

I feel nauseated. I sit down on my bottom in front of him, my legs crossed.

"So anyway. I tried to avoid her when she started coming around the shelter. But I'd dropped out of school and I was stuck with all these . . . these sad, sad people. And there was so much I'd never been able to say out loud, to anyone, about . . . all the stuff we'd been through. Me and my family, I mean. And Zahra just . . . she knew how to listen. I don't know how to explain it. I just . . . talking to her was so easy, and that kinda stuff's never easy for me."

"Yeah," I say. "I get it." It's starting to become a familiar story, as much as it hurts to realize. All these people, with all their pain, drawn to her, stunned by how easy it is to talk to her. Prickly Tabitha with her absent parents, and Ben, with the loss of his father. Me, on the heels of my own parents' divorce, and all the rage I'd been keeping inside for so long. Did we find her, or did she find us?

"She got you that bracelet?" I ask.

He touches his wrist. "Yeah. Yeah, we talked a lot about . . . you know, trying to move on, after something bad's happened. About the stuff my stepdad used to do and the way it just kept coming back again and again to fuck up my life, even after it was over."

"Trauma," I say simply.

"I guess." He rubs the back of his neck, like he's embarrassed by the word. "We were just *friends*," he says, more urgently. "She told me early on she had a boyfriend and it was serious. I knew. I knew it wasn't going to happen."

"But?" I say gently.

"But I'm a moron," he says. "And I fucked up. I kissed her. It was such a stupid thing to do, but we were up at Point Woronzof, and the sun was going down, and the way it lit her up . . ." He doesn't trail off so much as clamp his mouth shut, swallow the words back.

"How'd she react?" I ask.

"She . . . she kissed back for a minute. And I thought

maybe . . ." The look on his face is suddenly so young it's startling. All the rough edges collapse for just a second and he looks naïve. "But it was stupid. She pulled away and she freaked out. She blamed herself for it, which . . . killed me. She kept saying it was her fault. I told her it wasn't, I told her I'd never do it again. But that was the last time I spent any real time with her. She wouldn't talk to me after that. Wouldn't answer my texts, and if she saw me in the halls she'd dodge me, which really, really sucked. She was the one that talked me into coming back and finishing school. But then we started school and she wouldn't even . . . she wouldn't even talk to me."

"When was this?" I ask.

"It was right before school started. Like, mid-August."

I blink. "Wait . . . so you guys haven't been talking for . . ."

"A month," he says grimly. "She said she couldn't risk it. She said she liked me but her boyfriend was too important to her. And she couldn't trust herself, and she couldn't trust me, to be cool about it."

I frown. "Everyone made it sound like Ben thought she was cheating because of some guy who kept texting her," I say. Though now that I think of it I'm not sure who "everyone" is— if it's just the impression I got, or if it's something someone actually said.

He shrugs. "I texted her for maybe a week after it happened. In August. But I stopped. I figured if she was done, I had to just . . . let it go."

The sound of the warning bell echoes through the stairwell. He grimaces.

"Can I go now, officer?" he asks. "I've got a quiz in algebra I've got to get to."

"Just one more thing," I ask. "What were you doing the night she disappeared?"

He stands up, his long and spindly legs unfolding, and slings his backpack over his shoulder.

"Working," he says. "I do the night shift at Bauer's Donuts on the weekends."

He takes a step toward the door.

"Hey, wait a second," I say.

He pauses and sighs. "What now?"

"I . . ." I bite my lip. His back is still to me. That makes it easier. "I'm sorry," I say, in a sudden rush. "About being so shitty to you back then. I'm really sorry."

He gives a little shrug. I don't expect him to say anything else, and I'm half turned away when he finally speaks, one foot on the stairs.

"The really fucked-up thing is that I was trying to make friends with *you*," he says. His voice still has an acrid tang to it, like he's speaking around something bitter. "Not Zahra."

"What?" I stare at the back of his head, stunned. It makes no sense. Zahra was the one who was likable, who was magnetic, even. She was the one with the laugh that drew people in. "Why?"

He shrugs. "I don't know. Maybe just because you were so pissed off."

I laugh a little. "I wasn't pissed off! Why would you say that?"

"Just a feeling, I guess." He turns his head to look back at me from the side of his eye. "Some kids, you can just tell they've been through some shit. And I knew you guys had left your dad, so I thought . . . maybe hers is like mine. I thought maybe you would get it." He gives another little shrug. "But it was Zahra who seemed to get it, in the end."

He pushes through the door without another word.

And I'm left, once again, wondering what Zahra had been through that I couldn't seem to fathom.

CHAPTER TWENTY-TWO

"THIS IS THE MOST disgusting thing I've ever read in my entire life," Ingrid says, thumbing through her battered copy of Kafka's *Metamorphosis*.

It's early evening, and Ingrid and I are sprawled in the rec room doing our homework. I stare down at my biology textbook, my gaze skating over the surface of the words without really taking anything in. There's a circular flow chart on one page showing the citric acid cycle step by step—compounds consumed and regenerated in an endless loop of energy—but it's hard to concentrate. My mind, too, keeps moving in loops. Around and around and around.

Talking with Seb left me with more questions than answers—and it's not the questions about Zahra that are disturbing. I've always known that it's hard for me to make friends—always. But in my memories, I'm the one that gets bullied. I'm the one that's teased, or left out, or ignored. I'm not the one that goes on the attack.

Finding out that I may be oversimplifying the story is strangely jarring.

But I remember Mom telling me not to be such a snob, such a know-it-all. I remember when we moved to Walker Court and she acted like I was being a spoiled brat. The kids in the trailer park scared me a little—they were tough and independent, and they moved around in big brash groups that I didn't know how to deal with. So I'd withdrawn. Gone into my own world, at least until I made friends with Zahra. And maybe in the process, I'd been less than careful with the people around me.

Maybe in the process, I'd hurt some of them.

Ingrid heaves a sigh, sits up, and throws the book across the room. It lands in the corner behind the cable box. "That's it. I'm not reading this thing. It doesn't even make any sense."

"I think it's supposed to be absurd," I say vaguely. She shakes her head.

"Who wants more absurdity in their lives?" Ingrid asks. She grabs a pillow off the end of the couch and hugs it across her lap. "What's going on with you, anyway? You've been quiet all night."

I put down my pencil. She's right—there's not much point in studying right now. "Just thinking about Zahra, I guess. Wondering if Seb was honest about everything."

I've already told her about the confrontation with Seb—

about his claim that he'd been working the night she vanished, and about the fact that he said he hadn't spoken with Zahra in a few weeks.

"Did he ever . . . like, say anything, do anything, that creeped you out?" I ask. "At the shelter?"

She shrugs. "Have you ever been to a domestic abuse shelter? Everyone there's shell-shocked."

I try again. "Yeah, but did he ever cross a line?"

"I'm not really even supposed to be talking about this," she says, shifting her weight. "I signed a confidentiality agreement." Then, under my pleading stare, she sighs. "But no, he didn't. He was quiet and he kept to himself. He helped in the kitchen every single day and he was really, really sweet with the little kids."

"Hm," I say. "I wish there were some way to verify his alibi. Just so I know for sure."

Ingrid looks at me for a moment, then picks up her phone and dials.

"What are you doing?" I ask.

She holds up a finger. A moment passes. Then I hear someone pick up on the other line.

"Yes, hi." She pitches her voice down a little. "I'm Susie Jacobson with Merrill High's work program. Yes, I need to verify some work dates for one of our students so he can get school credit. Mm-hm. Yes, thank you, I'll hold." I watch as she bobs her head to the hold music. It'd almost be funny if it weren't so impressive. "They're playing Ariana's new song," she says to me over the receiver. Then she speaks into the phone again. "Oh, hi, yes. Yeah, I need all the shifts from the first pay period in September." She snaps her fingers at me; it takes me a second to realize she wants my pencil. When I hand it to her she starts jotting things down in the margin of my biology book. "Mm-hm. Yes. Yes. Okay, great, that's what he's reported. I just needed to get it verified. Thank you so much!"

She circles one of the dates she's scrawled down. "That Saturday he worked ten p.m. to ten a.m. He covered through the morning for a coworker who called in sick."

"It's as good an alibi as anyone has, I guess," I say. Since we don't know what happened to Zahra, we can't make a time line—which means no one's technically off the hook. He could have met up with her after getting off work—but anyone could have. In the end, it's just another scrap of useless information.

"This is so hopeless," I mutter.

Ingrid hesitates for a moment.

"I know you're . . . not into it," she says carefully. "But there's a Bible verse that always gives me comfort. When things are really messed up." She closes her eyes as she recites; with her round pink cheeks and her unfurrowed brow she looks for all the world like something that should be stuck at the top of a Christmas tree. "'Fear not,'" she says softly, "'for I have redeemed thee. I have called thee by thy name; thou art mine. When thou passest through the waters, I will be with thee, and through the rivers, they shall not overflow thee:

when thou walkest through the fire, thou shalt not be burned; neither shall the flame kindle upon thee.'"

Her eyes flutter open, and she looks a little shy. And maybe it's just because she's trying so hard to cheer me up, or maybe something about the verse itself, with its epic-sounding trials—a character walking through water and fire, protected by his god—but for some reason, it *does* kind of make me feel better.

"That's pretty," I say.

"Yeah. The poetic parts of the Bible . . . those are my favorites," Ingrid says. "The parts that are about . . . being protected, and putting down your burdens. And being loved."

There's no self-pity in her voice, but it makes me remember what Brandy told me, about the painful years of Ingrid's childhood. About how, somehow, religion had helped them find a ballast in their tumultuous lives. And I can't help it—I have to ask.

"I get that," I say. "I do. Finding something that makes you feel like you can survive the worst . . . I do the same thing, even if I'm not religious. When I read, when I write, that's what I'm doing, too. But there's something I don't get."

She cocks her head.

"Why Victory Evangelical?" I hold my hands up in question. "I mean . . . Ingrid, you're not a hateful person. I know you're not a hateful person. But Dale Worthen's spent his whole career telling people they're going to hell. He's a controlling, misogynistic, backward person. Why not find a church that's less . . . judgmental?"

She obviously doesn't like the question. She shifts her weight on the cushion. "You can't cherry-pick your beliefs. You can't decide not to follow the rules because they're uncomfortable."

"So you think women are supposed to do whatever their husbands say?" I ask.

"I think women should choose husbands who are righteous," she says defensively. But she's avoiding my eyes. "Then it won't be a big deal to do what they say."

"And you think people who have sex outside of marriage are evil? Or gay people? Or . . ."

"Look, Ruthie, my faith isn't a fairy tale," she says. There's a flush across the bridge of her nose; it's the first time I've seen a hint of anger from her. "I'm not some little kid who's been blindly believing all her life. I came to this and I tested it and I chose it, and it has helped me get through a lot. I don't expect you to get it."

"But, Ingrid, I . . ." I trail off as my phone starts to ring. I frown. "Who actually calls anyone anymore?" I say, looking down.

It's Tabitha.

My heart gives an anxious skip. If she's calling, it must mean there's news.

"Hello?" I lock eyes with Ingrid as I put the phone to my ear. She mouths *what?* and I shrug.

"Ruthless?" Her voice is oddly muffled; I hear something clatter against the phone, and then when she speaks again the sound is clearer. "Meant to call . . . Ben." Her words slur so badly it's hard to understand. I hold my breath, trying to make out what she's saying. "'S'okay. I'm okay."

"Tabitha? What's going on?" I shift the phone to my other ear. "Are you okay?"

"It's all so fucked up," she whispers.

"What is, Tabitha?"

I hear a raspy breath.

"Tabitha?" I ask again.

Silence. A distant sob. And more silence.

TABITHA'S FRONT DOOR IS unlocked when I get there. The lights are all still on—I doubt she's turned them off all week. The place is a wreck; the fresh flowers in the hall are wilted, the water brackish. Piles of dirty clothes lie scattered all over—I smell cat pee on one—and in the kitchen there's a tower of dirty dishes on the countertop. I look around the ground floor, then go upstairs to her room.

She's on the floor of her bathroom, slumped against the toilet. She's in sweatpants and a vomit-crusted T-shirt that says SCORPIO ENERGY. I kneel down next to her, reach out to see if she's conscious. Her skin is clammy; she starts when I touch her, opening her eyes to peer blearily at me.

"Sorry," she mumbles. "I shouldn't have called."

"Are you okay?" I look around for a clean washcloth, a towel, something to give her to wipe her mouth. She rests her head against the toilet seat.

"Better. I vomited," she croaks. "Worst of it is out of me now."

"Was it just alcohol, or did you take something?" I run some cold water into a glass and hand it to her. She just holds it, as if she can't quite figure out how to drink it but can't put it down either.

"Alcohol. No drugs." She closes her eyes and rests her head on the toilet seat.

"You've got to stop this, Tabitha," I say quietly.

I expect her to snap at me, to accuse me of being judgmental. But she just nods.

"I know," she says. Her tone is so utterly miserable, I don't have the heart to say anything else.

The bathroom has a slanted ceiling, just like her bedroom. In here it feels more claustrophobic than cozy. I feel like I should duck my head, even though I'm not close to hitting it.

"My mom's coming home Wednesday," she says suddenly. She looks around the room—at the mildewy towel, the empty whiskey bottle on its side—and gives a strangled laugh. "I can't wait," she says. "I can't wait for her to see the house. She's going to go nuclear."

"I bet." I pick up the liquor bottle. "Is this all just to punish her? Because she deserves it, but you won't be able to enjoy it if you're already dead."

She shudders and covers her face.

"You don't get it. I can't stop *thinking*. I just want to stop thinking for a little while."

"Yeah, but Tabitha, that won't help anything," I say. "Zahra will still be missing. Even if you manage to forget that for a few minutes, it's still true. We have to stay calm and keep looking."

But she lets out a long, low moan, tugging at her hair.

"There's no point. She's *dead*."

Something about the way she says it—so certain, so shattered—brings me up short.

"Why do you say that?" I ask slowly.

She doesn't answer me. She looks half mad, her hair wild, her long, lean body curled onto the floor. I think about everything she's told me this last week—how sure she's seemed that Zahra left of her own volition. My blood goes cold.

"Tabitha, do you know something?" I say.

"I didn't think she meant it," she whispers, so softly I have to lean down to hear. "She's always talking like that. 'I deserve to die. I just want to be done with all this. I just don't want to feel this way anymore.' I always try to be patient, always. I always try to ask what she's talking about and sit with her until she feels better, but . . ." Her gaze goes fixed for a minute. She stares at something only she can see, projected on the wall beside her.

"Tabitha?" I ask softly.

She shakes her head, like she's trying to clear her vision.

"This time she really meant it," she says simply.

I sink down from the side of the tub to the floor, grab her by the shoulders, and make her look at me.

"You think she killed herself," I say flatly.

Her face crumples, her lip shuddering into sobs. She

doesn't have to say yes. That's when I realize she's not trying to punish her mom with all this.

She's punishing herself.

"There's no reason to think she killed herself," I say, shaking her a little. "They haven't found a note, they haven't found any kind of evidence . . ."

"I never meant for her to get so upset," she says, as if she hasn't heard me. "I didn't mean for it to be so ugly."

I go silent again, watching her face. She closes her eyes for a moment, her lashes wet with tears, and then goes on.

"I just didn't want him to get hurt. And he just thinks she's so . . . perfect, like she's some kind of . . . angel, or something," Tabitha pleads. "I mean, I've been best friends with him since third grade, I'm allowed to want to protect him, okay?"

I let go of her then, sitting down hard on my bottom.

"You told Ben about Seb," I say softly. When she doesn't answer, I go on. "She told you about the kiss, didn't she? And you told Ben."

"It's not fair!" The words rend the air, a shriek of rage, her mood suddenly pivoting to anger. "Fucking everyone's in love with Zahra. God, I'm probably half in love with her. And she's . . . not perfect, okay? So yeah, fine, I told Ben about her kissing some other guy, and they broke up, and she killed herself. And I wish . . . I wish . . ."

But she never says what she wishes. She just gives a sob and lies down on the bath mat, spent.

I don't ask any more questions. I help her change into clean clothes. Then I get her to her bed. Mr. Pants comes over with an inquisitive trill, curls up by her neck, and goes to sleep.

I watch her for a moment, drool already gathering at the corner of her mouth. Could she be right about what happened to Zahra? I don't want to believe it . . . but at this point, Tabitha might just know her better than me. Tabitha might have a better idea what she's really capable of.

I shake my head, almost violently, and start to gather up the dirty clothes strewn all over the room, just to have something to do. I won't believe it. I can't. Until there's some new bit of evidence, some new sign, I can't.

If I thought Tabitha was right, I'd fall apart myself.

CHAPTER TWENTY-THREE

I STAY AT TABITHA'S all night, sleeping on a little trundle bed on her floor. She wakes up a few times, moaning in pain. I make sure she drinks water. In the morning I go down to the kitchen and rifle through her cabinets. There's a bag of bagels in the breadbox that are only mildly stale, so I take them upstairs, along with a large thermos of ice water, and put it all by her bedside.

She's pale and clammy, but it looks like she's through the worst of it. Her eyes flicker open, red-rimmed.

"Go back to sleep," I whisper. "I'll tell Ms. Yi you're sick."

"You stayed?" she mumbles.

"I'm heading out now. Go back to sleep."

She nestles back down under the covers with a sigh. I give Mr. Pants a little scratch on the chin and turn to start gathering up my stuff.

Outside, I sit in my car for a few minutes, my breath

billowing around me in the early morning darkness. It's almost seven. I'd promised Dad I'd make it to school on time today—last night I told him Tabitha was sick and home alone and needed some help, and he'd grudgingly agreed to let me stay over—but suddenly the idea seems impossible.

I look down at my phone, my hand pale and cold curving around it. Then, before I can second-guess myself, I text Ben.

> Saw T last night. She's convinced Z did something to hurt herself.

I pause for a moment, trying to figure out how to phrase my question.

> Where do you think she'd go if she wanted to be alone?

He replies almost immediately.

> Don't know why I didn't think of it before but I can think of one place we haven't checked.

My eyebrows shoot up. My hands start to tremble with the cold.

Okay, I text back. Let's go check, then.

———

"So tell me, what's the story with this place? Where are we going?" I ask, glancing at Ben in the passenger seat.

The sun is just starting to flare above the mountains. By the time I picked him up, topped off the tank of my car, and bought a bag of gas station snacks for the road, it was almost nine. We hit the highway, and I wonder vaguely what time the school sends out the automated phone calls reporting absences to parents. Will Dad know I'm skipping by now? Or will it be this afternoon, when we're already halfway to Glenallen?

"It's an island. It used to be a church camp, but they shut it down back in the nineties," Ben answers. "I guess there was some kind of accident. A kid died."

I raise an eyebrow. "Oh, come on, that's, like, the premise of every slasher movie of all time."

"No, I'm serious. Some kid wandered away from camp and got lost in the woods, and I guess he died of exposure."

"That's . . . awful," I say. Then I frown. "If it closed in the nineties, how'd Zahra even know about it?"

He smirks. "Guess who owned the camp?"

My stomach turns. "Dale Worthen."

"Right in one." He shakes his head, looking out the window. "Zahra'd never been up there before, but last summer a bunch of us drove up to check it out. Morbid curiosity and all that. But it's really pretty up there, and there are all these abandoned cabins you can stay in. It's kind of fun to explore—there's all kinds of old stuff left behind."

I smile. Because there's another glimpse of the Zahra

I'd known. The one who loves abandoned spaces, things left behind.

"We've been back a bunch of times since then," he says. "Sometimes with a group. Sometimes just the two of us." His neck reddens a little. My gaze jerks straight ahead, out the windshield. "Anyway," he says quickly. "We've got to at least look out there."

We sink into silence for a while. Soon, we cross the Knik River and pass the state fairgrounds. Looking up I see that the snow has made it halfway down the mountains. It won't be long before it starts to snow in town. And if we haven't found Zahra by then . . .

I try to block out the thought.

In a few more miles the radio starts cutting out. I plug in my iPhone and turn on a playlist—Chvrches and Bon Iver and Arcade Fire. He glances sidelong at me.

"Look at the Portland hipster," he teases. But his finger-tips tap along with the music, and he sings along when a Neko Case song comes on. "Do you have family there or something?"

The question jerks me out of my head with a start. "Hm?"

"You know. Why'd you guys end up there?" He leans his head back against the rest, watching me. I squirm a little under his gaze.

"Oh." I shake my head. "No family. Mom was just look-ing for a change after the divorce, and she ended up finding a pretty good job."

"Did you like it?" he asks.

"It's okay, I guess." I adjust my seat back a little, straighten up. "But I was always homesick."

He looks back out the window. "Yeah, I bet. I don't know what I'm going to do next year."

"Are you planning to go to college in the lower forty-eight?" I ask.

"Mom wants me to. I've got a chance at a good scholarship, depending on how this season goes, and a lot of the best cross-country schools are down there. But I don't know." He looks out the window. The Matanuska Glacier pops in and out of view, wedged between the mountains. "I'll miss my family. And it'll be weird, being somewhere without Natives. Or . . . being somewhere with different Natives, I guess."

I nod. Leaving was hard enough for me. I can't imagine how it'd feel if I had deeper roots, deeper traditions.

"Arizona State's been sending me love letters, but can you even imagine going somewhere that hot?" He grimaces. "I already sweat through my clothes running in fifty degrees. I don't even know how people do it other places."

"I don't even know how people do it, period," I say. "I used to feign twisted ankles in PE class all the time just so I wouldn't have to jog."

He snorts a little. "You and Zahra both."

I give him a surprised look. "Zahra's on the cross-country team, right?"

"The JV team," he says. "No shade, but she's kind of awful. I think she mostly does it because she likes the trails. She likes to be outside. She's poky as hell, and she doesn't seem to care much about winning." He smiles a little. "Last year she came in dead last at regionals, because she found an injured squirrel and stopped to try to help it."

There she is again—another little glimmer of the Zahra I knew, flashing like something darting between the trees. She'd never been very athletic, but she loved to walk the trails. She loved to explore and point out the plants and birds and things that lived there. I was always so preoccupied, so in my head, I didn't notice most of it. But she did.

"How long have you guys been dating, anyway?" I ask.

"A little more than a year. We were friends before that. She and Tabitha and I were in a group together for film class sophomore year. We made this dumb-ass parody of a noir movie. It was really cheesy, but it looked amazing, because Zahra turns everything she touches into art." He shakes his head, remembering. "I mean, she found the costumes at a thrift shop— these boring old church clothes. Nothing special. And I just remember her coming at me with a dozen safety pins and a necktie and suddenly I'm, like, Don Draper."

I can picture it so clearly. The look on her face, a little abstract, a little distant. The way she'd hum to herself.

"Does she still write?" I ask.

"Write?" His brow furrows. "Like, in a journal, or what?"

"No, like . . . like stories. Fiction," I say.

"Not that I know of. But maybe. She doesn't tell me everything." He goes silent for a few minutes. The radio thrums softly, just audible over the sound of the wheels on the pavement. "Sometimes I feel like she doesn't tell me anything."

GETTING ANYWHERE IN ALASKA takes forever. It's hard for most people to get that—after all, we're usually in a tiny little box in the corner of the schoolroom map, only slightly bigger than Hawaii. But it's enormous—a fifth the size of the United States as a whole.

It takes almost four hours to get to the lake. Ben dozes for a while, and I'm left alone, crawling along sheer cliff faces, driving alongside blue-gray glacier runoff. It's lunchtime when we make it to the Cormorant Lodge—a combination inn, restaurant, and boat launch that serves the lake.

I wait on the dock while Ben goes in to try to rent a boat. Gray-green waves slap up against the support beams, a handful of late-season boats rising and falling rhythmically. I don't remember having been out here before. When I was really little—before Dad's drinking got so bad—we went on a few family camping trips. One time he woke me up—pulling me out of the tent, my head nodding against his shoulder—to show me a fox that lurked on the edge of our campsite. I remember s'mores over a fire; I remember Mom trying to teach me how to cast a line at the edge of a lake.

"You okay?"

Ben's voice comes from right next to me; somehow I didn't notice him approach. I give a little shudder and then nod.

"Yeah. Why wouldn't I be?"

He cocks his head. "You just looked . . . I don't know. Sad, I guess."

"I'm fine." I hitch my backpack up a little. "Any luck with the boat?"

He nods toward a broad green fishing boat. There are three long planks for seats, rotten and splintered, and a motor that looks like it's about a hundred years old. "Our chariot," he says.

"Goody." I look down into it. There's a thin rim of water on the bottom. "You have everything you need?"

"Yup." He hops down into the boat, surefooted. In a bin near the rudder there are a couple of lumpy old life vests; he hands me one and I hook it over my head. Then he holds out his hand to me.

My fingers rest in his for only a moment. His hand is warm, compared to the sharp wind coming off the lake. I let him help me down. The boat wavers under my feet; I take a deep breath.

"Let's go," I say.

CHAPTER TWENTY-FOUR

THIRTY MINUTES LATER, OUR little craft bumps gently against a crumbling wooden dock. Ben jumps out and ties it off. Then he holds out his hand to help me out.

The island rises like a turtle's shell out of the water, steep on all sides, flat across the top. Trees bristle out from the sides, save for a wide path that looks like it used to be regularly cultivated. I stand for a moment, getting used to the unmoving ground beneath my feet, and look around.

"The camp is up that way," he says. "Come on."

It's a steep climb. Ben has to slow down a few times to wait for me. It's not long before my breath is short. The ground is dried mud, pitted and knobbed like an alien landscape. I stumble once, catching myself on my palms, and the hard crust scrapes my skin raw.

Ben helps me up. "Almost there," he says.

And then we're at the top.

A half dozen simple wooden buildings stand, paint peeling, wood splintering. Weeds grow in every crevice, and the pine trees are stark against the clouds. A row of abandoned mud nests hang under every eave, the barn swallows already gone for the winter.

"You should see the place in the summer," he says. "It's really nice then."

I can picture it. I'm sure it's beautiful. Now, the chill air feels almost tense with neglect. As if the place is holding its breath, waiting either for the campers to return, or for the wilderness to reclaim the island entirely.

"Come on," I say. "Let's get moving."

None of the doors are locked. We move in and out of the different buildings, looking for signs of life. A thick coat of dust and cobweb covers everything. Daddy longlegs skitter in the corners of the rooms. In one, there's an ancient pot-bellied stove and a long row of tables. A mess hall, clearly. A large chalkboard next to the cafeteria window still lists the last meal: enchiladas, green salad, rice. In a smaller building there are upended boxes of crafting materials scattered across the floor.

"Some raven's got a sequined nest now," Ben says, nudging one of the boxes with his toe.

A faded poster on one wall shows an angel with a sword dripping blood. When I look closer, I see that the angel has a grotesque leer on its face, a look of almost obscene pleasure. It points with its free hand to an image of a devil. The paper is tattered, nibbled by insects and animals, but I can just make out that the devil seems to have been disemboweled.

"Ah, now I see evidence that Pastor Worthen was here," I say.

"Yeah." He grimaces at the poster. "That guy's such an asshole. I've never been a fan, but especially not since I started dating Zahra. You know he used to come to our practices and meets and stuff? He'd just sit in his car and watch like some kind of creeper. Sometimes she'd go talk to him, sometimes she'd just ignore him."

"Really? I didn't think they had any contact after she moved out of his place freshman year," I say.

He shrugs. "I think he was still trying to get her to come back to church or something. Once he even got out of his car and shook her by the shoulders. I was out on the field leading stretches when it happened but I swear, I was ready to go beat his ass. But she pushed him away and he drove off before I could do anything."

"That's really messed up." I frown. "Did you guys ever call the cops or anything?"

"Nah. That was last year. He never came back again. And she didn't want to upset her parents." He exhales upward, and a lock of his hair lifts from his forehead before settling back down. "Her mom's super sensitive about it all."

I nod slowly. It's not a surprise—from what I saw of Worthen's preaching style, I'm sure he feels entitled to harass whomever he wants. Especially a young woman; especially one related to him.

Classrooms, study rooms. A chapel with pews and a podium of rough-hewn wood. A storage room full of weird props—a moth-eaten papier-mâché tombstone, a rack of dusty costumes, a handmade puppet that looks like it could either be a dragon or a green dog. A few unspeakable outhouses—there's no plumbing out here. It's all silent and still.

"What a romantic getaway," I say.

He gives a lopsided grin.

"It's a little different when it's nice out." He points toward a path. "The cabins are this way."

He leads me toward the center of the island. Ahead of us on the trail I see an ermine scuttling away into the trees, its black-tipped tail sweeping behind. It looks like it's molting for the winter; there are patches of white along its legs. A camp robber screams from a nearby branch as we pass.

The path opens up into another large clearing, with a dozen painted wooden cabins arranged in a circle. At the center there's a small rusty playground that can't help but remind me of the abandoned one in Russian Jack. Maybe Zahra is just drawn to the neglected, the damaged.

We walk slowly around the ring of little A-frames. He points one out, a yellow one across from us, on the far side of the playground.

"That's where we used to stay. I think it belonged to her grandparents. Still has some of their old stuff in there. If she's been here . . . it'll be in there."

But something is off. I get a sharp whiff that stings my nostrils. At first I think it's come off the playground—there's a tang of rusted metal to it. It gets stronger as we approach the cabin, tinged with something else. Something hot, and heavy.

Ben halts in his tracks, reaching out an arm to stop me. And I can see from his expression that he knows what he's smelling—that he recognizes it, a moment before I do.

Blood.

The world goes sideways, my vision blurring with vertigo. I know what we will see next. I know what's behind the door to her cabin. Tabitha was right. Tabitha, and Ben both, because she came here to do it—to this place she loved. Alone. Where no one could stop her.

A sharp pain shoots through my arm. Ben is squeezing, hard. His face is still as a pillar. And then I hear what he does.

A low grunt. And then a horrifying crack, like wood being broken. And the wet, messy sound of eating.

It's coming from my right—from between a splintering red cabin and a blue one. I don't want to look. But I have to look. I have to know.

The first thing I see is movement. It's hard to make out what's happening; my eyes can't assemble it into a picture that makes sense. Something large and bloody on the ground. Bone jutting up. And perched on top, a behemoth. Thick neck twisting as it pulls meat from the bone. Hair bristling along its back. Muzzle dark and wet.

A bear.

It's maybe forty yards away. The size of it . . . it's hard to fathom. You see bears on TV, filtered through a lens, and you don't have any real clue. It's enormous. All muscle. All tooth and claw.

Ben's fingers dig into my arm.

"Don't run," he says. His voice is stunningly calm. "Walk. Slow. Come on, this way. Walk."

I can't lift my feet. He pulls at me, and I stagger a few steps after him.

The bear lifts its massive head and looks at us.

"Come on, Ruthie. We're just going to walk over here to this cabin, and we're going to let ourselves in. Okay? Don't run. Breathe. Just walk." He talks loudly, clearly. Some part of me recognizes what he's trying to transmit to the bear: *We're no threat. We don't want your food.* I take a deep breath and force myself to start walking.

The bear takes a wary step away from its meal. I follow Ben blindly as he cuts a wide arc away from the two cabins to either side of it, toward one a few doors down.

"No need for anyone to be scared." Oh, God, his voice sounds like it's coming from so far away. "We're just going over here."

My neck wrenches around as we walk away. I can't tear my eyes from it. It takes another few steps toward us.

"*Ruthie,*" Ben says. Beneath the calm I hear the urgency. "Stop staring at it. Don't make eye contact."

I force myself to turn away. My body is mechanical again, but it's slow to respond to my commands. And somewhere in that large empty space, in that rattling tin-can robot body, an alarm is going off, shrill and repetitive.

We're on the wooden porch. Ben's fingers curl around the doorknob. He twists, but it doesn't turn.

"Fuck," he says.

I turn to see the bear coming closer. For a moment it seems confused by the playground equipment—it stands before the swing set, huffing and grunting. Then its small, dark eyes fix on us again.

"I know Zahra's is unlocked," he says, nodding at the yellow cabin. It's not far—twenty feet, give or take. Not far—but then, the bear isn't far, either. "Nice and slow. Come on now." We move toward the yellow cabin. The alarm in my head is getting louder and louder. I can't stop to worry about that. I can't stop to think about the . . . *thing* I saw, back there on the ground. The bear's made its way through the playground now and nothing stands between us and it. It's building up to a charge, its gait clumsy and lopsided but shockingly fast, faster than anything so large should be. We're a few feet away now, Ben's hand already outstretched to the brass doorknob in front of us, and behind us the bear lets out a low, guttural bellow, and I'm certain I can feel its breath on me, I'm sure of it, and still we're walking, walking, walking so slowly . . .

And then the door is open, and Ben shoves me inside. I fall to the dusty plywood floor, bracing myself on my hands. I crane my head in time to see Ben jump in behind me, flinging the door shut.

A moment later, a great weight slams against the side of the cabin.

CHAPTER TWENTY-FIVE

I AM ON THE floor, something hard at my back, staring at the door. I can't move. It's odd—it feels just like when something terrible happens and I go very calm and very quiet, but this time—this time I can't move. Some connection seems to have broken. Some circuit has been fried. I can't make myself move, no matter how hard I try.

I think of the thing. The thing on the ground. Blood and gristle and bone. It'd been impossible to make out details in the midst of the mess. It'd been impossible to see what it was.

No, not impossible. Because I know what it was. It was death.

My eyes are wide and staring at nothing and I keep trying to will them to blink, to focus, but they don't obey any more than any other part of my body. My hands are limp against my legs.

"Ruthie. *Ruthie.*"

Ben's voice is calm and hard and insistent. He is some-where to my right. He takes my hand in his and squeezes hard.

"Was it her?"

I don't even recognize my own voice for a moment. My eyes are still fixed and I can't refocus; I don't even look toward Ben as I speak. The words come grating out of my throat, rough and slurred.

"Can you say that again? I didn't quite catch it." He sounds like the search-and-rescue people that came to get Mom out of the ravine—almost condescendingly composed.

For a moment I sit in silence. My breath is heavy—this body reflexively dealing with fight or flight. And then I blink, slowly, and look up at him.

"The body. Was it her?"

He is crouched next to me, still holding my hand. There's a look of forced calm on his face, but his pupils are wide in his already dark eyes.

"No. It was a moose. Well . . . half a moose," he says. "I saw the hooves."

And that's when I snap fully back to my body.

I curl forward, nauseated and shaking, heart shuddering. My whole body begins to tremble, starting at the top of my spine and spilling downward. For a moment I think there's something wrong with my lungs—my breath is coming in weird hitching starts and stops. Then I realize I'm sobbing.

"Shhh shhh shhh." Ben's hand flies over my mouth. "Ruthie . . ."

The cabin shudders again, the bear slamming against the wall. There's a splintering, cracking sound.

"We don't want to agitate it," he whispers. "No loud noises, okay?"

I choke down the noise and nod. When he takes his hand away, I press my own palms to my mouth.

It's not her. It's not Zahra out there. The terror leaves me in hot, heavy tears, spills down onto the dusty floorboards. I take deep, desperate gasps of air, but I do it silently.

It's only several minutes later that the fact registers: we are trapped here.

By a seven-hundred-pound apex predator.

With serious personal boundary issues.

"Oh my God," I whisper. My voice is strained and shrill. "We almost died."

"There's still time for that," Ben says with a grim smirk. He's standing next to a grimy little window, peering out. "It's gone back to that moose for now. But it can knock this cabin down like tissue paper if it wants to."

I think about all the stories I've ever heard about bear encounters. Most of the time bears avoid humans—but if you startle them, especially when they're protecting their meal, they'll go berserk.

We are very, very lucky.

"We may be here for a while," Ben says. He looks down at his phone. "Do you have a signal?"

I pull my phone out of my backpack. "No."

"Me neither." He glances back to the window. "We're about to lose the light. I think . . . I think we're here for the night."

I look around the little cabin. It's a small single room, most of the space taken up by a double bed pressed against one wall. The mattress is old and water-stained. There's a rough wooden table littered with old camping detritus—bug dope, sunblock, a broken pair of sunglasses. The only light comes from the two little windows. In the corner is a ladder to a loft.

"It could be worse," I say.

"In so many ways," he agrees.

He puts his backpack down on the bed and opens it up. Inside is one of those super-light synthetic jackets back-packers use—extra warm, without taking up much space. He unfolds it and tucks it around my shoulders, over my hoodie.

"I'm not cold," I say.

"You're kind of in shock," he says. "Just humor me and wear it for a little while, okay?"

"Okay." It smells faintly of wood smoke and conifer.

He sits down next to me, exhaling heavily. "She hasn't been here."

"How do you know?" I ask.

"Nothing's been moved." He gestures around the cabin with one hand, without looking up. "This is where we usually spend the night. That bug dope over there, we left that here in July. It's dusty." He's quiet for a moment. I feel his breath, slow and even, next to me. "I knew she wasn't here the moment we landed. She usually leaves her shit all over the place. Towel on a porch rail to dry, boots by the stove to warm. The dining hall stove hasn't been used and there's no ash in the bonfire pit. Even if she came out here to hide and keep a low profile, there'd be some sign of her."

We sit in silence for a few minutes. Outside, I can hear huffing, grunting. The bear back at his meal. The birdsong starts up again around the cabin.

"I just feel like if I knew her better, I'd be able to find her," he says. "And it pisses me off so much. Because I showed up. Every day. I showed up, and she kept putting me off."

Maybe I'm just raw from the unaccustomed crying fit— or maybe an actual bear attack is the only thing that can leave me vulnerable. But my breath catches a little at his words. His feelings send a resonant shiver through my body.

I speak slowly, carefully. These aren't the kinds of things I'm used to saying out loud. "Ever since I got back to Anchorage, I've been trying to figure out just who Zahra is. She's changed. Or . . . she was always someone else, maybe, and I just saw a side of her that no one else did. I don't know which. For the last few years, I've thought I knew her so well. And it's been really hard to find out that's not true. The girl everyone keeps telling me about seems so strange to me."

He rolls his head to the side to meet my eyes. We're close enough that I can see the thin gradient of color between his iris and his pupil, the place where the deep brown gives way to black. I catch my breath, inch ever so slightly away.

"Tell me about her," he says. "The version you knew."

So I do. I tell him how we met, when she saw me reading

Abhorsen in the little postage-stamp yard outside my trailer and asked if I had the other books in the series. How we would hang out talking about books for hours on end. How I'd show up at her door at ten most mornings—that was when she rolled out of bed—and eat cereal at her cluttered kitchen table while her mom read us our horoscopes. How we'd park in front of the TV to watch *Star Wars* or superhero movies. How we'd bike to the mall and try on the ugliest dresses we could find and take selfies in the fitting room. And how, more than anything else, we worked on our own writing together.

"I've never told anyone about it," I say. "And I guess she didn't, either. It's kind of . . . God, it's almost embarrassing how into it we got. We had these characters and they were, like . . . they were us, basically, but with superpowers." I'm purposely glossing the details—how, at a certain point, we'd call each other *Lyr* and *Starmaiden* anytime we were alone. How I could sometimes feel the weight of my sword in my hand. How our secret clearing in the woods felt truly like another world sometimes, how it felt literally like we were a million miles away and if we just pushed a little harder at the stubborn membrane of reality we might break through and *become* those characters, with all their strength and all their sense of purpose.

Instead I focus on the way we'd sit, so close I could feel her curls on my own shoulders, passing a notebook (wide ruled; I preferred college but we had to accommodate Zahra's wide, looping letters) back and forth to write scene after scene in purple glitter pen. I tell him about the outline we made for a whole trilogy—we only ever made it halfway through book one, but we had *plans*. I tell him we were going to mail the manuscript to Tamora Pierce to ask if she'd help us find an agent.

I don't mention the playground. Because that's ours. Mine and Zahra's, and nobody else's.

By the time I stop talking, the light has gotten low. Outside the window the sky is striated in lines of pink and gold and blue. The sun's down, but its rays die slowly.

I can just make out Ben's face—his small, thoughtful smile. There's nothing in his expression that comes off as mocking or amused. I'm grateful for it.

"She was always . . . dreamy, I guess. To be honest, she had the better imagination. I just had the discipline to get things down on paper. Zahra was like a will-o'-the-wisp. Sort of . . . wandering and capricious." I shrug a little. "But Marcus and Jeremy and Tabitha talk about her like . . . like she's sort of a mess. And you talk about her like she's an ice princess. And . . . I don't know. Are they all true? Or was I wrong all along? Or . . . has something happened to her?"

He shifts his weight. I can feel his arm next to mine, warm through the sleeve.

"Don't you think that's how we all are, though? You only see what you want to see in other people. Or maybe you only see what you *can* see in other people. And everyone acts a little different depending on who they're around. So maybe what you saw as her free-spirited side just looks messy to Tabitha. Or maybe you brought that free-spiritedness out in her."

I laugh a little. "I seriously doubt that's it. I'm the opposite of a free spirit. I'm always so in my head about everything."

"But that's why," he says. "Because some part of her, conscious or not, knew that was what you needed. I mean, I'm not saying she was playing it up for you or anything. I'm just saying, maybe the way she related to you has to do with what she saw in *you*."

I consider that for a moment. It's not the way I'm used to thinking about people. "That feels . . . I don't know, kind of cynical. Like everyone just performs for each other all the time?"

He gives a little laugh in the darkness. "It's only cynical if you're trying to manipulate someone. Which I don't think Zahra on her worst day would do. I think maybe it's more about finding the best way to connect. Whether you realize it or not, you show them the part of you they most want to see. You do it because you want them to like you."

I let his words sink in. I understand what he means—and in a way, he's right. But for some reason it hurts, too. Hurts to think that the connection I shared with Zahra might not have been as unique as I'd thought.

"Did Zahra have mood swings?" I ask, a little abruptly. "Tabitha says . . ."

"Tabitha is not the ultimate authority on Zahra," he says.

"Yeah, I know. That's why I'm asking you," I say, a little shortly.

He sighs, gets to his feet. I see his outline against the square of the window, stretching.

"I guess you could call them that," he says. There's something so profoundly sad in his voice, so aching. He's looking out the window now. The light is pale blue, the moment in twilight when it gets somehow lighter on its way to getting darker. "She had really bad panic attacks sometimes. I don't know why. But they were awful. And she'd get depressed after them. Shut herself in her room, refuse to eat or bathe or anything. She'd never talk to me about what was wrong."

"That must have been . . ."

"Awful. It's really fucking awful to know the person you love doesn't trust you," he says.

"Yeah," I say. "I bet."

He runs his hands through his hair. "She wasn't like that with you?"

"Honestly, she never told me much about her feelings. But that might have been my fault. I was more interested in talking about imaginary things. I was avoiding my own feelings. So I don't know that I ever asked her much about hers."

"She was good at deflecting," he says. "She'd redirect the conversation without me even noticing it until later, if she didn't want to talk about something. And I never wanted to invade her privacy. I figured she'd tell me what was wrong if she wanted to. But . . ." He trails off for a moment. "Fuck. Now I just wish I'd pried."

"You can't make people talk about things." I rest my head on the mattress behind me. "Trust me."

"Yeah." He moves quietly in the darkness. I hear the rustle of his clothing, the creak of his shoes on the wood. Then,

216

suddenly, he's right next to me again, his leg against mine on the floor. "I guess you'd know that."

"What do you mean?" I hate the sound of my voice, tremulous in the dark. It sounds rough, oddly sensual, and the very thought makes my cheeks burn.

"You know. After we got away from the bear. You were, like, shut down for a little while there. It was spooky."

"Sorry," I whisper.

"Don't apologize. It's not an accusation."

We're quiet for a moment. I imagine I can hear his heartbeat, just a foot or two away. I imagine I can hear the bellows of his lungs.

"It happens when things get really bad. I've done it since I was a kid," I say softly. I've never talked about this, either, but here in the dark, the only humans on the island, it feels all right. It feels safe. "I don't know why. I guess maybe it helped me survive. My dad was a drinker. He never did anything really awful, but there was a lot of yelling. Things were unpredictable. I think I went a little robotic sometimes, just so I didn't have to deal with it."

"So that's what you meant when you said you were avoiding your feelings," he says.

"Yeah, I guess," I say.

Something touches my shoulder. His arm. It slips around me. I am not usually a hugger—I don't like feeling constrained, pressed down. But this is different. It doesn't feel like I'm trapped. It feels like ballast, like it's keeping me here. Rooted.

The light finally leaves the sky. A few early stars poke

through the dark in the windows. I don't hear the bear any longer. I wonder if it's bedded down somewhere out there. I wonder if the other creatures on the island are starting to poke tentative noses from their dens and nests. I lay my head against his shoulder.

"I'm glad we came, anyway. Even if Zahra isn't here," I whisper.

"Really? Even if we almost got mauled to death?"

"Yeah. I feel closer to her when I'm with you. Maybe that's messed up. But I'm glad that, if nothing else, I've met you."

"Me too," he says.

We're quiet I don't know how long. At a certain point we both get up on the bed. It sags, and the mattress smells like mildew, but it's more comfortable than the floor. Any other time it'd freak me out to be on a bed with a boy—it seems like a big deal. But that's the thing about near-death experiences: they really leave you open to new things.

We don't want to waste our cell phone batteries, so once it gets dark, it gets really, really dark. The stars are bright in the little windows. Outside the birdsong has quieted; now it's just the waves and the wind, beating up against the little island.

I don't know if it's an accident or not. I move, or he moves, or the bed itself moves, the island, the earth moves, and our lips touch. My fingers brush his stomach, those hard ridges of muscle, the soft cotton of his shirt. There's a tug at my hair. He has a handful of it, knotted around his fingers, and I don't know if he's trying to get free of it, caught in the long loose mass, or if he's holding on for dear life. But then I am—holding on for dear life—and our lips play against each other, soft and then hard, hungry. And it's strange, it's so strange. I keep waiting to disappear down in my body the way I do, to become a giant mech suit with a tiny pilot inside, because this is new and it should be terrifying, it should send me hiding deep inside, but it doesn't. It doesn't. Every part of my flesh remains alive, aware, electric. Every inch of me trembles, waiting in breathless hope that its turn is next—toe, knee, shoulder, sacrum, all of it suddenly desperate to be touched.

And then maybe the earth shifts one more time, and we draw that much apart—enough to catch our breath, enough to think maybe we need to stop now before it goes any further. I push my face against his shirt. I listen to the quiet rhythm his heart beats out, and I feel his arms tuck around my waist, no longer groping and eager but strong. I hear him fall asleep first, his breath going soft. I lie there for a little while, dizzy with it all, almost drunk on it. My body feels impossibly awake to everything. But finally, I drift off, too.

CHAPTER TWENTY-SIX

I WAKE UP SHIVERING and ravenously hungry on the bare mattress, my body aching all over. It takes me a minute to put it all together, to believe that my memories are memories and not bad dreams: yes, there was a bear. Yes, it chased us.

Yes, we kissed.

We. That's when I sit up sharply. Ben's gone, and I'm alone in the cramped and musty cabin, wrapped up in a bundle of threadbare quilts. The sky outside is sallow with low, streaky clouds. I kick the covers off and half roll, half stumble off the bed.

According to my phone, it's just after six a.m. Everything that felt warm and intimate the night before looks ugly in the naked dawn—the wooden walls raw and splintering, the cabin a dirty little box. I'm still wearing Ben's jacket, and I hug it around my shoulders against the cold. Where is he? Did he leave me here? Am I going to have to figure out how to get out of here on my own, past that bear, across the lake?

I'm kneeling down next to my backpack, rummaging for an extra jacket, when the door opens softly behind me. Ben comes in, his hair wildly mussed, the legs of his jeans covered in dust. I jump to my feet.

"*There* you are," I say.

He gives a crooked smile. "Sorry. I was trying to get back before you woke up."

"What were you doing?" I ask.

"Looking around, trying to see if it's going to be safe to get back to the boat today." He chews on the corner of his thumbnail. "Bear's gone. So's the carcass. It looks like he dragged it toward the woods. So . . . it's not what I'd call 'safe' out there, but I think we can make it down to the boat if we're careful."

I stare at him. "That's a bad pep talk," I say. "You're bad at pep talks."

"I'm a runner, not a cheerleader. Besides, the alternative is to stay here all day not knowing where it is or what it's doing." He gives a little shrug. "We'll go slowly. There's lots of shelter between here and there, so we'll be able to get into the cabins or the classrooms if we hear it along the way."

"As long as the doors aren't locked," I say. I close my eyes and take a deep breath. "But I guess you're right. We don't have much choice."

I catch my breath as he steps closer to me. My lips pulse with the memory of his. But he doesn't look at me; he picks up one of the blankets and starts to fold it neatly. Blushing, I grab another. We pack them away in the bin under the bed.

"There," he says. "Now the next people in here hiding will have clean, dry blankets to sleep under."

The next people, I think, or him and Zahra, if they get back together. It's coming to me, with the hard light of day, that this is the cabin where he usually comes with Zahra— that they've slept in the bed together, wrapped in these quilts. That they probably did more than sleep.

That I came out here to find her, but instead I made out with her ex in the same bed where they've probably done more than sleep.

No wonder he won't look at me. We crossed a line.

The walk back down to the dock seems to take forever. We move slowly and deliberately and talk loudly as we go—but our conversation is all strained and superficial, made only for the sake of the bear. Everything easy and comfortable about being with him has disappeared in the last twelve hours.

"So do you think your dad's going to be mad?" he asks.

"Definitely," I say.

"Yeah, I'm probably grounded forever," he says casually, looking around as we move past the dining hall. "Either that or Mom's already rented out my room."

"I'm probably going to be packed off to a reeducation class at Victory Evangelical," I say. "With any luck they'll realize I'm not good Handmaid material. Maybe they'll let me empty the wastebaskets instead."

We stop at the dock for a moment, turning our glances

back up the hill, to the empty cabins and overgrown forest. We didn't cover everything we could have—not by a long shot—but Ben seems certain she's not here.

"We're running out of places to look," I say softly.

He doesn't answer. Just hops down in the boat and starts readying the motor.

"Maybe it's not that we don't know her well enough to find her," I say. "Maybe . . ."

I stop. I don't want to say it out loud.

But it's not like it's a stretch to imagine a random stranger hurting her. It happens all the time—all over the place, but especially in Alaska, especially where there's a lot of people on drugs, a lot of people who pass through town on their way to seasonal work. This place has been a hunting ground for evil men plenty of times before now.

Ben gets the motor started, and I jump down into the boat next to him. He doesn't need me to tell him all this. He knows it. So I sit on one side of the boat, and he takes the rudder, and the island gets smaller and smaller behind us.

The lodge isn't open for breakfast yet. We get to my car and scrounge in the cooler for the rest of our snacks—granola bars and beef jerky, Cheez-Its and gummy bears. It's the most satisfying meal I've ever had.

"Nothing like almost dying to put the savor in your processed food item," Ben says, cramming a handful of crackers in his mouth.

My phone is out of battery, so we don't listen to any music as we turn onto the road. But somewhere just beyond Long

Lake, where Dall sheep dot the mountainside overhead like patches of snow, his hand finds mine. We don't speak for the rest of the drive, but my fingers burn as if the contact has rubbed away the skin. As if touching him makes me raw.

IT'S LATE MORNING WHEN we get to my house. I expect everyone to be gone; it's Wednesday, the middle of the school day. But when we get to my house, Dad's truck and Brandy's car are both in the driveway—and there's a cop car parked on the street.

Ben and I look at each other. I realize abruptly that he's let go of my hand.

I don't have time to wonder why the cops are there, though. Because that's when Tabitha pulls up behind us in her dented blue crossover. She gets out and leaves her door hanging ajar. I watch with surprise as Ingrid gets out of the passenger seat behind her.

Tabitha gets to us first. I'm in the middle of climbing out of my car, and my foot is tangled up behind me as she strides over to me. Her jaw juts aggressively. Her amber eyes flash.

"What are you guys . . ." I start to ask, but she talks right over me.

"Where the hell have you been?" she hisses.

I look at Ben, then back to her. "We went to Shosubenich Lake. To look for Zahra."

She makes a sound in the back of her throat like she's choking on something small and hard.

Ingrid's caught up now. Her face looks unusually dour as she sizes me up. I wonder if she's going to write me off the way she has Tabitha, just because I spent the night with a boy I barely know. But she just glances at the cop cars.

"Did you even stop to think how this would look?" she asks.

"God, Ingrid, I don't care how it looks," I say. "It was totally innocent, but even if it wasn't, you can mind your own . . ."

"No, I don't mean . . ." She stomps her foot like a child, looking impatient. "God, Ruthie, that's what you think of me? I'm not talking about sex or whatever. I'm talking about the fact that you *disappeared*. At the same time as the guy who was there the night Zahra disappeared. People are freaking out."

I look over at Ben. The blood has left his face. His mouth falls open. "You thought that I, what, snatched Ruthie?"

"*I* didn't think that," she says, though I'm not so sure I believe her. "But you guys were both missing, and no one was answering texts . . ."

"No service," I say. "And then the phone died anyway."

"Yeah, well, that's why people usually tell their friends and family where they're going," Ingrid says, looking aggrieved. "Mom and Rick called the cops first thing this morning. Tabitha and I have been driving around looking for some sign of you."

Tabitha's just glowering, staring across the top of my car at Ben. I feel, like I often do, that she's trying to tell him something. But he doesn't even look at her. He's looking at the house.

"I'd better go in and explain, then," he says.

Surprisingly, all three of us jump to stop him at the same time.

"You'd better not," Ingrid says. "Rick's ready to have you arrested as it is. If he sees you . . ."

"You need to get home to your mom," Tabitha puts in. "She's left me about five hundred messages. Come on, I'll drive you."

He glances at me. I nod.

"I can handle my dad," I say. "Your family's probably really scared. I'll talk to you later, okay?"

For a moment he doesn't say anything. Then he gives a short nod and picks up his backpack from the back seat.

Tabitha gives me another long, hard look before following him to her car.

I stand motionless as they drive away. A miasma of bug dope and sweat clings to me, and I can smell the sharp chemical tang of my own terror, the remnant of the adrenaline from last night. I realize suddenly that I'm still wearing Ben's jacket.

"So, you and Tabitha went out looking for us, huh?" I say, tossing my car keys from one hand to the other. "That's kind of the team-up of the century, huh?"

Her lips twist downward.

"I called her. I knew she'd want to find you, too. And I didn't have a car to go looking for you."

Right. "Ingrid, I'm so sorry I left you without a ride . . ."

She shakes her head. "I don't care. It's fine."

"And thank you for looking for me," I persist. "With Tabitha, of all people."

"Ruth, it's fine," she says, more firmly this time. She turns to go into the house. "I just wish you'd realize that people actually care about you."

I follow her to the house in silence.

Upstairs, Dad and Brandy are both at the kitchen table. Officer Sapolu is there. With him is a white woman in a neat black pantsuit, her thin blonde hair tied at the nape of her neck. She's sipping from a steaming mug, her legs crossed in front of her.

When I come in, the reaction is immediate and over-whelming. Brandy's the first one to me. She puts her arms around me and pulls me up against her so my face is in the crook of her neck. Her arms tremble around me. I don't move away. I can sense already that she is my only protection in this room, without even looking at my dad.

"Where. In God's name. Have you been?"

His voice is low and controlled. Beneath the careful enunciation, I can hear it—that deep, almost subaudible thrum of anger. That through-gritted-teeth snarl that always came before one of his rages, back in the old days. Usually it was my mother on the receiving end. Sometimes, though, I got it, too.

"I'm sorry," I mumble against Brandy's neck. I look up, turn to face the rest of the room. Dad's risen to his feet, but he stays back, as if afraid of what he'll do if he comes any closer. Officer Sapolu and the woman exchange glances. "You guys aren't going to believe the night I had. We were looking for Zahra on this island, and there was a bear . . ."

"Island?" His voice goes up a few decibels. "What *island*? Where did you go? In what world did you think it would be okay to vanish like that?"

"Mr. Hayden," says the woman. I turn to look at her face. It's deeply lined, especially along the forehead. She's older than I thought at first.

"I know how upset you must be," she says gently. "And I don't want to interfere in family affairs. But Officer Sapolu and I have a few questions for Ruthie. If we could take a moment, we'll get out of your hair as soon as possible."

Dad's face is mottled and red, and looks for all the world like he's been downing vodka since dawn. Something about it makes my spine snap straight. I feel my armor going up.

He gives a little nod. The woman smiles up at me.

"It sounds like you had quite a night," she says. "We haven't formally met. I'm Detective Lucy Teffeteller. I'm assisting with the search for Zahra Gaines." She pauses. "You gave everyone a real scare."

"I'm . . . sorry," I say. "I didn't really think."

"Obviously," snaps my dad. My gaze shoots up toward him, but before I can say anything, Detective Teffeteller is speaking again.

"So you've been spending time with Zahra's friends?" she asks.

I give a little shrug. "They're my friends, too." I don't know if that's true anymore. Tabitha could be done with me now that she's seen me with Ben. And Ben . . . I have no idea how Ben thinks of me.

"You were out of town with Ben Peavy. Her ex-boyfriend, right?" the detective says.

"Yes," I say. "We went looking for her together. We planned to be back late last night, but there was a bear on the trail and we had to hide in one of the cabins."

Dad gives a snort like he doesn't believe me. I roll my eyes, but I don't say anything.

Teffeteller's eyes widen, but it comes off as performative, as if she's humoring me.

"Can you tell me everything that happened?" she asks.

I don't have a good reason not to. I sit down across from her and tell her everything that's happened since we set out for the island. Dad makes little scoffing noises every so often, but I don't respond to it.

While I'm talking, the detective watches me from pale blue eyes, rimmed with lashes so short and light you can barely see them. Officer Sapolu is making notes in a small book. When I'm done, Teffeteller leans forward, forearm on her knees.

"So you and Ben talk about Zahra quite a bit, then," she says.

"Yeah, I mean . . . we're both really worried," I say.

"Has he told you much about the night of the party?" she asks. "Has he talked about the fight they had, or . . ."

"I don't know anything he hasn't told you," I say. "He accused her of cheating. They broke up. He stormed off. He went caribou hunting after. When he came back she was missing." I look around the table. "Look, Ben's trying to find her as hard as anyone."

The detective holds up her hands placatingly. "We all want to find Zahra, Ruth. And that's why it's so important for you to think about whether Ben said anything that struck you as odd. Did he describe the argument? Did he talk about his hunting trip at all?"

I shake my head. "No. But I did track down the guy they were fighting about."

"Tracked down?" Sapolu's heavy brows shoot upward. He looks almost amused. "What, are you running a separate investigation?"

I feel Teffeteller's eyes sharpen on me. She is obviously *not* amused.

"They were fighting because he . . . he heard a rumor. That she was cheating. So I thought . . . well, whether she was cheating or not, that's another person that might know something. So I asked around. The guy's name's Seb Collins." It's so odd to me how calm my voice can be in a time like this. As long as I don't look at my dad, my voice is slow and matter-of-fact. "He had a crush on her. I guess he kissed her, and she freaked out."

Teffeteller runs a hand across her forehead. "Okay. Look, Ruth, I'm going to need you to back off. I know you're trying to help, but you don't really know what you're doing, and you could be tainting the witness pool, or giving away pieces of information that need to remain as private as possible without meaning to."

"Did you know about Seb before I told you about him?" I ask, the faintest edge of heat to my voice.

"As a matter of fact . . ." she starts, but before she can finish the statement my dad jumps in.

"That's not the point," he snaps. "You're going to stop this, Ruthie. You're going to mind your own business from here on out, do you hear me?"

"Everyone hears you," I mutter.

I can feel the tension in his limbs, radiating outward across the kitchen. Brandy puts a hand on his shoulder. It's a light touch—it's not like she's holding him back—but it seems to help. He turns away abruptly, like he can't even stand to look at me anymore.

"It seems like you might need a little time to talk," Teffeteller says. Her voice is cold and clipped. "Ruthie, don't pull any more vanishing acts. The town's on high alert as it is. And look . . . I know you're worried about your friend. But the best thing you can do right now is to let us do our job. If you hear something, even if it's just a rumor, give us a call and we can look into it, okay?" She hands me a card.

I fight the urge to throw it down. "Sure. Sorry for scaring everyone."

The cops are in the doorway when Teffeteller turns to

speak one more time. "There's going to be a press conference later today," she says. "But you should hear it first. The tests from the blood on Zahra's cell phone came back."

My fingers clench against my legs; I'm tight-shouldered in my seat, waiting.

She grimaces, gives a helpless little gesture with one hand. And I know before she says it.

It's Zahra's blood.

CHAPTER TWENTY-SEVEN

THE FIGHT IS QUICK and nasty and predictable. Dad snarls; Brandy cries. Ingrid makes herself scarce.

"You're grounded." He's standing in front of me, looking down at me. We're still in the kitchen. "For the next two weeks. You'll go to school and come home. And you'll stay away from that Peavy kid."

"Okay," I say automatically. I see his lip curl, see him trying to see if I'm sassing him somehow, if this is some kind of deep sarcasm. I take a little pleasure at that. Good; let him be confused.

But the truth is, I just don't care. I'm letting him bawl it out to get it over with. All I can think about right now is Zahra. Zahra's blood.

"And . . . no phone," he says. He sounds like he's fishing now, trying to get a rise out of me. Trying to figure out how to make me as upset as he is. But I hand over my phone silently.

Brandy touches his shoulder. "Rick, no. What if there's an emergency? What if she needs us?"

For a moment, he looks like he might blow up at her next. I see it flit across his face. I remember the hole he left in our wall when I was a kid, after Mom asked how many drinks he'd had before she'd let me in the car with him. But he takes a deep, shaky breath, and hands me back the phone.

"Car keys, then," he says.

I shrug. I hand him the keys. "Are we done?"

"We're done when I say we're done," he snaps. I nod silently and wait. I distantly, vaguely realize that my lack of response startles him, maybe even scares him. There's a moment when he doesn't really seem to know what to do next.

Brandy steps in. She takes me by the hand. "We'll talk more later, okay?" she says. "Why don't you go clean up, get some rest. It sounds like it was a long night."

"But don't think for a minute I believe that bull honky about the bear," he shouts after me as I make my way downstairs.

Bull honky. It seems such a waste to hear that right now, when I can't laugh at anything. When hope rides so low it scrapes the floor.

Ingrid's sitting on the sofa in the rec room, playing with her phone in its pink glitter case. The TV's on, set to some random nature show—fennec foxes skittering across the desert floor, chasing rodents and hiding from humans. I sit down next to her.

"It's her blood," I say.

She's quiet for a long time. She's not wearing make-up today, and her hair is limp against her scalp. She looks exhausted.

I try again. "I'm sorry if I scared you," I whisper. "We really did plan to be back last night, but . . ."

She throws her phone down on her lap. It's a gentle toss, but it's so uncharacteristic I go silent.

"After Mom sobered up they put me in therapy for a while," she says. I don't ask who "they" were; from what I know of her mom's past, it was probably a court order of some kind. "And the therapist had this poster in the waiting room. It was this chart, of all the different kinds of roles kids take on in dysfunctional families. You know—'the Hero,' who has to succeed at everything in order to pretend things are okay. 'The Scapegoat,' who acts out and takes on all the blame. 'The Mascot,' who makes everyone laugh to cut the tension. I knew without having to be told that I was 'the Caretaker.' The one that tries to smooth things over, that tries to keep everyone calm so things don't escalate."

I'm not sure why she's telling me this. I'm not sure what it has to do with anything. But I don't interrupt.

"Anyway, it's a role that sounds very sweet but it's pretty self-serving," she says. "You bend over backward to make peace, no matter what happens. It's not because you care about anyone else's well-being. It's because you're scared. It's because you've figured out how to make this awful situation work for you, and if it changes, you don't know what you'll do. Even if it changes for the better. Better not to fight or let things come to a head, because if they do, if your mom hits her bottom and has to get clean, all these systems you have worked out are going to fall apart." She gives a little toss of her head. "It's not like I was aware of all that while I was doing it, obviously—I was just a kid. But it's something we talked a lot about in therapy. How I'd accommodate every crappy thing Mom did so I didn't have to face the truth."

"Okay," I say slowly.

She looks at me then. Her eyes are wide and blue and clear as glass. But somehow, in all that transparent depth, there are things I can't see.

"There's another role on all the posters. The Lost Child," she says.

My body goes tense. I wait.

"The one that opts out. That disappears. That writes the whole thing off," she says. "The one that makes herself small and assumes no one wants her or needs her."

Anger starts to crawl up my spine. "Are you seriously going to throw some psychobabble bullshit in my face right now?"

She doesn't flinch. She takes a deep breath.

"You owe it to me to listen for a minute," she says.

She's right. I do.

"I'm just trying to tell you . . . we want you, Ruthie. We need you. Okay? So don't just . . . vanish." She looks at me another moment, then she stands up.

"Where are you going?" I ask.

"School," she says. "It's lunch, I can go in for the last couple classes."

She picks up her backpack from where it's slumped against the ancient wood paneling. Then she slings it over her shoulder and heads up the stairs.

I watch her go, thoughts lurching and stumbling through my mind. Her words hit harder than Dad's ever could. His just made me angry. Hers did, too; but they also made me feel guilty.

Never mind the guilt I've been carrying already. My skin burns with it; it lingers in the memory of Ben's touch. Now in the light of day I can't believe it happened. I can't believe I *let* it happen. My best friend's ex. What's wrong with me?

But even thinking about it makes my breath catch. I close my eyes. The way he touched me . . .

How can I still want that so bad, with the fact of Zahra's blood in front of me? How can I be almost dizzy, wondering where he is, what he's doing, knowing what that might mean?

I pull out my phone. First I text Tabitha.

I'm really sorry, is all I say.

Because I am, and because she came to look for me. And because now I have no leg to stand on; she may be the one who's got a crush on Ben, but I'm the one who made out with him.

Then I text Ben.

Are you okay?

He doesn't reply. I head down the hall to the yellow-and-white bathroom and plug the phone into the wall. Then I get into the shower.

I crank the water up as high as it can go, so it stings my skin, so it turns me lobster-red. After our night shivering in our own sweat, it feels good. And maybe it burns away some of what we did. Maybe if I can scorch my skin, it'll stop wanting what it can't have.

The text alert comes just after I've soaped up my hair. I don't wait; I pull back the curtain and look.

> Cops here too. they have a warrant now. Tearing the house apart.

My heart sinks. Now that they have blood evidence, Ben will be locked in their bull's-eye. If they even think they can win a case against him, they'll make his life a living hell.

The only way to fix this is to find her. And time is running out.

CHAPTER TWENTY-EIGHT

WE HAVE TO TAKE the bus the next morning. Ingrid's stoic about the whole thing, which almost makes me feel worse. *I'm* grounded, so *she* has to ride the bus with the rowdy, ungovernable freshmen of our neighborhood. She keeps her eyes on her phone while spitballs course overhead, ignoring the kid that calls her a fat-ass when she has to squeeze down the aisle to find a seat. It's really not fair. Dad should have at least given *her* a ride.

We're the last stop, so we don't have a chance to sit together, and when we get off the bus she gives me a quick wave before disappearing into the crowd. I wonder if she's mad at me, or just preoccupied, but it leaves me feeling weirdly lonely.

Inside, I make my way down the wide checkerboard hallway. I'm almost to the stairs when someone grabs me by the hand and jerks me to one side.

It's Ben. He pulls me into a room and shuts the door

quickly behind us. The momentum sends me crashing into him, up against his chest, and he puts his arms around me to steady me.

He clears his throat, moves away slightly. "Sorry. I'm not supposed to talk to you. I didn't want anyone to see us."

"It's okay," I say, smiling. "I'm not supposed to talk to you, either."

We're in the athletic supply closet. It's huge but cluttered, and the air smells like old sneakers and bleach. There are a handful of football dummies clustered in one corner, and mesh bags full of balls slumped against the walls. A broken gymnastics horse sits on its side. The only light comes from the gap under the door, dim and distant.

He looks down at me, and I wonder fleetingly what it is he sees. A co-conspirator, an ally in the search for his ex-girlfriend? Or something else . . . something beyond the relationship we both have with Zahra?

"Are you okay?" he asks.

"Yeah." I set down my guitar case, bite the corner of my lip. "I'm grounded until I die. But it's fine. What's going on with you?"

"I'm going in this afternoon to make another statement. Mom wouldn't let them talk to me without the lawyer present. So instead they just tore up the house." He grimaces. "I guess you know about the blood?"

I nod. "They told me."

"They don't know for sure if that means she was hurt," he says. "The phone was broken and the blood was along one of the shards. She might have just cut herself on the screen."

I nod. But then we fall silent. Outside, the normal noise of the pre-class crowd swells for a moment, then subsides again. I bite the corner of my lip. It's a big closet, but we feel impossibly close.

"My dad didn't believe me about the bear," I say, more to have something to say than anything else. It's a mistake, though, because as soon as I mention it, we're back in the cabin, pressed together and frantic. For a second I think it's just me—that I'm the only one imagining it, reliving it, wanting it again. But then he steps toward me and grabs me in one quick movement, one hand on my hip and the other cradling my face, and my body goes vibrantly, brilliantly alive again.

I lean up, ever so slightly, and that's all it takes. Our mouths are already so close, so hungry. His lips are dry, slightly chapped, but I don't mind. I run my fingers across his hair, the short-shaven sides and the longer locks along the top. I feel the rhythm of his lungs and his heart through the soft cotton of his shirt.

I can hear, vaguely, an announcement coming over the intercom, muffled through the door. Then his hand glides around my hip, resting on the small of my back, and I don't care. I wish I could turn off the sound as easily as the light. I wish I could stay in here forever, learning the textures and shapes of him.

But outside the door, a commotion is building—a long wail, a shouted curse. The quick-building rumble of a crowd. We pull back from each other, eyes wide in the dim light.

Then we step out into the chaos.

The hallway eddies and swirls with activity. Everyone's looking at their phones. A few people are crying.

I pull my phone from my pocket to see what's going on. But before I can check my alerts, I hear Ben's voice. "Tabitha!" he calls. I look up and see her there, down the hallway.

She turns around slowly. I half expect her to see us together and make a nasty face, but she looks numb. She holds up her phone. I can't make out what's on it, but I don't have to. She tells us.

"They found her body," she says.

CHAPTER TWENTY-NINE

ANCHORAGE, ALASKA—*Anchorage Police discovered human remains buried near an abandoned playground in Russian Jack Springs Park Thursday evening.*

APD officials have declined to comment further, stating that the investigation is ongoing, but sources did confirm that the body was found with the help of cadaver dogs requisitioned in the search for Zahra Elizabeth Gaines, the seventeen-year-old who has been missing since the night of September 16. Gaines was last seen at a friend's party fewer than four miles from the crime scene.

Anyone with information is asked to call the tip line at . . .

SOMEONE'S LEADING ME THROUGH the halls of the school. There's a hand on my elbow, not gripping, just touching. I let them propel me forward.

"Ingrid Bell, Ruthie Hayden, where do you two think you're going?"

"Sorry, Mr. Thatcher, Ruthie's . . . not well. I'm taking her home."

They talk for a moment, somewhere to my left, their voices low. I'm aware of the great press of the crowd around me. I hear Zahra's name on everyone's lips. Everyone seems to have heard about the body.

The words of the article—so short, so succinct—drum through me on repeat. *Human. Remains. Buried. Abandoned. Playground. Investigation. Cadaver.* I can see the clearing in the park, our old refuge. The bare swing set frame like a giant daddy longlegs poised over the weedy ground. The crumbling playscape, wooden platforms ravaged by insects and weather. The faded animals lying in the overgrown grass, the springs that used to mount them long pillaged.

I can see, so clearly. Blood spattered across the dirt. Soaking down into it, making hot, sticky mud.

"Come on, Ruthie." Ingrid's voice. Weirdly calm. The Caretaker—the great soother. She was right about that, of course. Right about me, too; I am a lost child. I have never been so lost in my life.

She takes me by the hand. "Let's go."

A thought stirs. "We don't have the car today."

"I called Rick. He's coming to pick us up."

I nod robotically and follow her outside, my eyes unfocused. I don't really want to see my dad; I am mad at my dad. All these thoughts, though, are like rocks falling into a well. They hit the water with a splash and then sink out of sight.

Dad's energy is frantic, frenetic. At one point he comes into sharp focus in front of me, his blue eyes the only color in his face. He stares down at me, and he's saying something, again and again, his voice urgent.

"Ruthie. Ruth. I'm so sorry, Ruthie, I know you must feel . . ."

I just nod, nod, nod. Except I don't feel. I don't feel anything.

At home I lie on my bedroom floor. I didn't quite make it to the bed, and now I just don't care. The floor is cool and quiet, the cheap carpet bristly against my skin. I don't fall asleep but I can't seem to move. I lie there and listen to the sounds around the house. Ingrid and Dad talk quietly in the kitchen upstairs for a while. I hear Dad leave—maybe heading back to work. I hear Ingrid's steps on the stairs and then her soft knock at the door. When I don't answer, she goes away.

Outside the high window I watch time pass. Clouds thread across the sky. The light moves in its sallow autumn arc.

My phone clangs periodically with text alerts. It's in my backpack, a few feet away. I don't bother to check. I'm sure it'll be Marcus, Jeremy. Maybe Soo-Jin or Margo. Maybe Ingrid, hoping I'll at least message her from a room over. They don't need me. They're just trying to get me to step into the river with them, to be carried on the current of grief and gossip. I can't. I just can't.

The playground. Our sanctuary. Ancient ruins in the middle of the woods, excavated, explored. It was a place not to hide but to be seen, in the most vital way. To be seen by each other, to be seen by ourselves, without the noise and chaos and ugliness of the world polluting our personalities. Who are you really, when you walk away from the world, when you don't have other people's mistakes governing your every move?

It had only been a matter of time before it would be invaded by the outside world. Before the noise and chaos and ugliness of the world found us. It felt like such a secret place— but after all, it was barely a quarter mile from civilization.

Blood in the dirt. Blood on the equipment—a spatter on the metal slide we sometimes used as a mirror, bright against the dented metal. I can't shake the image.

I don't know what time it is when I hear a knock at the door. "Ruthie?"

My eyes snap open. I must have dozed off. Clouds have coalesced outside; it's still light but there's a looming dark.

It's Ingrid's voice. "Ruthie, please say something."

She waits for a second. Then she pushes the door open.

She stands over me, her forehead crinkled. I stare blankly back at her. "It's dinnertime," she says.

I close my eyes again. "I can't."

"Rick said we can stay down here. In your room, if you want. Or at the couch," she says. "Come on, Ruthie, you need to eat. It's just a little soup and toast, nothing heavy."

"What time is it?" I ask.

"Five," she says.

"Can we watch the news?" I ask.

She hesitates. "Sure, if you want."

"Okay. I'll meet you there in a sec." When she's gone I take my time, getting slowly to my feet. My body's stiff, a low ache in my back. In the bathroom I wash my face, run my fingers through my hair. I stare into the mirror. The girl who stares back at me is a mystery.

Down the hall I hear the drums and trumpets of the local news. I make my way to the rec room. Ingrid has our food set up on two little TV trays; she's laid it out with cloth napkins and a small blossom in a bud vase. She smiles at me nervously as I take a seat.

"Tonight's top story." The anchorwoman has been the same woman my whole life; the only thing that's changed is her hair, the style flitting alongside current trends. Now it's a long, sleek bob, dyed a shade too pale for her complexion. "Anchorage Police have released the identity of the body found in Russian Jack Springs Park, discovered yesterday afternoon during a search for missing teenager Zahra Gaines." Here the screen flashes to Zahra's picture. "Gaines was last seen at a party in Rogers Park, when she left after a fight with her boyfriend, and her disappearance is currently being investigated as a crime."

I can feel Ingrid's eyes on me, wide and nervous. I stare straight ahead and wait.

The screen cuts to a press conference. Detective Teffeteller stands at a podium, her name on a chyron along the bottom of the screen.

"We're still waiting on forensics for a lot of information, but at this time I can confirm that the body is that of Bailey Sellers, who went missing in the summer of . . ."

"It's not her?" Ingrid's voice cuts across the detective's, shrill and ringing. "Wait, it's not ... but ..."

"It's not her," I answer, closing my eyes tightly. Something inside me shifts. I breathe slowly, almost afraid to move. "It's not her."

"Yes, we are currently investigating this as a homicide," Teffeteller says, in answer to a question from the reporters. "As to whether it's connected to the disappearance of Zahra Gaines, it's too early to say for sure. But the girls did live in the same trailer park, and I understand they were friends."

"Does that mean this might be the work of a predator?" someone asks from the crowd.

Teffeteller sets her jaw. She speaks slowly, carefully.

"At this time, I can't speculate," she says. "But we are asking young women to take the same safety precautions we always encourage: travel in pairs, or even better, in groups. If you are out at night, stay in public, well-lit areas. If you feel unsafe, don't hesitate to call for help."

The crowd erupts in questions.

"Detective Teffeteller, can you tell us ..."

"Is there a serial killer in Anchorage?"

"Do you think ..."

Ingrid's already on her phone, texting someone. Back in my room I can hear my phone chiming again, too. In just a moment I'll have to move, and there will be a million questions to ask, a million things to think. But for now, I just sit and breathe.

CHAPTER THIRTY

"SO . . . STILL NO UPDATES?" Dad asks.

It's Sunday morning, and we're at the Cup and Saucer before church. Brandy, Dad, and Ingrid sit around the little table with me, sipping their coffee, picking at blueberry muffins and croissants.

"Nothing," I say. "No news on Zahra, no news on . . . on Bailey."

The café is still papered with Zahra's image. Now Bailey's has joined it. Seeing their faces side by side, the contrast is jarring: it's not like Zahra's is a picture of opulence, but Bailey's is so clearly a portrait of want. Her cheeks are pinched, her oversized T-shirt stained. There's a tough little smirk playing around her mouth. Her hair's combed back into a tight, savage ponytail.

She looks younger than I remember.

Ingrid shakes her head, looking around the room. "I can't believe no one even knew she was missing. It's so . . . it's so messed up."

I've gotten most of the details from Zahra's dad. Apparently Bailey's mom was the kind of person who'd vanish for weeks on end and you'd only later find out she had a new boyfriend she was shacked up with, or that she'd been in jail, or that she'd been facedown in some strange drug den the whole time. According to him, Bailey hadn't even known where her mom was for much of that summer. The other families in the trailer court tried to look out for her—they invited her over for dinner, brought her groceries, checked in on her—but they weren't the kind of community that called the Office of Children's Services. And Bailey was almost fourteen, and was pretty independent, so they just let her run wild and made sure she ate every now and then. When she vanished, most of them assumed she'd either gone to live with her mom elsewhere or that she'd landed with a foster family.

The media's been all over Walker Court, asking around about her. One station made a big show of looking into how many registered sex offenders live in the trailer park, though they neglected to mention that the numbers were about average (I checked). Every story I watch or read manages to find the most neglected trailers, the filthiest cars, the most methed-out-looking people, the reporters coming off like smirking anthropologists exploring an alien culture. It's gross. Especially when I know how many people are truly devastated by the news—the Gaineses in particular.

"It's so sad," Ingrid says, staring at the flyers posted next to us. "She never had a chance, did she?"

Up at the counter, Soo-Jin's ringing someone up. As soon as she's made change, she steps over to us, standing at the corner of our table. We hadn't had much of a chance to talk when we ordered—there'd been a line.

"How are you guys holding up?" she asks gently.

"Been better," I say, fidgeting with my spoon. My appetite hasn't really come back since they found the body. "How're you?"

"Ditto that," she says. She sits down at the corner of the table. "Did you know Bailey?"

I nod. "Not very well, but I met her. Zahra hung out with her sometimes."

I remember thinking that three, somehow, didn't work right. Two was perfect. Two could find a comfortable equilibrium—almost symbiotic, even. But three? Three people would triangulate. Three people was drama of a kind I didn't like. Bailey always seemed a little jealous when Zahra hung out with me. And maybe I was a little jealous, too. I remember the handful of times Bailey would crack a joke that I didn't get, that'd make Zahra laugh. Or the seamless way they pocketed lipsticks at Fred Meyers, with one intuitively serving as lookout while the other did the deed. If I complained, or said it wasn't a good idea, suddenly their heads would duck together and they'd both be giggling. I hated that.

"Do you think . . ." Soo-Jin bites the corner of her lip. "I mean . . . do you think the same person . . ."

I know what she's trying to ask. The same question half the town is asking.

Is there a predator, picking off girls from Walker Court?

Ingrid answers before I can. "The police only found one body. Unless they find more . . . there's no way to tell."

Brandy makes a strangled noise in the back of the throat. I glance at her, realize she's looking pale and stricken. Both her and my dad, actually. Soo-Jin looks a little embarrassed.

"I'm sorry. I didn't mean to ruin your morning, guys, I just . . . it's been hard, waiting for news."

"Of course," Dad says softly. "It's okay. Don't apologize."

"I've got to get back to work," she says, glancing at the counter. "I'll text you guys later, okay?"

We mumble our farewells. She slips back behind the counter and whispers something to the other barista.

I'm startled when Dad reaches across the table and takes my hand in his.

We haven't really talked much since our fight. He's been giving me space this week, letting me hide in my room when I want to, letting me set the tone. I've been out of school since we got the news, without a peep from him, and the few times I've gone out there's been no talk about the fact that I'm supposed to be grounded. But now he gives me an anxious, aching look.

"I'm so happy I've got another chance," he says. "I don't know what I'd do if . . . if I . . ."

And that's when I realize. For Dad, for Brandy—what happened to Bailey isn't just what happened to Bailey. It's what happened to her mom. It's the worst-case scenario for an addict parent, being so out of it that you lose your kid forever. And I don't know why this is what does it—I don't know why it has to be the actual worst-case scenario for me to open up even a little—but the tiniest spark flares up somewhere in my chest. It's not quite forgiveness, but it's something that feels similar.

I squeeze his hand back.

"Me too, Dad," I say. "I'm glad, too."

VICTORY EVANGELICAL IS PACKED when we arrive—even more so than usual. I'm guessing some people are here because they heard about Zahra's connection to Dale Worthen and are hoping for a show.

It's weird—I feel like, in a way, we should be relieved. As ghoulish as that sounds, it's Zahra that we love—Zahra that we care about. And we still don't know where she is. But it feels like everyone has decided that Bailey's death means that Zahra must be dead, too. I guess I can see why. The connection between them—their friendship, their proximity—is one of the only pieces of information we have. So of course everyone is jumping on that.

But I'm still clutching at hope. I'm not ready to give up. Not yet.

"Spare the rod," booms a voice from the pulpit, "and spoil the child."

Pastor Worthen stands at the podium. I blink a few times to clear my vision; everyone around me is sitting up more sharply, craning their necks to see him. He's flushed already, mopping his head with a handkerchief.

"One of the most well-known verses in the Bible, of course. Everyone knows that one. But how many times do we treat it as a metaphor?" His hands grip the edge of the podium. "How many times do we treat it as a little poetic advice? 'Oh, the Lord didn't mean it literally!'" His voice goes cloyingly high as he speaks for some hypothetical Christian. "'The Lord doesn't truly want us to spank our children!'"

He looks around the cavernous space with a fierce gaze. In the front row I spy Grace Worthen. I can't see her expression from where I'm sitting, but there's something fragile in her frame.

"The Lord is clear that we are to train our children up, not just to keep them safe, not just to form them into responsible Christian adults—but for the sake of their salvation!" he shouts. "'Thou shalt beat him with the rod, and shalt deliver his soul from hell.' The stakes could not be higher, brothers and sisters. We are not just keeping them from the darkness of this world, but from the darkness of the next."

The room is perfectly silent. Next to me Ingrid's clutching the fabric of her skirt in both fists, her eyes wide. Down the pew I can see Brandy's and Dad's fingers knotted together.

"It's not easy," he says, lowering his voice a little. "Of course it's not easy. Why would we expect it to be easy? It's a war between good and evil. Every time you strike your child, every time you force them into submission, you are battling the devil. It is one of the hardest battles we face. Much harder than contending with our own sins. But it is because we love our children that we must triumph. Even if they fight us. Even if they're not willing."

This—this is the message he has chosen to deliver the Sunday after a girl's body was discovered buried in the woods. This is the message he's chosen while his granddaughter is missing, possibly dead. It seems beyond contemptuous. It seems cruel.

"I hear parents all the time, making excuses for their children's transgressions." He pitches his voice high again. It's not lost on me that it's clearly a woman's voice he's emulating. "'Oh, but Pastor Worthen, it's such a minor thing. Pastor Worthen, it can't possibly matter. Pastor Worthen, he's only a little boy, he's just a baby, he doesn't know what he's doing . . .'" He slams a fist against the podium. "It is because they are so young, so vulnerable, that we have to force them to see the light."

My mouth feels dry. I stare up at him—the man who drove Charity away, the man who followed Zahra around in the months after she rejected his religion, harassing her, maybe even assaulting her. I can picture it too clearly. I can see the pleasure he'd take in forcing someone to submit to his will.

"If we do not act," he says, "your children are lost. Again, this is not a metaphor. They will wander without light, unable to find their way. The Bible is not vague on this point. Beat him with the rod, and deliver his soul from hell. It's worth it, even if you have to beat him again, and again, and again."

He stares out across the crowd, and I know it's my imagination—it has to be—but for a moment I'm sure he locks eyes with me.

"It is worth it, even if you have to beat him bloody."

CHAPTER THIRTY-ONE

THE FUNERAL SERVICES ARE held on Monday, at a local nondenominational funeral home. They're calling it a "Celebration of Life," but it's pretty clear that there's not much to celebrate. There's a slideshow that plays throughout the service, but there are only about twenty photos, and they're all badly framed and out of focus. In one, a preschool-aged Bailey has an obvious split lip and black eye. In another, a syringe and a spoon are visible on the coffee table while Bailey opens a birthday present on the floor beyond. Whoever edited this thing apparently didn't notice, or didn't care.

Her junior high English teacher speaks first. She reads "Nothing Gold Can Stay" and claims Bailey wanted to grow up to be a veterinarian. Then a woman in a dark gray suit leads the room in prayer. There's music, all generically sad. I remember watching Bailey and Zahra dance to Fetty Wap in

Zahra's bedroom; I don't know if Bailey ever even heard "Wind Beneath My Wings" in her short life, but here we are.

Ingrid sits next to me in her black wrap dress, hands folded in her lap. Dad and Brandy both offered to skip work to come, but I told them we'd be all right alone. Besides, the place is packed, standing room only.

I'm fighting to stay present. I didn't want to come, but I knew I had to. Charity, Ron, and Malik are here, a few rows ahead of me. I recognize a few other families from the trailer park—including Seb and a younger girl that has to be his sister, they look so alike.

Near the end of the service a woman in the front row starts to sob convulsively. I can only see the back of her head—thin dishwater hair hanging limp down her bony back—but I know instinctively it must be Bailey's mom. And that's what does it—what sets off an irrational blast of anger. Because it's fucking pathetic. She didn't even know Bailey was missing. Or she didn't care. Or it was actually a relief, an unlooked-for blessing, because with Bailey gone she could do whatever she wanted without guilt. Who even knows. And now she has the nerve to grieve. Hell, can you even call it grief? It's just self-pity. Poor me, my daughter was murdered. But will she even miss her?

None of these people knew her. None of them cared when she was alive. And before I can stop myself I'm on my feet, and I'm making my way for the door, my breath coming fast and sharp, and I'm tumbling out into the lobby beyond.

I brace myself against the wall. The world feels very far

away now, the lights gray. I can still hear the sound of the music inside. Inside I'm pushing the levers again and again and again, trying to make this body move, but it won't. It can't.

I see his shadow moving into mine, merging with it, before I hear him. His hand falls gently on my shoulder. He smells of winter air, pine needles. His voice is low and rich.

"It's okay," he whispers. "Ruthie. It's okay."

I close my eyes. It all runs together—all the visions of blood in the dirt, blood on the slide. The memory of my bike snapping under my dad's tires, of him slamming his fist into my dollhouse so hard the roof caved in. The memory of Bailey, her chip-toothed grin, her knobby knees. The memory of Zahra. The memory of my mom, her eyes flaring wide as the earth slipped out from under her feet.

He puts his arms around me and I lean into him. We stand that way for a long time. Then he pulls back a little.

"Come on," he says. "Let's get out of here."

We drive for a little while, past the seedy motels along Fifth Avenue, past the currently abandoned tourist traps downtown, past the giant whale mural on the side of the JCPenny building, to the park that looks out over the inlet. I sit in the passenger seat, staring out the window. I focus on breathing slowly and deliberately. On staying calm and present. It's hard.

He reaches over and takes my hand. Tears sting my eyes, sudden and sharp. How can his touch do that to me every time? Make me raw, make me real? It takes my breath away. But I know this is it; I know we can't do this anymore.

"I'm sorry I haven't texted more," he says. "Everything's been kind of . . ."

"Yeah," I say. "I get it."

"The cops are still looking at all my stuff, but they've let up a little bit. Now that . . . you know, now that Bailey . . ."

I nod. "They think Bailey and Zahra were taken by the same person."

He darts a glance my way. "You don't?"

I just shrug. "I still have hope."

He nods and looks out the windshield at the level gray water. The tide's out, and half the inlet is mudflat, wet and shining in the weak sun.

"I'm not sure I do," he says. "Have hope, I mean." He shakes his head.

Then, suddenly, out of nowhere, he's beating on the dashboard, his face twisted in an agony of rage. He clutches the edges of the steering wheel and screams.

"It's so fucked up," he snarls. "God, this can't be real. It can't be real."

I realize then that he hasn't been able to sit with the idea of her death. He's been angry—angry at the suspicion on him, angry at her for leaving him like this. Angry, and scared, and trying desperately to solve the problem. As if he could bring her back by knowing her, understanding her, well enough. There hasn't been time in all that for him to really truly consider the worst.

But now, two weeks on, now it's hard not to.

I put my hand on his arm, and he crumbles. His hands

on his face, he leans up against me and sobs. We cling to each other for a long time that way, without talking. And while it's nothing like before—nothing like the kissing, the touching we did in the cabin, in the supply closet—it still leaves me feeling charged.

"I just . . . I keep thinking of the things she might have gone through," he says.

"Don't," I whisper. "Don't think about that. We don't know. We just don't know. You can't torture yourself like that."

He takes a ragged breath.

"Tabitha came to see me last night," he says. "She's the one who told me, by the way. About the kiss, between Zahra and that other guy."

I nod. "I know."

"She's a mess right now too. She said . . ." He shakes his head. "Well, some of what she said is private, I guess. But she told me the thing with Zahra and that guy wasn't even a thing. That he kissed her and she put a stop to it."

"I know," I say.

He gives a harsh chuckle "Tabitha's blaming herself. She thinks Zahra wouldn't have freaked out, run off in the woods, if not for that fight. But fuck, I'm the idiot that bought in."

"You're not the first jealous boyfriend to overreact about something like that," I say softly.

"I know, I know." He tilts his head against mine. We're sitting side by side now, facing the sunset, his arm around my shoulder. "I just mean . . . things were obviously not good between us, if I believed it so easily. And it's killing me that I can't figure out why. Because I love her so fucking much, and that should be enough."

I think about all of the things I've heard about Zahra since moving back. Those mood swings, those anxiety attacks. I think about how hard it has always been for me to connect with people—even with people I like, even with people I love. How hard Ingrid had to work to win me over. How hard it's been for me to trust.

"Sometimes it's not enough," I say. "Sometimes ... people are broken, Ben. That's not on you."

"Yeah, but you know what is? Not realizing it. Not understanding it, until it's too late," he says.

I shake my head, but I don't argue. Sometimes you can't argue. Sometimes people just have to hurt until they're done hurting.

He plays with a lock of my hair idly, then suddenly jerks his hand away. I close my eyes. I know what's coming, but knowing it doesn't make it less painful.

"I'm sorry, if I took advantage of you," he says.

I give a little laugh. "Took advantage?"

"You know what I mean. At the lake."

"No. You didn't," I say.

I hesitate for a moment before going on.

"I know it can't go anywhere, Ben. I know ... I know it was wrong. But I don't regret it."

"Neither do I," he whispers.

He kisses me on the temple, one last time.

Then we watch in silence as the tide starts to come in.

CHAPTER THIRTY-TWO

TUESDAY AFTERNOON INGRID AND I get permission from our parents to go to the Gaineses'. Charity and Ron have invited a handful of Zahra's friends over to eat dinner and strategize our next steps.

When Ingrid and I get there the street is lined with cars. Yukon and Deshka are in the yard, barking wildly, tripping over each other as they run up to the gate to meet us. I scratch Yukon's ears, Deshka's nose. Even after so long, I remember their preferences.

There are already about fifteen people crowded into the trailer. Soo-Jin and Margo sit on the sofa, leafing through picture albums, pulling out photos they think they could use for flyers. In the kitchen, a couple of cross-country kids stand by the counter, drinking soda and talking. Ben's not here yet—it's his grandma's birthday, so he'll be arriving late—but Jeremy and Marcus both sit at the oversize table, working on the Find Zahra website. Ron's at the counter, ladling chili from a gigantic crock pot.

"Hey there, Ruthie-girl." He gives me a little squeeze around the shoulders when he sees me. "How you holding up?"

"Doing okay. This is my stepsister, Ingrid. I hope it's okay that I brought her," I say.

"More the merrier." He looks around the room with an odd little smile on his face. "Half the reason we're having everyone over is to get some noise in this damn place. It's been too quiet."

"I can only imagine." I look around. "This would be a good party if we weren't missing the guest of honor."

"You know it." He gestures toward the crockpot. "You girls hungry? There's cornbread on the counter, soda in the fridge. Help yourselves."

"Thanks," I say. "Maybe in a bit." I look around, frowning. "Where's Charity?"

"Lying down." He looks like he's about to say something else, but a couple of kids step up to get some food, and he's distracted.

I look around the room again. Strange how normal this is becoming for all of us. At the table, Marcus laughs at something Jeremy says. I overhear some snatches of conversation from around the room—someone's talking about Cardi B, someone else wants to know if they should get bangs. It's surreal. I get it—I of all people get it, the way you sometimes have to compartmentalize, to distract yourself, so you can keep going. But a part of me feels very lonely. Very cut off. Am I the only one that really, truly needs Zahra?

My eyes fall on the kitchen doorway, and I give a little start. Tabitha's just arrived. And Ingrid, instead of making a face or muttering under her breath, gives a little wave and trots over to her.

Did I miss a memo? I know they made peace to search for me and Ben the night we were stuck at the lake, but I'd thought . . . well, I'd thought that was all about me. Now I feel like an idiot. Or a narcissist. They're *friends*. Somehow, they've become friends. I hang back for a moment, watching them talk. Ingrid puts a hand on Tabitha's shoulder, as if she's comforting her.

I look around the room again. Something about it feels different, suddenly. That loneliness of a moment ago, the tug in my heart, has calmed. I look at Ron, in his REAL MEN COOK apron; at the kids crowded around their stacks of photos, cooing over pictures of baby Zahra; at Tabitha and Ingrid; at all these people that love Zahra, and for the first time I don't feel like it's some kind of competition, like more love for them means less for me. For the first time I just think . . . thank you, Zahra. Thank you for creating something like this.

Now come back, so you can be a part of it.

I suddenly want to see her room again—to sit in the space she occupied for a minute. I slip down the hall. No one seems to notice me go. The sound fades behind me.

When I get to the bedroom, though, I'm not alone.

Charity's curled up on the bed, on top of the covers. She's

hugging Zahra's pillow, staring out in space. I stop in the doorway, make to turn and head back, but she sees me before I can.

"What happened to my baby?" she asks. Her voice is high and soft.

I hesitate, then come in, shut the door behind me. She sits up and pushes her hair out of her face, setting the pillow to the side.

She looks like she's aged about ten years; her roots are gray, and the bags beneath her eyes bring out all the shadows and lines of her face. I see that she's been looking through Zahra's things—a portfolio sits open on the desk, a bunch of black-and-white photos spread out across it. Photos of places and people. I recognize a few of the island.

I sit on the edge of the bed and take Charity's hand. She squeezes.

"Nothing's been right for a long time now," she whispers. "And I don't know what happened to change it all. She stopped talking to me. She had secrets."

I nod slowly.

She shakes her head, wipes at her eyes. "This isn't what I wanted. Everything I've ever done has been to make this family . . . different. To make our life different."

"From what you grew up with," I say gently.

She nods. "I didn't want her to have to hide things from me, the way I had to from my parents. I didn't want her to be scared of us."

"She wasn't," I say. "There's no way."

"Then why don't I know anything about her?" She gestures

to the photos on the desk. "I don't know most of those kids. I don't know anything about her. And there are pictures of that fucking church camp in there—Jesus. I never even knew she went out there. But she did—dozens of times. And she never told me."

"Maybe she just thought it was beautiful," I say carefully. "Or . . . maybe she liked it because she went with her friends."

Charity blows air through her lips. "It's a horrible place. If she knew the things I knew . . ."

I draw in my breath a little. "You were there," I say softly. "When it was open."

She doesn't answer, but I already know I must be right. I haven't had a chance to look into the story Ben told me— the dates, the details—but if it closed in the nineties, she'd probably have been a teenager.

Her eyes have a faraway look, and I think . . . God, another Lost Child. "'He that spareth his rod hateth his son: but he that loveth him chasteneth him betimes,'" she says. Her voice sounds strange and soft, almost like she's in a trance. "Dad always believed it was his responsibility to break our spirits."

I believe it. I think about the sermons I've heard from Pastor Worthen—the emphasis on sin and punishment, blood and pain. The anger emanating from the pulpit. He is a man who enjoys punishment. He is a man who wants to control the people around him.

"You know about Josh?" she whispers.

I shake my head. "Who's . . ."

"Josh Forster," she says. "The boy who . . ." She closes her eyes and shudders. "He was my age. Thirteen? Fourteen? It was ninety-four, so I guess fourteen. Just a kid. Funny. Always telling these bad Fozzie Bear–style jokes. But nice, too, a nice kid. He wasn't even a repeat offender."

She's speaking in wide, elliptical loops, but it's not hard to follow her—because I have a feeling what's coming. My stomach tightens as she talks.

"Nothing like me. I was always in trouble, at home and at camp both. I squirmed through church. I was obsessed with pop music—Madonna, Mariah Carey, Janet Jackson. All those fallen women." She snorts. "I was always asking questions that Dad didn't like. And he was determined to correct me. Beating me, locking me in a closet to 'pray on my sins.' That's how I know I'm not telekinetic, by the way. Because I would've gone Carrie on that house every day of my childhood if I could've."

She stands up and goes to Zahra's desk, picks up one of the photos. In it, Zahra's friends sit along what I recognize now as the dock on the island, dangling their feet in the water.

"It was the same at camp," she says. "Dad made sure of that. The counselors whipped us with PVC pipe, they made us run laps or tread water in the lake, they made us dig latrines. One time they made a girl hold buckets of water out at either side for hours. Hours. If her arms dropped they reset the clock. That was just for using God's name in vain." She shrugs. "And one year, the thing they came up with was to make us stand outside all night."

I shiver slightly, remembering the conversation I'd had with Ben about it.

"Josh got in trouble," she says, closing her eyes. "We both did. We'd gone out after lights-out. We met in the dining hall because it was cold that night, and we wanted to huddle up by the embers in the old wood stove. We talked for hours, and then . . . you know. We kissed. It was innocent. We were just kids." She takes a deep breath. "It was Dad that caught us. And he . . . he was livid. He made all the other campers get up out of bed to hear him lecture. Stood there in the middle of the cabins, preaching about fornication and the sins of the flesh."

She shakes her head. "Poor Josh. He wasn't supposed to die. He was supposed to be humiliated and cold. But a storm blew in. Rain and howling wind. I remember lying in bed, staring at the ceiling, sure they'd let him back into his bunk. But they didn't, and the next morning . . . he was gone. Disappeared. It took two days to find him—I guess when the hypothermia set in for him, he got disoriented and wandered into the woods."

She falls silent. I can hear the *tick-tick-tick* of Zahra's wall clock, the distant sound of conversation in the kitchen. I can hear the thud of my heart.

"Didn't they get in any trouble?" I ask. "I mean . . . did anyone investigate, or . . ."

"My dad's good friends with half the politicians in this state," she says bitterly. "And the cops, and the troopers. They're not going to mess with him."

"What'd they do to you?" I ask suddenly. "When they caught you both. Why weren't you outside, too?"

Her eyes go bright with scorn.

"Me?" she says. "Oh, they beat the shit out of me. Made me take my pants down in front of everyone so they could spank my bottom. Josh had to pay for his sins, sure. But he wasn't supposed to die. He was supposed to stand in the cold for a little while praying for his soul. *I* was the temptress. I was the one who was supposed to suffer."

I swallow hard. His sermon from the other day echoes in my ears. *It's worth it, even if you have to beat him again, and again, and again. It is worth it, even if you have to beat him bloody.* I think about his ugly sermons, and the fact that he's done nothing to help look for his granddaughter. I think about the prayer where he asked God to save Zahra's soul, but not her body. I think about Zahra's failed experiment living with him. Think about him following her to cross-country meets and . . .

I've been assuming she went to her grandparents because of whatever happened.

Dale Worthen would rather kill a child than allow him, or her, to sin.

I stand up.

"I have to go, Charity," I say. "I'm sorry. I'll . . . I'll be back."

Then I get up and hurry for the door.

CHAPTER THIRTY-THREE

THE WORTHENS' HOUSE IS enormous, bursting from the midst of a copse of trees like a ship crashing through waves. Its multistory windows reflect the low, woolly clouds as I pull up in front of it. Out past the trees, Cook Inlet stretches flat and gray.

It was easy to find in Brandy's address book; I guess she and the Ladies Auxiliary must come here for meetings sometimes. I wonder if this is the house Charity grew up in—if this is what she fled. It's easy to imagine. The place may be large, but it has the same dour, looming sense as Worthen himself. The siding is the color of slate, and the only adornment on or around the house is a large wrought iron cross hanging near the door.

For a second I think I see movement from one of the windows. Then I see a bird fly past, and I wonder if it was just a reflection in the glass.

I take a deep breath; I have to be steady. I can't jump at the slightest movement.

I ring the bell.

Everything is quiet. You can't even hear traffic, the way you usually can in town. A raven screams from somewhere in the woods. I stand very still on the doormat.

It's a few minutes before the door swings open.

Grace Worthen looks much the same as she did at church—pale blonde hair pulled up, a thick shawl wrapped around her shoulders. Her lashes bat in a quick little tic when she sees me there on the doorstep. "Can I help you?"

"Hi, Mrs. Worthen," I say, forcing a smile. "I don't know if you remember me. I go to your church, and . . ."

"Yes, you're Zahra's friend," she says. "I remember you. Ruth, isn't that right?"

"Yes, ma'am," I say. "Is Pastor Worthen in this afternoon?"

"I'm afraid he's still at work," she says. She hesitates for a moment, her eyes flickering behind me, to my car in the driveway. "Is there something I can help you with? Or maybe I could give you our youth pastor's phone number, he's very . . ."

"No, no, thank you," I say quickly. "I was actually hoping to talk to you."

Her frame stiffens, ever so slightly. Somehow, slender as she is, she manages to fill the doorway. Her shoulders are bony epaulets, angling sharply to block my view.

"I was talking to Charity," I say softly. "Your daughter?"

"Yes, I know my own daughter," she says, an edge creeping into her voice.

"And she says you haven't been in contact with her. It just strikes me as kind of weird. Wouldn't you reach out to her in the middle of a crisis like this? Even if you don't really get along?"

Her lips go thin.

"My daughter has made it very clear she doesn't want me in her life," she says.

"Sounds like *you* guys made that clear to her, honestly," I say. "Beating her, locking her up? You didn't like that she was a free spirit, so you tried to break her. Right?"

"Young lady . . ."

"And now . . . now you're doing the same to Zahra," I say.

She goes extremely white beneath her makeup. Her eyelid flicks again, that little nervous flutter.

"Why would you say a thing like that?" she whispers.

Because I go to Victory Evangelical. Because I've seen the way Worthen talks about sinners—about women. Because he killed a boy once for kissing his daughter. Because Zahra has been wracked with some heartbreak since the last time she saw you. Because something hurt her, and I think it must have been him.

"Because . . . because I saw her in the window upstairs," I say softly.

It's a bluff. I don't even know what I saw, not really. But Grace Worthen turns to look at me for the briefest moment. Then she slams the door shut.

Almost.

I manage to wedge my knee in before it clicks shut. The

door cracks against my kneecap, but I ignore the pain. I push my way through into the foyer.

"Where is she? Upstairs? Locked up somewhere?" I ask.

She gives a strangled cry. "Nobody's here!"

I run toward the stairs. I'm four or five steps up when she grabs me, her hand gripping the fabric of my sweater. How's she so fast? She doesn't look like she should be. I try to twist away but she reaches her other arm up and grabs my elbow.

"Get off me!" I hiss.

"You can't go up there. Get out of my house, or I will . . ."

"GET OFF OF ME!" The words tear out of me in a blast of rage. I turn and shove her, quick and sharp, in the chest.

There's not enough time to register the look of surprise as she falls backward.

The sound is stomach-turning, a crunch, a sob. I turn away from her again. I run up the stairs, two at a time.

On the second floor I throw doors open wildly. Linen closet, bathroom, office, guest bed. I kick things out of my way. I feel Zahra's name in my mouth, again and again, and I realize distantly that I'm calling for her.

"Zahra! Can you hear me? Zahra?"

I stand on the landing for a moment and look down. Grace Worthen is sprawled on the floor. Her hair is matted with blood; she must have hit her head. I watch as she stirs, her hand creeping up to wipe at the blood on her face.

There isn't much time.

Up another floor, I find the room where I saw the curtain move; I'm almost sure of it. A small guest room, bed made;

a fireplace that doesn't look like it's ever been used. Nothing personal on the surfaces or walls. I go to the window and look down at my car. Yes; this is right. But she's not here. No one's here.

Then I turn to see the closet door. There's a knob lock on it; why is there a lock on a closet?

Slowly, I step closer to it. It's not locked. Not right now. I grip the knob and throw the door open.

She's curled up on the floor, in the fetal position. She opens her eyes and squints up into the light.

"Zahra," I whisper.

CHAPTER THIRTY-FOUR

SHE TRIES TO GET up but collapses on the weight of her arms, and my eyes are running over her, looking for signs of pain, of injury, but maybe her hand just fell asleep, maybe she just got caught on the yards of fabric she's swathed in. Her skirt is long and full, and she's wearing a gray sweater that hangs off her narrow shoulders. I kneel down next to her. "Zahra," I say again. "It's okay. I've got you."

She scrambles away from me, pressing her body to the back of the closet. She's silent except for her heaving breath. My heart gives an unsteady lurch. "It's okay," I whisper. "It's me, Ruthie. Zahra. I'm here. I found you." The words don't seem to calm her. She looks up at me, uncomprehending, blindly terrified. My hand goes to my mouth.

"What have they done to you?" I whisper.

She makes a noise that's somewhere between a wail and a sob. It spikes the hair on my arms. My mind races through scenarios, through all the half-remembered stories of cult discipline and brainwashing and ritual abuse I've ever heard. They've broken her. They've left her unable to speak, to move, to be a human being. All because she was beautiful and un-tamed and they couldn't abide it.

I push myself up, run to the bedroom door, and look down the stairs.

There's a smear of blood on the bottom three stairs. But Grace Worthen is nowhere to be seen.

We have to move.

I scramble back to Zahra. "Can you walk?" I ask, trying to sound gentle. "We have to go, Zahra. Your grandma . . ."

"Grandma?" Her voice sounds like a child's. "Where is she? Is she . . ."

"She's coming. We've got to go. Come on." I wait for a half second, but Zahra's not moving. I'm going to have to help her. I reach down to take her hand and she recoils with a sob.

"I can't. Please, please, just leave me alone . . ." she cries.

"Never," I whisper. "Never again." I kneel down and grab her by the forearm, pulling her up. I expect her to be weak, pliant, but all of a sudden she's all muscle, thrashing and wild. She pulls away and stares at me with burning eyes.

"Don't touch me!" she screams.

"I'm sorry," I whisper. "We can't wait. We have to move. I'm sorry."

I grab her again, this time more forcefully, and pull her toward the door. She lets loose a scream that makes the window shudder in its frame, throwing her weight backward, but I don't let go. I hear the sound of sirens. Grace must have called the cops, or hit a panic button. The sound is far away, a distant echo. My fingernails catch on Zahra's skin—I feel them scrape, and I'm sorry, I'm so sorry, I don't want to hurt her, I don't want to touch her when she's so afraid and so lost, but we have to move, because now, louder than the sirens, so much louder, I hear footsteps on the stairs, and they're quick, quick, quick . . .

Grace is a horror, straight from a slasher movie. Blood covers her face and mats her hair. She holds a rifle in both hands. Her grip is awkward, cringing, but the barrel is aimed right at me, and her finger is on the trigger.

"Let her go," she says, her voice shaking.

I freeze, my hand still tight around Zahra's wrist. Behind me Zahra moans softly, but she stops struggling.

"I won't let you have her," Grace says. She takes another step into the room. Her face is a grim red mask, pale blue eyes peering half-mad from behind locks of bloodied hair. I keep my eyes trained on her, but my mind is spinning around the room, trying to remember what's in there. If there's anything I can use as a weapon. If there's anything I can use to get us free.

"She's not yours to keep, Grace." I mean the words to sound defiant, but they come out in a strangled squeak. Still, a look of fury blows across her face.

"You . . . will . . . not . . . leave . . . this . . . house!" she screams, lifting the gun up to look through the sight.

An explosion tears through the room. A lamp explodes behind me as the bullet hits it. My fingers slip free of Zahra's arm; she falls to the floor. Grace slumps against the wall; for a minute I think she somehow shot herself, though that makes no sense. Then I realize the recoil of the gun has knocked her back.

And then my body's moving, and it's almost like it's outside of my control. I lunge toward the fireplace, my fingers fumbling at the wrought iron stand to its right. The poker is cool in my fingers, my muscles thrilling a little at its weight. I raise it high. And I don't hesitate. I don't wait to see her face, or telegraph my intentions, beyond the simple, swift downward stroke. I bring it as hard as I can across Grace Worthen's head. And even when she falls to the ground, I keep it clenched tight in my hand.

The sirens are loud now. Blue and red lights start swirling through the window. Downstairs I can hear someone calling out. I hear the word *police*. I don't look at the end of the poker. At what is dripping from its hook. I don't look down at the woman on the ground, her blood seeping into the carpet.

Zahra's crouched next to the bed, crying softly. She looks so small, somehow—as if some part of her has been chipped away, worn down by the blasting winds. My heart wrenches dully in my chest. Because I've found her . . . but what if it's too late to save her?

But then she looks up, and the tears on her face are illuminated red and blue, and they glitter as bright as stars. As bright as magic. And I smile. Because there she is—my dearest friend. The Starmaiden.

CHAPTER THIRTY-FIVE

WEDNESDAY AFTERNOON THE CLOUDS are dark, the mountains hidden behind a gray mist. There's a chill in the air. I hunch into my peacoat as I walk up the trail to the playground.

Finally. Finally, I'm going to get a chance to talk to Zahra.

The world has been in a tumult ever since the moment I arrived at Grace Worthen's house yesterday afternoon. After the police arrived, Zahra was loaded into an ambulance and whisked away. I was taken to the station to make my statement. Again and again, I sat across from Detective Teffeteller and told her what'd happened. That I'd gone to the Worthen house on a hunch, more or less. That I'd seen Zahra in the window and hadn't thought twice, but had pushed past Grace to get to her. That I'd been desperate to get her out of there. That she hadn't wanted to leave—but that the Worthens had a history of abusing, manipulating, gaslighting, and brainwashing people.

She'd refused to tell me how Zahra was doing or what she was saying. It was all confidential, "part of an ongoing investigation." But she told me they'd arrested Dale Worthen at the church. She also told me Grace Worthen was in the hospital, in stable condition.

By the time I got home it was almost one in the morning. My phone was blowing up with texts—mostly from Tabitha and Ben and Marcus, Soo-Jin and Margo, but some from people I didn't even know. I don't have a clue how the news made it out there so quickly. I sent a few messages—I'm okay, Zahra's okay, I will tell you everything as soon as I can—but the only person I really wanted to talk to was Zahra.

She texted me from her mother's phone this morning, unprompted.

This is Z can u meet at Pedo Park 4pm

It was nine and I was still lying on my bed, not sleeping—I hadn't really slept all night—but resting, waiting for an update. I held the phone in front of my face for ages before I could quite process what I was seeing. A text. From my best friend. For the first time since I touched ground in Anchorage. It's everything I've wanted. The only thing I've wanted. And now . . . now I don't know how to feel. Who will she be? The girl I dragged, screaming, from the closet yesterday afternoon? The one I've been chasing for the past few weeks, through rumors and half-heard stories? Or someone else entirely?

But she was reaching out to me this time. I'd been

planning to wait a few days, to let things settle down. To let her talk to her parents, to let her sleep and eat and regain her strength after whatever she'd been through with the Worthens. The fact that she wanted to see me made me feel hopeful for the first time in weeks. The fact that she wanted to see me at our old haunt? *That* made me feel happy.

So here I am, a few minutes early. I crest the hill, then cross down into the little clearing. The deciduous trees are all bare now. Only the conifers stand, shaggy and dark in their coats of needles. The investigators that found Bailey last week trampled a lot of the undergrowth flat, and the playground is still festooned with police tape. I walk to the center of the equipment and look around at the damage—the slide uprooted from the earth, resting on its side; the enormous tire gone entirely, pillaged or removed. There's evidence of intruders other than the cops, too. Empty beer cans litter the damp earth, and someone's spray-painted RIP BAILEY on the playscape in bright green.

Under the highest platform on the playscape, there's a patch of dirt recently turned, a scraped-looking place where someone has filled a hole.

Slowly, I start to unthread the police tape from the equipment. They've already learned everything they'll learn from the playground. At the most recent press conference, Detective Teffeteller said that the crime scene was so old, and so contaminated, anything they found there was of limited value. Vagrants have come through, and kids looking to party, and urban explorers, and plenty of other people.

The police will have to rely on other methods to find out who killed Bailey Sellers.

I look around the clearing. We're too old, now, to turn this place into a hideout. But I wonder if any of this—the playground, the Precipice, the long-ago connection between two lonely girls—can be pulled from the wreckage. If we can excavate some tiny, glowing seed from all that's happened since. I get the last of the tape off the playscape and crumple it into a little ball.

When I look up, she's there.

It's almost stunning to see her there, in the flesh, after so long. Yesterday I didn't even have time to process it. But I've gone over and over my memories, tracing her face in my mind for so long, and now, here she is, braced at the edge of the woods like a doe considering flight. She's wearing the same baggy sweater she wore last night, but she's traded the skirt for jeans and boots.

There's something so fragile about her face. I keep thinking of stone formations in the desert, left behind by the water that wore them down. Something in the angles of her cheekbones, the jut of her chin, reminds me of that. As if some great and terrible force has carved some piece of her away.

Her eyes meet mine. I'm not sure if I should smile, or look serious, or what, so I just raise a hand to wave.

She steps over one of the metal bouncy animals, looking around the clearing. "Wow," she says. "This place is . . ."

"Pretty trashed," I say. "Yeah. They tore it apart."

She doesn't answer. Her hands drift over the surfaces of

things—the slide, the swing set. I watch her face closely, trying to see what she's thinking. Once it would have been easy. Now she's impossible to read.

"Are you okay?" I ask. "I mean . . . did they hurt you?"

She doesn't answer for a moment. But after a moment she looks at me again. Her gaze is so direct, so bold, it startles me a little.

"What did you tell the cops?" she asks.

For some reason I'd expected her to sound robotic, like she's in some kind of trance. Like she's been brainwashed. But she doesn't. She sounds . . . like Zahra. Like the same girl I knew three years ago. And somehow, that's almost more frightening, though I'm not sure why.

My voice is slow and even when it comes. "I told them that I went looking for you, after your mom told me how abusive your grandparents were. That I saw you in the window and I pushed your grandma out of the way. That I ran upstairs to find you. That she pulled a gun on us."

I take a step toward her and stop when I see her tense. We stand on either side of the fallen slide, facing each other. She's taller than me now—we used to be around the same height, but she's gained a full two inches on me, at least.

"This isn't how I imagined seeing you again," I say. And the moment the words are out, something in me throbs in pain. All the scenarios I've spun—the homecomings I've imagined, both of us back here at the playground—are all flat, lifeless things now, as two-dimensional as the notebook paper we used to write on.

Her lips push together into a sneer, but there's a look of curiosity in her eyes, too.

"What did you think would happen?" she asks.

What did I think? I don't know. Not this. Not that I'd be squaring off across a broken slide, my shoulder still sore from swinging a metal poker at an old woman, my best friend's face twisted in scorn. I feel my lip start to quiver, and so I bite it down to hide it.

"I don't know," I say softly. "I guess I hoped it'd be less complicated."

She just smirks. My heart gives a sharp stutter.

"What happened to you, Zahra?" I take another step closer to her. I watch her eyes narrow, but I don't move away. "Something changed you. Something . . . hurt you."

There's something uncertain in her eyes. No—not uncertain. Incredulous.

"You're kidding, right?" she says. When I just look at her, she laughs. "Come on, Ruthie. You remember. I know you do."

She gestures around the playground.

"What happened to me?" she asks. "You did, Ruthie. You happened. You fucking psycho."

CHAPTER THIRTY-SIX

ZAHRA

I'VE BEEN RUNNING AWAY from her for so long. Now she stands in front of me, a figure from three long years of nightmares, a stricken look on her face. And it's just so ridiculous, so absurd, so terrifying, that for a moment I can't stop laughing.

But Ruthie—this poor, lost monster, this demon from hell—just looks at me, and her face is so wounded, so shattered, the laughter finally dies in my throat.

"Why would you say a thing like that?" she whispers.

THAT SUMMER IS NEVER far from my memory.

"Let's say the Starmaiden has a—what's the word? Like, someone she kind of loves and kind of hates?"

It was August. Ruthie and I were in the woods. At the

playground. I sat on one of the wooden platforms on the rotting playscape, the notebook on my lap. Trying to come up with the right word.

"Nemesis," Ruthie replied.

"Thanks," I said. Ruthie always had the right word. It impressed me no end. I read nonstop but I had a tendency to skim right over things I didn't know or didn't care about. I never bothered hunting down a dictionary or even typing a word into my phone; I scanned for what I was interested in. The love, the magic, the friendship, the laughter. The fight. The big win. But Ruthie paid attention to words.

I'd never known anyone like her before.

I jotted down the idea in the notebook, my handwriting large and loopy under her all capitals. There'd been rain that week, and the leaves around us were heavy with it, but now the sky was periwinkle blue, the clouds lit pink and gold. A cotton candy sky, a cartoon unicorn sky. The kind of sky that stood over a magical world.

I was going to be fourteen in a week and a half. Way past cartoon unicorn age; way past the age of playing pretend. And we'd be heading back to school, and I had no idea what our friendship would look like in school—it made me cringe a little to think about it, to imagine, say, Tabitha Morgan's face if she saw us out here like this. Or even Bailey's. Either of them would think this was crazy.

And they'd probably be a little bit right.

Ruthie was . . . brilliant. Smart, and intense, and

determined. And she had the aura of someone who'd seen real pain. I didn't know the story, and she didn't talk about it, but it gave everything she said and did a kind of weight.

But she was also undeniably *weird*. And it was hard to put your finger on how. It wasn't anything obvious. She looked normal—she was prettier than she thought she was, even if she dressed a little frumpy. And it wasn't her obsession with books, or movies, or stories. That was normal fangirl devotion. That was just fun.

No. It was something else. Something just behind her eyes that stayed untouched by laughter, or emotion. I'd seen it, felt it, and I assumed it was a part of whatever pain she'd been through. It didn't matter to me. But I wondered what it'd be like when we were in school, surrounded by other people.

For now, though, we were alone. Ruthie knelt on the ground, hammering another nail into the bookshelf she was building. We'd had the idea to fix the place up a little, and for the past few weeks we'd been smuggling my dad's tools out here, stealing stray nails and screws and making plans. It was a little goofy—we were too old for a fort, honestly. But it felt exciting to carve out our own little space. To *make* something.

"What you doing?"

My pen froze above the page. I knew that voice. I knew that voice, and I knew what I'd see when I looked up, but I still dreaded it.

Bailey Sellers stood at the edge of the clearing.

She stood with her arms folded over her chest. Her hair

was the color of a black cherry—she dyed it a week or so ago. It was ratty, and the color uneven. She stepped onto the playground, her body language meek but her chin jutting.

I glanced over at Ruthie. She'd halted her work, the hammer hanging loose in her hand. She was looking at Bailey with that hard little smirk she got sometimes, usually when she felt insecure.

Crap.

Bailey'd always been a "summer friend" more than anything—during the school year we were in different circles, different classes. But we lived a few blocks away from each other, so in the summer we were friends on the merits of proximity. One year we'd spent every afternoon sunning ourselves on my trampoline and reading gossip blogs on our phones. Another, we developed what we thought was the clever trick of buying a ticket to a movie matinee and then sneaking into other movies for the rest of the day. We'd ridden bikes to Goose Lake and watched older kids smoke and flirt. We'd eaten candy until our tongues were patchy and green from the sugar.

But Bailey wasn't interested in making things up or indulging flights of fancy at all; she didn't look for cloud shapes, she didn't talk in funny voices for her pets, she didn't make up little stories about the people we saw on the bus or at the mall. She didn't read. Worse—she acted like I was a freak show when I did those things. Half the stuff I liked she dismissed as "weird." It didn't really bother me—I just shrugged it off—but when I met Ruthie, it was an almost shocking relief. All the things I'd done alone suddenly had another person to fan the flames. I didn't want to stifle them anymore.

So I'd been neglecting Bailey for the better part of the summer. Dodging her, hiding from her sometimes. Or worse, letting her tag along with me and Ruthie and giving her a kind of patronizing smile whenever she tried to change the subject to one she cared about. Sometimes I felt awful about it; I'd pass by her trailer and see a single light on in her bedroom and wonder what she was doing, if she was okay. I'd see her slinking around the neighborhood alone, looking scruffier by the day.

Now I quickly slid my notebook under my hoodie. I didn't want to have to explain that to her.

But Ruthie, still smirking, stepped over the planks she was working on, toward Bailey.

"Preparing for the sacrifice," she said nonchalantly.

Bailey's left eyebrow arched up. It was her best fuck-off face; I knew it pretty well. "What?"

"We're building an altar," Ruthie said, gesturing toward the half-made bookshelf. "That's where we'll put our offering. It's the only way to pass into the Darkness."

I still hadn't moved off the playscape. The language was from our stories. In one, a cult of blood mages, driven mad by the constant daylight, was trying to bring about nightfall by sacrificing innocents. It wasn't even the light that made them unhinged. It was the exhaustion of anticipation—the fact that the sun moved so low on the horizon but never dipped down below it. In the book, Lyr killed their leader, and the Starmaiden banished the rest of them to a system of underground caves to sleep for fifty years.

Bailey looked at the bookshelf. "Okay. What you gonna sacrifice?"

She tried so hard to sound game. It made my heart ache. She didn't care about any of this, but she was so lonely. She was trying. I was about to hop up off the playscape, to pad over on my bare feet and talk to her, when Ruthie grinned cruelly and said, "Oh, don't worry about that."

Then she swung the hammer high overhead.

Bailey let out a strangled cry, covering her head with her arms, but the hammer stopped a half inch away from her head. I let out my breath all of a sudden.

There was a long moment when nobody moved. Then Ruthie started laughing. She lowered the hammer, twirling it in her hand, and walked away. Bailey looked up and lowered her arms, her expression changing slowly from terror to rage.

"Fuck you," she screamed. Her cheeks were passing quickly through red to purple. I'd seen that before. Bailey was prone to sudden rages. I'd seen her tear a neighbor's fence down with her bare hands once; I'd seen her throw rocks at a girl who'd called her "dirty."

"Calm down," Ruthie said. "It was a joke."

"It's okay, Bailey," I said. I jumped up from the playscape, thinking I could distract her and defuse the situation. "We're just fixing the place up. Want to see?"

Her eyes met mine for just a split second. That's one of

the images that comes back to me a lot. That moment when we looked at each other, and her eyes said, *Why? Why are you hanging out with this girl? Why did you leave me behind?* For a second it hurt. Then it made me mad. I didn't deserve a guilt trip. I was allowed to hang out with whoever I wanted. I was allowed to be happy.

Then she looked around the little clearing. She kicked at a flowerpot we'd placed out there; it fell over but didn't break, the dirt sliding out.

"Hey," I said. "Don't do that."

She flipped me off and kicked it again. The ceramic cracked as she stomped down. Ruthie took a step toward her to grab her, but Bailey slipped quickly away. She looked around the clearing at all the other things we'd done. The doodles along the equipment in multicolored Sharpie. The sheet I'd hung for shade. The little ceramic incense burner in the shape of a cat; the stack of books on the playscape. "Fuck your dumb little clubhouse," she screeched. She grabbed the edge of the sheet and pulled at it; there was an awful tearing sound. She threw it to one side without even looking at it, ran over to the slide and kicked over the old coffee can that held my nail polish. She punched the slide one, two, three times, denting it more than it already was, leaving her knuckles bloody.

Ruthie was staggering after her, trying to catch her. I didn't know what would happen if she did. I had to get there first—I'd calmed Bailey down before. I took a few steps toward her. Then I felt the notebook slipping from under my hoodie, falling down onto the damp gravel below.

Bailey saw it. She couldn't have known what it was—we never worked on it in front of her—but she knew I'd been hiding it. She knew it was something secret. So she dove for it. I heard Ruthie give a wordless scream as Bailey grabbed the notebook and started to tear the pages. Somehow the sound of it, the crumple, the rip, was so loud. I grabbed one edge and pulled. "Give it back. Give it back." But she wrenched it from me, tearing at it wildly, throwing paper every which way. I tried to catch her, but Bailey'd been dodging blows her whole fucking life. All our work, the words that made the Precipice real to us—the magic spell that kept this beautiful, aching, desperate place our own—was being destroyed.

Then came a sound that drowned out the sound of tearing paper. A sharp, heavy crack. A gargling scream. I watched as Bailey fell to the ground. I couldn't figure out what was happening. Then I saw Ruthie behind her. Her face twisted with rage. The hammer in her hand. She raised it up high again and brought it down onto the back of Bailey's head. And then again.

And then, everything was very, very still.

CHAPTER THIRTY-SEVEN

No. No. No. I had to stop this. I had to fix this. There had to be a way to fix this. But it took forever for me to move. It took long, long seconds for me to dive toward Ruthie, for me to wrestle the hammer away. How many more blows did she get in while I stood there, gaping? How many minutes did Bailey lose while I begged and pleaded with any higher powers out there to make this be a dream?

But then I had the hammer, and Ruthie was scrambling around on the ground, picking up the scraps of paper, an awful, long keening sound coming from her throat. And there was something on the hammer and I didn't want to look at it, so I threw it as far as I could away from me. And Bailey was lying very still. And it wasn't a dream, and there was no way for me to fix it, and that moment—that moment on the Precipice—is the one that stays with me the most. The moment when the worst had already happened, but when nothing had started yet.

"She destroyed it. She destroyed it." Ruthie's voice barely sounded human. It was a choked, retching snarl and a whine all at once. "Help me!"

I didn't make a decision to move. My body went into motion, a runaway horse, wild and spooked. I ran. I ran across the earth, half-blind with terror, careening off trees, stumbling over roots. Breathing so hard I thought I might be drowning. I didn't know where I was going, or why.

But then Ruthie's hand clamped around my wrist and she pulled me so sharply I fell.

My mouth and nose were full of dirt. My palms burned, the skin skimmed off the surface in the fall. I couldn't think. I couldn't speak. All I knew was that I had to get away. From the park. From her.

"Where are you going?" Ruthie was kneeling down behind me.

"Help." The word was a pathetic gasp from somewhere in the bottom of my lungs. "We . . . have to get help."

"No!" Ruthie's face came close to my ear. I could feel the heat roiling off her. "She's dead. We killed her and she's dead and no one's going to help us."

No, no, no, it's not true, it can't be true, it's not . . .

But she was already pulling me to my feet. I looked at her and she looked at me, and I saw the truth there in the blood flecked across her cheek. I saw it in the fierce gray eyes behind those smudged glasses.

"She shouldn't have come here," Ruthie said. "She should never have followed us."

Ruthie was always so good at telling stories. I could already hear that she was telling herself this one.

"Come on," she said. "We have to go back. We have to fix it."

"No," I begged. "Ruthie, I can't, I can't go back there, I . . ."

She shook me by the arm. Her fingers were strong, her nails jagged where she bit them. "We have to hide it," she hissed.

And I didn't know what else to do. Because I was afraid of Ruthie. But also—oh, God, it hurts to even think about—I didn't want to get in trouble. I didn't want to have to tell what had happened.

So I followed her.

The playscape came back into view. It looked like a cardboard cutout of itself, like an ugly, flimsy model. It wasn't a magical place anymore. It looked like a gallows in the dim sunlight. Bailey—her body—was where we left it, unmoving. I didn't think I could stand to look. Except then Ruthie was dragging me over, and I collapsed by the crumpled little form, and I put my hand on her motionless back.

"I was supposed to be her friend," I gasped, staring down at her. "I . . . I can't . . ."

"We'll hide it," Ruthie said. Voice deadly calm. "We've got to."

We had a lot of tools. Hammers, screwdrivers, shovels. We started to dig. Under the remnants of playground gravel the earth was hard-packed. It took a long time, and by the time it was wide and deep enough we were working in the flashlight of her phone because the sun had disappeared entirely, and my arms were weak and limp, and my body was exhausted from crying. It was cold. My arms were covered in gooseflesh; it was almost the end of summer.

Ruthie went toward the body, but before she got there, I said, "No!" She turned her head to look at me, and her expression was like the moon, pale and blank and white. I went over to Bailey and tried to pick her up. She was tiny for her age, but still too heavy for me to lift alone. I ended up half carrying, half rolling her into the hole.

Before we started to shovel dirt over the top of her, I got one glimpse of her face. Her eyes were open, staring up at the star-scattered sky. I had a vision that was so strong for a moment I thought it might really be happening—of me climbing into the grave, lying on top of her, putting my head on her shoulder. Of me closing her eyes, closing my eyes. Of the dirt falling down on both of us, taking us both to darkness.

But I didn't climb in, though for a long time I would wish I had. I picked up a handful of dirt and dropped it onto her.

"We don't tell anyone," Ruthie said. "Not a word."

"Her mom . . ." I whispered.

Ruthie's fingers dug into my arm.

"Starmaiden," she hissed. "The secret must be kept. Remember what happens to oathbreakers. Remember when King Lorcan betrayed the Precipice to the Elodea?"

The threat wasn't even thinly veiled. She was talking about a scene in the book—oh my god, that fucking *book*, it seemed so stupid now—where the king destroyed a magical seal that protected his city from the creeping evil force we'd called the Elodea. He did it because the Elodea promised to spare his family. But Lyr had fought her way through his entire palace guard and killed him. She'd killed him on his throne, and then killed his wife, too, for talking him into it. It'd been a dark scene, even for Ruthie.

A dark scene. But not just a scene. Not just a book. Not anymore. Because Ruthie would kill. Had killed. And she'd do it again, if I didn't do what she wanted.

I was so bone-tired. It already felt like a bad dream, like it hadn't really happened. Like there'd never been a Bailey in the first place—we'd imagined her and written an awful story.

"Zahra?" she asked. There was a warning note to her voice, almost singsong. "Are you on my side here?"

The sky was going pale along the mountains. The sun would be up soon. We had to get out of there.

"Yeah," I said. "Yeah, okay."

CHAPTER THIRTY-EIGHT

I NEVER MEANT TO hurt so many people.

First Bailey, obviously. Bailey, who I still see when I close my eyes. Sometimes I see her alive, her hopeful, pugnacious little chin jutting forward fiercely. Other times . . . I see what we did to her. Her blood, spattering the slide, soaking into the dirt.

But then, a few weeks ago, I got that text from Ruthie announcing that she was coming back, and everyone else—everyone I love—got pulled in, too.

I'd been so grateful when she moved to Portland, just a few days after Bailey's death. I knew nothing would ever be all right again, even then—but at least Ruthie would be far, far away. At least she wouldn't be able to hurt me, or my family. But soon she was texting me, sending these chatty little messages as if we'd been in the middle of casual conversation when her mom had just happened to take her to Oregon.

> This isn't fair, she's uprooting me just because she wants a "fresh start." what does that even mean?

And a few days later:

> You have to visit soon. You will not believe the trees here. It's not the Precipice but it could be a cool setting of its own.

And then, finally:

> Fucking reply already, oathbreaker

So I had. I'd replied. **Sorry been busy with school. Miss you girl.** I'd replied that time, and the next time, and every time, and I'd learned how to find the exact balance: how little could I say to her before she'd freak out? How vague could I stay, how long could I stretch the silences, before she threatened me? I hated it, every second of it, but I knew I had to keep her calm. And besides, I deserved to be punished for my part in what'd happened. If this was my punishment, I got off pretty light.

I stayed away from social media. I kept my head down. I tried to get away, as far away as I could. I tried to become someone else. First I thought maybe Jesus would help. Mom never liked talking about her childhood or her parents, but Grandma and Grandpa had been nice enough to me the few times we were together. It wasn't until I moved in with them that I understood even a fraction of what she went through.

Jesus seemed like a good guy. My grandpa, on the other hand, refused to let me wear a sleeveless shirt to school and referred to my hair as "nappy." And as much as I wanted to change, to be a better person than I was, I knew I couldn't do that with him.

Back home I tore down all my decorations and took box after box of books to the curb. I painted my walls smooth and clean and gray. I threw out all my crumpled art projects, all my half-used glue sticks and my pinking shears and the origami animals that littered every surface in my room. My parents were terrified. I could see it in their eyes. They didn't understand what was happening. I caught my little brother fishing a bunch of my stuff out of the trash one day. "You still want it, I know you do!" he'd fumed, as I crammed it all back down in the bin.

But I couldn't ever change enough to outrun the truth. Images of Ruthie, spattered in blood and brains, would spring up to claw at me out of nowhere. Or worse—images of Bailey. Bailey laughing, scraping the bark off a tree with a rusty penknife. Bailey stealing money off my kitchen counter, never realizing that my mom left it there for her to steal.

Bailey convulsing on the hard-packed ground, her hair matted with blood.

Even when I did start coming out of my shell a little, the memories ambushed me. Even when I was lucky beyond belief, making friends. Falling in love with Ben. Learning how much I liked to take pictures. Finding the island my grandpa's church had abandoned. Everything happy and good got touched, eventually, by my own dirty, bloody memories.

Then this September she sent a fresh flurry of messages.

> Send me some pics? I'm so homesick.

> What have you been reading lately? Did you see Naomi Novik finally finished Temeraire? I think you'd like the last one.

> Everything okay?

I didn't answer fast enough. I knew I was cutting it close. Maybe I was getting complacent. She was in Portland, after all. It'd been three years. How long was I going to have to be her pen pal to keep her happy? I thought, maybe, if I just ignored it a little longer, it'd be over, done, gone.

Then I'd gotten her last text. And it wasn't the rage-filled screed I expected. It was far, far worse.

> Arriving in Anchorage this Sunday. Can't wait to see you.

I'd gone into a blind panic. I had to run. I had to hide. I never had a good plan but there wasn't time to slow down and come up with one. First thing was to vanish. I thought disappearing from a party would help to cover my tracks. So I hid my bike in the woods down the street from Tabitha's house. I was going to slip out when everyone was drunk. Then I could use the bike trails to get to Grandma's house, where I'd beg her to let me stay.

But then Ben found out about Seb. And everything went wrong.

He blew up. He'd never blown up like that before. Ben was endlessly patient with me, with my panic attacks and my mood swings, with all the ways I tested his boundaries, with all the ways I lashed out blindly. But something about that stupid kiss was too much for him to take. He paced the lawn. He called me names I'd never even heard him use. And I just sat there, sobbing—partly because it hurt so badly, but partly because I knew it was the worst possible thing he could be doing. I knew it'd make it look like he had something to do with my disappearance.

And I still did it. I still did it, knowing full well what it'd mean for Ben—the last person in the world I wanted to see hurt. I went back to the party and pretended to get drunk. I made sure to stay late, as late as I could—I didn't want anyone to think I'd left with Ben, though they of course thought that anyway. And then, when the party was at its wildest, when people were making out in the corners and breaking vases in the living room and stumbling blindly around, I slipped out the door and headed to the trail where I'd left my bike. It was out there, while I was groping around in the dark woods, that I tripped on a root and broke my phone's screen, the shattered glass leaving a shallow cut on my palm. And I'm so stupid, I never thought about the blood—I just didn't want the cops to be able to track me with my phone. So I left it there, next to a tree, hoping it'd be another misdirect to keep anyone from finding me.

And it was. For a while. Though it scared my parents, my brother, my cousins and aunts and uncle out of their minds.

Everyone's been dragged into this now. Because of me, because I couldn't face my crimes. My parents thought I was dead. Dad can't even look at me without breaking into tears right now—all morning long he's been leaving the room whenever I come in. And Mom. The whole thing has broken something inside her. She thinks Grandma and Grandpa did something unspeakable, when all they really did—at least, all Grandma really did—was trust me. I showed up at her doorstep at three in the morning, without warning, and she brought me in, and trusted that I needed to hide. I told her someone wanted to hurt me. I was vague, but I made it sound like maybe I owed someone money, like maybe I'd gotten involved with drugs or something. It made me look sketchy as hell, but it was better than confessing to murder. She told me I could stay as long as I needed. She told me she'd handle Grandpa.

Now she's in the hospital. And if I don't do something to fix things, Grandpa's going to jail. And it's all my fault.

She's torn through everyone I love on her way to get to me. But then, I should've known. Lyr always hated oath-breakers.

———

"YOU HAVE NO IDEA what I've been through," she says now. "You have no idea what I've had to do to get back here to you."

I'm trembling, with anger, with terror, with all the adrenaline I've been swallowing like poison for the last three years. "It can't be worse than what you did. To Bailey."

"That was an accident," she says.

"You beat her with a hammer!" I nod toward the now-empty grave. The place Bailey'd been hidden for so long.

"You helped," she says.

"I helped you *bury* her," I say. "I helped you keep the secret. But you were the one that killed her."

"Why do you keep saying it like that? She *attacked* us. She shouldn't have followed us." She looks at me, almost exasperated. "I've had to fight my way through so much to get here. I had to figure out a way past my mom. I had to retrace your steps, I had to learn who you'd become, I had to get past your grandma . . ."

"You beat my grandma half to death," I say.

"I did it for you, though," she says. There's a pleading note in her voice, like she's trying to reason with me. But there's something under that—something flat, and cold. I shift my weight a little, onto the balls of my feet. In case I have to move. "I came back for you. I missed you so much, Zahra. And you weren't writing, or texting, or . . . I felt like I was losing you."

Something in what she's said suddenly hits me. *I had to figure out a way past my mom.* But her mom had died in a hiking accident—I'd seen it in the newspaper. I'd set up a Google Alert for both of their names after they'd moved away, to keep track of where they were, and I'd seen the obituary. An accident in the Columbia River Gorge.

"Your mom . . ." I say. "She fell."

"She *had to fall*." She emphasizes every word. "It was the only way I was ever going to get back here. I don't know how she knew about Bailey, but she did. Or at least she suspected. She wouldn't let me come back, even when Dad got married."

"You . . ." I feel sick, dizzy. I feel the tug at the bottom of my stomach that usually signals a panic attack. Not now. I can't afford it—not now. "You killed her?"

"I did what I had to do," she says.

I can picture it. Because I've already seen it. The way a switch goes on, and then she moves, faster and stronger than you'd ever expect. The way it comes out of nowhere.

And the way she can push it back down, after. The way that cold, reptilian thing inside of her takes over and lets her act like everything's normal, everything's all right.

"Why, Ruthie?" I ask. "Why did you come back here?"

"Because you're my best friend." Her voice is soft, not quite calm—I can hear the tremor—but matter-of-fact. Her *best friend*. After what I saw her do. After what she made me do to hide it.

"No," I say. "I'm not, Ruthie. I hate you. You ruined my life."

Her lower lip starts to tremble, but she bites down on it hard.

"You're my best friend," she says again, louder this time.

I can't help it. I laugh. I laugh hard, right in her face. It comes from the bottom of my stomach, all acid and bile. From all the bitterness of everything I've lost and everything I've destroyed. I laugh hard and hot and watch as she gets paler and paler.

She lunges at me across the slide. Her fingers dig sharply into my shoulder. We fall down together, scuffling in the hard-packed dirt. I grab a lock of her hair and twist it hard around my fist, and she screams and lets go. I scrabble away on hands and knees, then jump up onto my feet a few yards away.

I run.

My tendons and muscles are tight from a few weeks of disuse. I feel the impact shoot up through my body every time my feet hit the earth. For a second I think I've left her far behind, that she's still back there at the Precipice.

But then I hear her breath. I risk a glance behind me and see her there, barreling down the trail toward me.

She will follow me. She'll follow me anywhere I go, until one of us, or both of us, is dead.

CHAPTER THIRTY-NINE

IT STARTS TO RAIN.

I can hear her footsteps. Her furious whimper. And for a second I lose track of the line between memory and the present moment. I'm running away, and she's behind me, and both of us breathe in panicked heaves, and there's a body behind us in a pool of blood.

But no. That was a long time ago. That is a mistake long since made.

I'm taller and stronger than I used to be. This is part of why I joined cross-country. Not to compete, but to flee. To get hard and lean and fast and to be able to run forever. Her breath is fading behind me and I think, *It's working, I'm getting away . . .* but then I turn and look, and my foot snags against the root of a tree. I go tumbling. My lungs go flat as the air is knocked out of me. For a moment I gasp like a landed fish.

Above me, Ruthie's face looms in.

"I thought you understood," she says. Her face is a mess of tears and blood.

The rain is coming in hard, stinging darts now. Her hair is plastered to her head, and drops fleck the lenses of her glasses. Her fingers close around my neck and she starts to squeeze. Her hands are freakishly strong. I try to wrench myself away but she tightens her grip.

My vision is fuzzy and gray. I claw at her hands. My lungs burn.

I don't know how it happens, but suddenly I've hooked her leg with mine and tugged her off balance. Her hands loosen and I gasp for air; now we're both on the ground, scrabbling at each other with fingers struggling to find purchase.

I close my eyes. I argue with my body, this unwieldy thing that has never obeyed me. *Get up*, I think. *Get up and run*. But it won't.

So I guess I have no choice but to stay and fight.

I drive my fist into her stomach and she gives a low groan. I sit up and punch her again; it sends pain shooting up through my fist, but I grit my teeth against it. She screams, and it's a banshee sound, whipped away on the wind.

A few feet away, my eyes fall on a jagged piece of rock, sitting to the side of the trail. And for one split second I imagine it: picking it up and bringing it down with all my might against her face.

It'd be over then. Over for good.

But not really. Not ever. Because even if she died right here, at my hands, she'd never be gone. I'd never be free. We're tied together. We have been since we killed Bailey. I'll never be able to look myself in the mirror without seeing what I've done—without seeing Ruthie, standing just behind me in my reflection. And killing her? That would only make her stronger.

I look down at her. Her long hair sprawled across the mud, one lens of her glasses broken. Her face is mottled purple, and she's crying, a whole-body sob so violent I'm afraid she'll shake herself to pieces.

"You were the only person," she cries.

I wait for her to finish the thought. But that's all she says.

The fight seems to have left her, but I keep her pinned beneath me nonetheless—even though all I really want to do is check the phone in my pocket to make sure it's still recording. That's the only reason I came out here, to this awful fucking place. The only reason I forced myself to face her. I wanted her to confess. I wanted to make sure I had it on audio, so I could give it to the police, so I could finally help to put her away where she couldn't hurt anybody ever again.

Even if it puts me away in the process.

I can hear the sirens now. I'd called 911 from the trail. I told them to come to the park, that someone was hurt, and then I hung up. I figured no matter what happened between us, it would be true. Someone would be hurt. Someone had been hurt.

Underneath me, Ruthie continues to cry. All around us, the rain pummels the earth, making the forest tremble beneath its fury.

CHAPTER FORTY

"WHO'S A GOOD GIRL? Who's a big dumb good girl?" Malik holds an end of a knotted old sock, Deshka tugging on the other end with all her might. Her long, shaggy tail sweeps back and forth.

The dog freezes for a moment, then gives a sudden tug that sends him tumbling. And even though it's late April, and it's been almost seven months since everything that happened with Ruthie, my laughter is still so rare that it startles me when I dissolve into giggles, watching.

I'm sitting on a lawn chair, Yukon curled up next to me. It's not actually warm yet. But the daylight has started coming back to us, and that means we can't help but drift outside, out of the cramped little trailer and into the weak sun. The snow has mostly melted, except for a few dirty mounds lingering in the shadows.

Normally Malik would be out on his bike, racing around

the neighborhood with his buddies. They have a track they've made in an empty lot at the edge of the trailer court, where they go to do tricks and jumps. He's good—I've seen video of it. I've never been over there to watch him, though. I can't really go far with the house arrest monitor on my leg. But he's been spending more time at home lately, and even though he doesn't say it, I'm pretty sure it's to keep me company.

"What's so funny over there?" Malik pulls himself up, trying and failing to brush the crumbling mud off his shorts. "Oh, you think you cute? Deshka, get her. Go on." He snaps his fingers and points, and suddenly I'm covered in ninety pounds of muddy dog, her feet trampling across my sweatpants.

I shriek. "No!" But I can't stop laughing. She keeps trying to give me the wet sock and I finally take it and throw it as hard as I can toward Malik. She takes off running, and Yukon jumps up to chase after her. Their feet tear up the dirt—poor Dad is never going to have a lawn.

Here we are, normal teenagers playing with their dogs on a raw spring afternoon. Regaining daylight after the dark and the cold start to lift is usually enough to make me feel giddy— but add to that the fact that I haven't been out of the house all winter except for court dates and therapy appointments, and for a little while, I almost feel weightless. House arrest means I can't do much of anything. I can't leave the property, can't go to work, can't go to school—though Dad's making me study for my GRE. In a lot of ways that's probably a blessing—I'm not exactly Miss Popularity these days. I'm the girl everyone was so worried about who turned out to be a murderer.

Or, at least, an accessory to murder.

I've been on house arrest since September now, and honestly I'm lucky; Aisha, my lawyer, went to the mat to get that for me. The prosecution wanted me thrown in jail, and most black girls would have been. It took about thirty character witnesses to convince a judge to let me wait at home while the legal proceedings drag on.

Ruthie, on the other hand, is in jail—adult jail, now, because she turned eighteen a few weeks ago. She's being charged with Bailey's murder and with Grandma's assault. It's possible she'll have to go to Oregon to stand trial for her mom's death, too. Her lawyers are trying hard to get the confession I taped thrown out of the trial. If I have to, I'll testify—it's a part of the plea deal Aisha worked out for me—but I really hope they don't call me to the stand. I don't want to have to look at her again.

I watch my as my brother runs around the yard, all gangly limbs. I was just a little younger than him when Ruthie murdered Bailey. The thought makes me feel suddenly protective. He's so young and so goofy and so vulnerable, and I wish I could protect him from all the mistakes just waiting to be made.

But they're his to make. And maybe—maybe he'll be lucky, and smarter than me, and know better how to do what's right.

"Hey."

I look up to see Tabitha standing just beyond the fence. She's holding a garment bag in one hand. Tonight is Merrill

High's senior prom, and even though I'm obviously not going, I'm going to help Tabitha get ready.

"Hey! Come on around," I say.

She looks at the dogs capering through the muddy yard and purses her lips. "Uh . . . maybe I'll meet you in your room. Hey, Malik, what's happening?"

He smirks and shoves his hands in his pockets, suddenly all fourteen-year-old attitude. "Hey, Tabitha, not much," he mimics.

She heads for the front door, and I stand up to follow.

"Tabitha!" says my dad, when we come through the kitchen. He's still in his work clothes, his pants flecked with paint, but she goes in for a hug anyway.

"Hey, Ron. Hey, Charity," she says to my mom at the table.

Mom smiles up at her. She's got her most recent project— a line of lip balms she's still trying to perfect—spread out in front of her. "You ready for your big night?"

"Not yet," Tabitha says. She grabs a Coke from the fridge and opens it. "How's the recipe coming?"

"I can't quite get it right," Mom says, sticking her finger in her mouth. "I'm going for raspberry and it still tastes like cough syrup."

I stand back for a moment, still a little bemused by the image: Tabitha, in my home, making small talk with my parents, comfortable enough here to grab a soda from the fridge without asking. For a long time she barely came here if she could help it. She always acted like it was because we had more privacy at her house—undeniably true, since her parents are gone a lot and her house is enormous—but I knew that part of it was that she didn't want to hang out in a trailer park. She didn't want to spend time with my weird family.

And it's not like she's done a total one-eighty. There's still something a little forced in it, a little awkward. But she's trying. Plenty of people haven't bothered. I haven't seen most of the kids on the cross-country team since I got home.

"Come on," I finally say, tugging her by the arm. "We've got to get started."

I love her for trying not to look relieved as she waves good-bye to my parents. "Gotta go," she says. "Thanks for the Coke!"

MY CRAMPED BEDROOM ISN'T the most convenient setup, especially compared to Tabitha's en suite bathroom and expensive vanity mirror that mimics natural light—but we turn on some music and set up our makeup on my desk and soon it feels so cozy it doesn't even matter.

"How the heck do people get it so close to the lash?" Tabitha asks, liquid eyeliner trembling in her hand.

"Practice," I say. "And lots of eye-makeup remover, so you can do it again when you mess it up. Here, let me help." I step close, pivoting her toward me. "The key is not to think about it too much."

"Oh, like denial?" she asks. "I'm good at that."

"Me too. Look down." I draw a thick black line across one lid. It's intimate, putting on someone's makeup. I don't know that I've ever done it before.

Or . . . not with Tabitha, anyway. A memory surges up, the way they do, the way they have done for three years now. Bailey Sellers on the edge of my bed. Me with a stolen Wet n Wild lip pencil, giving her the absurdly over-lined lip that was in that year. "Now we look like twins," she said, looking at our faces in the mirror, at my thicker lips next to her ridiculous drag queen ones. It hurt, but I never said anything. Because Bailey was so hapless, and so dumb, and had no way to know better.

I breathe in, breathe out. Focus on the feel of the air in my throat and lungs, moving and circling in and out. It's one of the very basic exercises Dr. Mabry gave me, to work through my flashbacks. Sometimes it helps. Sometimes, I have to try something else.

But this time, I come back. Tabitha's face is angled up toward me, her eyes closed. I breathe, and I do the other eye, flicking the line up at the edge. "There," I say. "It looks good."

"Thanks," she says. She looks into the mirror. Her hair is curled around her chin, thirties-glam style. She's wearing black cigarette pants and a green glitter halter that is in no way seasonally appropriate, but that looks amazing. "So do you."

It'd been Tabitha's idea to dress me up, too. It's kind of silly, since I'm housebound, but after a half year in sweatpants and T-shirts, it's fun. My dress is dark blue, strapless, and rustles around my ankles like a whisper. "Believe it or not, Grandma got it for me."

"Grandma *Worthen*?" she asks, disbelieving.

I laugh. "Yup. She got me a bunch of stuff for my court hearings—you know, boring stuff. And then she pulls this thing out and is like, 'I know it's not terribly appropriate right now, but I saw it there and I couldn't walk away from it. I could just picture it on you!'"

"She must have hidden it from your grandpa," she says wryly. "He'd throw a blanket over you if he saw you in that thing."

She's right, of course. The whole time I'd stayed with Grandpa he'd insisted on long skirts, heavy sweaters that would cover my whole body. When the three of us prayed together, it was always about chastity and decency and modesty. I remember once, a few years ago, when he showed up at a cross-country meet and told me I looked like "a harlot" in my track shorts.

Once the truth came out, that Ruthie'd murdered Bailey, that I'd helped, and that Grandma and Grandpa had kept me hidden, there'd been some brief backlash against Victory Evangelical, some talk about charging them with obstruction of justice for helping me. But their lawyers managed to get them out of legal trouble, and Grandpa's actually managed to turn the whole thing around from a PR standpoint. "Should we not love the sinners among us, and try to save them?" he says. As if he hasn't talked thousands of times about punishment and shame. It's actually ended up bringing him some new followers.

I wrote him, and Grandma, a letter to apologize. I hadn't been sure they'd want to see me, after all I'd put them through.

And while I haven't seen much of him, except at a few of the court hearings, Grandma's been coming around a little bit. The first time she did it my mom hid in her room and refused to come out, so I just sat with Grandma at the kitchen table and talked with her. I tried to tell her how sorry I was, how badly I felt that she'd been hurt.

She just took my hand in hers. "Let's not talk about it, dear," she said.

Let's not talk about it. A true Grandma response. Better to not discuss how my murderous ex-bestie tried to bash Grandma's head in because she went out of her way to take care of me. Which was of course the entire root of my problem—and my mom's problem, and my grandma's problem, for that matter. Not talking about it. Burying it deep and ignoring the way it made the floorboards buckle and heave beneath you.

But all I can take charge of is my own life, so I didn't press the issue. I squeezed her hand. I told her I was glad to see her.

"Where are you guys going for dinner?" I ask now, smoothing my dress. I try not to sound jealous. Tabitha's going to prom with Ingrid Bell—which is a surprise, but not actually as much of a surprise as either of them thought it'd be—and she's meeting her and a bunch of our friends to eat.

"Some new place. I don't know. Ingrid was going to set it all up." She looks up at me, her expression suddenly tentative. "I'm sorry, Zahra, is this, like, salt in the wound?"

"No!" I shake my head. "This was my idea, anyway, remember? I wanted to help you get ready."

Okay, yeah—maybe a part of this is painful. Watching Tabitha get ready to go out and do the normal senior girl thing with all our friends. Knowing that I will miss it. But that part of my life is over. Aisha's still working on my plea deal, and I'm not sure what my sentence will look like . . . but I know it's not going to include a lot of formalwear.

"I wish you were coming," she says. "It's not fair."

"Yes, it is," I say automatically.

She makes a face. She always acts like I'm blameless in all of this, like I'm a victim of circumstance. Or of Ruthie.

"That little bitch . . ." she starts. But I shake my head.

"Come on," I say.

"She pulled you into this . . . this nightmare," she says. "She fooled me, she fooled Ingrid, she fooled Ben . . ."

"I fooled you, too," I say. I sigh. "Leave it, Tabby."

Ruthie didn't make me complicit. I could have confessed anytime in the three years she was in Oregon. I was a coward. And no matter how much I wish things were different, there's no changing it. Scared as I am about what may happen, I'm less frightened than I used to be, before the truth was out. Because now I'm not waiting for the other shoe to fall. Now it's all in the open.

The court-mandated therapy with Dr. Mabry probably helps, too. Turns out PTSD is real, and not just something soldiers deal with.

"Should we get Mom to take a picture?" I say. "You probably have to go pretty soon, right?"

"Yeah, let's go." She gets up, tosses her curls. "Come on."

I follow her down the darkened hallway. "You know, this is actually the best of all worlds. I get to wear the sexy dress but I don't have to put on the high heels or deal with some slob spilling shitty spiked punch on . . ."

My voice drops away as we step into the kitchen.

The lights are off, but the room glows with candlelight. Candles flicker from every surface. The table is draped in deep burgundy, china plates and wine glasses laid out at each place.

Ingrid's at the counter in dark red velvet, opening the lids on a bunch of caterers' containers. I see prime rib, scalloped potatoes, green beans with almonds, fresh steaming bread. And at the table . . .

At the table is Ben, in tuxedo and tennis shoes, pulling out a chair.

"Your parents took Malik out to Moose's Tooth for pizza," Tabitha says softly. "We've got two hours."

"I know you can't go to prom," Ingrid says, smiling at me as she slides an arm around Tabitha's waist. "But we thought we'd bring the pre-dance dinner to you."

I hear them both distantly. My eyes meet Ben's.

He's been at the house almost every day. He's come over with cupcakes, with books, with stuffed animals. He's come over with board games and puzzles. He's come with flowers. I don't deserve any of it. I'd like to believe I would've come out of hiding before the cops got too serious about looking at him . . . but I'd also like to believe I wouldn't let someone get away with murder. It sucks to know the very worst things about yourself as a fact.

He told me what happened with him and Ruthie. He'd been so serious, so anxious about telling me—he'd said that he'd been caught up in the emotions, that he was so sorry. "I feel like a moron for letting her manipulate me," he'd said.

"You're not the only one," I said, putting my hands on his cheeks.

We're not back together. Not really. We have kissed a few times since I came back. We've . . . done more than that, too, once or twice. But I won't let it get more serious than that. For one thing, he's going to University of Oregon in the fall. And if I do go to prison, I don't want him to think he has to wait for me.

And then, too . . . he has forgiven me, but I haven't forgiven myself. Which is exactly what the problem between us has always been.

But now he smiles, and I melt a little, my shoulders going soft. I take a step toward him, forgetting about the girls behind me.

"You look beautiful," he whispers.

"Thanks," I say. "You do, too. I mean . . . you look . . ."

He grins, and it knocks the words right out of my mouth.

"You guys didn't have to do this," I say, looking around at them. "You should be out, at Bootlegger's Cove, or . . ."

"Please," Tabitha says. She puts a bowl of bread down on the table. "Every single boy I have ever made out with is at Bootlegger's Cove right now with his date. I don't need that shit."

"But the prom . . ."

"Oh, we're still going to the prom," Ingrid says calmly. "After we eat."

"Right. I didn't manage a perfect liquid cat-eye just to sit around here all night," Tabitha says. She looks at Ingrid, a trace of a smile quirking one side of her mouth. "I'm arm candy, girl, I've got to make the rounds."

I glance at Ben. He's watching me, smiling faintly.

"Well, they're going," he says, when he meets my eyes. "I'm not going to that shit-show. Are you kidding me? There's a Fast and Furious marathon on USA tonight."

I mock groan. "Oh, no."

"Believe it," he says. "I've got your dad's permission to park on your couch all night and watch."

"Ben, you've got to go to the dance. Weren't you nominated for prom king?" I ask.

"Yes, but I dropped out of contention. This prom will be a democratic system. Or at least a constitutional monarchy. I would accept the crown in name only. The people will rule." He gestures grandly.

Tabitha rolls her eyes. "That's what he says, but really he doesn't want to lose to Javonn Carter. The fix is in."

"Anyway, we can argue about it—and I'm sure we will— after dinner," Ben says, patting the chair. "Right now I'm starving."

As I sit down, the memory flickers before me. The image of Bailey, cradled by dirt. Her eyes wide-open, her mouth slightly parted. Fragments of that night have come back to me plenty of times over the years, but this is the one that waits for me, anytime I risk a moment of happiness.

I focus my breath. Breathe in, breathe out. Don't fight it; acknowledge it. Easier said than done. I feel sweat start to bead along my hairline. I feel my heart pick up speed. My body braces for it all to come flooding back.

But then I open my eyes, and I look around the table. I look at what my friends have done for me. I look at the way they've made the night a thing I could be part of. I look at their faces—these people who came for me, who looked for me, and who didn't turn away once they'd found me and seen me for what I really was. Tabitha, brittle but fierce, and strange, brave Ingrid. And Ben. Ben, who I've loved since I met him, though I've never told him so. Ben, who's been trying to find me for years. Who still hasn't given up on it.

We all look at each other in the wavering candlelight, and for a second I believe that we see each other clearly. All our flaws, all our fragility and fear and pain, and all our hope and strength and our desperate attempts to change. We see it, and we accept it, and we still love each other.

"Let's eat," I say.

EPILOGUE

LYR

THERE'S AN ALMOST COMFORTING sameness to every day. Get up. Brush teeth. Brush hair. Get dressed.

Follow other women down the long linoleum hall to wait for meds. They come in a small paper cup. The nurse checks under your tongue, and then it's time for breakfast.

Breakfast, class, crafts, yard time, free time. They watch you all the time to make sure you are not wandering from the path.

I steer my body through the days and the nights. For the most part it's easy. Push this button, and the body's arm lifts. Push that one, and the legs move. I am far down inside, a tiny pilot operating the controls, and in here very little bothers me. It's all simple and mechanical and doesn't ask much of me. And the meds help. The meds make everything seem so calm and muffled and buried.

They also make it so I can't read, though. Which I hate.

Sometimes a woman visits. Dark blonde hair, scarred face. She sits across the table and speaks softly. *Your dad's not ready to come,* she says. *He's trying. He's . . . trying to understand. He told me to tell you that.*

Dad, a man with a black circle for a mouth. The yelling man. I don't miss him. It doesn't matter that he won't come.

The other one, though—the woman's daughter. With her doll-like eyes. Ingrid. I miss her. She won't visit, either, and when I ask, the blonde woman just looks sad. If I dwell on that too much it's like pressing down hard on a bruise.

So I try not to.

Get up. Brush teeth. Brush hair. Get dressed. Meds. Breakfast. On and on, every day.

A man in a suit asks, *Ruthie, do you understand what I'm telling you?*

We're in a private room—not the visitation room. I blink a few times, I try to focus on what he's saying. He has a large folder in front of him, full of paperwork. At one point he's shuffling through pages and I catch a glimpse of a picture. It's gruesome, a decomposed body, bits of black hair sticking to the scalp.

The thing we will have to do is to show that you were delusional, and Zahra . . .

That name. It shakes everything inside of me loose so the world becomes cloudy and impossible to see, the way a lake looks when the sand at the bottom is stirred by a storm. My insides are full of sand and bubbles and rocks, cloudy and opaque, and when it all settles again the man is gone and I am alone, strapped to a bed.

After that, no one says the name.

But I think about her. I think about her all the time. The Starmaiden. Gone forever, eaten by the Elodea. How I will miss her.

Get up. Brush teeth. Brush hair. Get dressed. Meds.

And then, one day, I figure out the precise place in my cheek to tuck the pill so the nurse doesn't find it.

It takes a little while for the drugs to leave my system. I'm still foggy. I'm still clumsy. But soon, I'm clear-headed again. I look around at the other women in my unit—most of them are much older than me. Most of them don't even read. There's no one I care to talk to.

Until one day.

The girl is about my age. Her head's shaved and she's got tattoos all over her arms, flowers and bees and birds. I see her reading in the library. A book I've read a dozen times, with a dozen small dragons circling the cover.

That's one of my favorites, I say.

The girl's eyes, dark as pitch, glance over the top of the book and meet mine. A thief, I think. The girl could be a thief, a rogue, stealthy and sharp. Or maybe an assassin.

Yeah, the girl finally says. *I like dragons.* There's something almost shy in her voice. She hesitates for a moment, then adds, *Want to see my drawings?*

And I just smile.